FORBIDDEN READING

'She needs properly pleasuring,' Marie told Pierre sternly. 'Imagine you are taking me.'

Justine shivered as she listened to the command. The decadence of being naked and surrounded by glamorous strangers heightened her arousal and expectation. She was acutely aware of the soft fabric against her back and buttocks and delighted by the way it soothed the heat of her febrile flesh. Pierre placed himself over her while the two maids delivered hungry kisses to Justine's breasts and pussy. The end of his erection brushed against her sex lips and she realised one of the maids was holding his length and teasing its tip against her labia.

'You are here in pursuit of pleasure?' he whispered.

Not trusting herself to speak, Justine could only nod.

'I think you might have come to the right place,' he said and grinned.

By the same author:

THE BLACK ROOM
THE BLACK GARTER
AMAZON SLAVE
FAIRGROUND ATTRACTIONS
THE BLACK WIDOW
THE BLACK MASQUE
DANCE OF SUBMISSION
THE SLAVE AUCTION
SLAVE SENTENCE
THE TORTURE CHAMBER
THE BLACK FLAME
PROPERTY
ORIGINAL SINS
HOT PURSUIT

FORBIDDEN READING

Lisette Ashton

This book is a work of fiction.
In real life, make sure you practise safe, sane and consensual sex.

First published in 2006 by
Nexus
Thames Wharf Studios
Rainville Road
London W6 9HA

www.nexus-books.co.uk

Typeset by TW Typesetting, Plymouth, Devon

Printed in the UK by CPI Bookmarque, Croydon, CR0 4TD

ISBN 0 352 34022 3
ISBN 9 780352 340221

You'll notice that we have introduced a set of symbols onto our book jackets, so that you can tell at a glance what fetishes each of our brand new novels contains. Here's the key – enjoy!

cp (traditional)

cp (modern)

spanking

restraint/bondage

rope bondage/hojojutsu

latex/rubber/leather/enclosure

fem dom

willing captivity

medical

period setting

uniforms

sex rituals

Before the Journey

'You're a dirty little bitch, aren't you?'

Justine held herself still when she heard the voice.

The vault was underground, designed without windows and lightless save for those few stray rays that filtered from the floors above. It was always a challenge to find the light switch and, as her fingertips scoured against the aged wood panelling, she began to believe that this time her hand wouldn't fall on the vital plastic button. Her heart raced, the inside of her mouth turned bone dry, and she struggled not to panic at the thought of being trapped in the unlit room with a menacing stranger.

'You're a dirty little bitch, aren't you? You're a dirty little bitch who needs a damned good thrashing. Is that why you've come down here? Have you come down here to have your backside thrashed?'

Justine didn't know who had spoken – she couldn't decide if it was a male or female voice – but she understood every syllable of the filthy suggestions. Fighting to appear brave, not wanting to be intimidated by the intangible combination of darkness, rude words and her own apprehension, she drew a deep breath and squinted into the shadows. 'Who is that? What are you doing in here? Don't you know this is Mrs Weiss's personal vault? Only authorised personnel are permitted in here.'

'Take off your blouse, Justine,' the voice whispered slyly. 'Let me see your breasts.'

She considered running then shunned the idea. The timer switch for the hall had already blinked off and everything behind her was unilluminated gloom. If she did choose to run, Justine knew she faced a terrifying race along a narrow passage. When, or if, she reached the end of the corridor, there would follow a frantic search for the right key from her bunch as she tried to open the locked door that led back to the sanctuary of the library. Fear threatened to overwhelm her and she struggled to find the light switch before the mounting panic won.

'Go on, Justine,' the voice coaxed. 'Take off your blouse. Show me your tits. I'm aching to see them. Don't you want to show them off to me?'

From out of nowhere a hand touched her breast. Unseen fingers stroked the swell of one orb and her nipple pulsed softly as though responding to the vile stimulation. Startled by the contact, Justine dropped her keys to the floor. The jangle of metal striking stone was drowned out by her exclamation of despair and surprise. Without the keys she had no way of escaping the vault and, in the darkness, she had little hope of finding the fallen keys. Her search for the light switch was renewed with almost frenzied haste.

'Go on,' the voice insisted. 'Take your blouse off and show them to me.'

Justine still couldn't decide whether the voice was male or female – or if there was something familiar in the tone or if that was just her imagination – but those details were immaterial. Her main objectives were to turn on the light switch, find her keys, and finally flee from the vault as fast as she was able. She repeated those three goals inside her head like a personal mantra for survival.

Light, keys, run. Light, keys, run. Light, keys, run.

Going into the vault was her least favourite part of a job that had lost its allure many months earlier.

Working in the library she had soon grown weary of cataloguing endless tomes – filing, stamping, repairing, re-filing and re-cataloguing – but those elements of her day-to-day routine were manageable even if their monotony had transcended the mundane. A long time before this incident, well before she had found herself trapped in the inescapable vault with an unknown stranger, her weekly visit there had been the one chore that she truly dreaded.

'Unfasten a couple of buttons,' the voice urged. 'Show me a little cleavage. I want to see the milky white pallor of your tits so I can picture sinking my teeth into them. I'd love to bite you, Justine. I'd truly love to taste your ripe, plump flesh.'

Justine shivered and placed a defensive hand across her chest.

Light, keys, run. Light, keys, run. Light, keys, run.

She continued to claw at the wall, terror making her ill as she scrabbled to find the switch, but she kept her other hand fixed firmly over her breasts. The insidious touch she had suffered before had been unnerving and she was determined not to feel that loathsome caress for a second time.

Almost as though the stranger understood her fears, a hand traced against her backside and squeezed a buttock. 'Be a good girl and take your blouse off, Justine. I'm aching to get a proper look at you.'

Forgetting her search for the light switch, Justine slapped the hand away and pressed her back against the wall. She couldn't recall being more terrified. Her breath came in rapid, nervous gasps, pure adrenaline pounded through her veins, and her skin was suddenly clammy with perspiration.

Light, keys, run. Light, keys, run. Light, keys, run.

She tried to focus on her three-step plan for escape but it was impossible to think past her hatred of the room that had now become her prison. She had always despised the vault, and finding herself trapped within its secured walls was like the realisation of her every nightmare. The library's patron, the local philanthropist Mrs Weiss, retained this vault beneath the main building for her own private collection. It was used to house a spectacular hoard of rare works, first editions and original manuscripts. There were a couple of hand-written Wordsworth poems, untidily made priceless by their fascinating corrections, additions and deletions; complete collections of Dickens, Poe and Hemingway in first editions, several of the titles signed by the authors; as well as a host of personal diaries from those historical luminaries whom Mrs Weiss revered. Yet, in spite of the priceless treasures it contained, and going against her professional appreciation of their importance, Justine still hated the vault.

'Get them out for me, Justine. I want to see them. I need to touch them.'

The room was always claustrophobically dark. Even when the meagre lights were switched on the shifting shadows held dominion over its airless realm. And there was something in the solitude and silence that made Justine yearn for the comparative bustle and companionship of the library above. But it wasn't just the loneliness or the lack of light that she truly disliked. Being honest with herself, she had never understood the point of the room. For a book-lover like Justine, keeping such a marvellous collection hidden in the lightless gloom of the vault seemed tantamount to sacrilege.

'Take your blouse off, Justine, and then I'll turn the light on. How does that sound for a fair exchange?'

'Who are you?' She could hear the spiralling lilt of hysteria in her tone and tried desperately to squash it before it became too noticeable. 'Who are you? What are you doing in here? And why are you tormenting me like this?'

'Take your blouse off.' The whispered instruction returned from the depths of the shadows. 'Do that and I'll turn the light on.'

'I don't want to take my blouse off,' Justine complained.

'Maybe you don't want to,' the voice agreed. 'But you'll do it if you want me to switch the light on. Why don't you give in now and save us both the trouble of this senseless argument?'

She held her breath for a moment, wishing she could think of an appropriate reply, but only one response seemed right. She didn't want to take her blouse off but she was less inclined to spend any longer in the vault than was absolutely necessary. Sure she had no other option, quietly promising herself that she would allow things to go no further than this one simple act of acquiescence, Justine said, 'All right. I'll take it off.'

The stranger drew an excited breath and, for the first time, Justine began to suspect that she might be trapped in the vault with a woman. She didn't know where the idea came from – she couldn't understand how it was possible to ascertain the stranger's sex from an excited breath when she hadn't been able to detect that much from the insidious questions and lewd suggestions – but she felt sure she was right. The thought did nothing to help ease her nerves or stop her fingers from trembling as she tried to release the buttons from her blouse, nor did it do anything to curtail her blushes as she shrugged the cotton garment from her shoulders.

'Beautiful,' the voice whispered. 'Truly beautiful. Now take off the bra.'

'You said you'd turn the light on,' Justine exclaimed. 'You said, if I took off my blouse, you'd turn the light on. You promised.'

'I'll turn the lights on once you've removed the bra.'

In the oppressive silence that lingered between them, Justine could feel her resolve fading. She didn't want to

5

expose herself to this unknown woman, although it was so dark in the vault she couldn't properly call it exposing herself, but she had gone so far as to remove her blouse and she didn't think it was such a great step to go that one step further and take off her bra. A sly voice at the back of her mind suggested that the woman's night vision would be used to the vault's gloom, but Justine shut those words off, unable to listen to their salacious suggestions. Treacherously, her nipples stiffened within the lacy cups of the garment, as though the tiny beads of flesh were trying to sway her with their own decision.

'Take off your bra, show me your tits, and then I'll turn the light on.'

Justine sniffed with disgust, most of it aimed at the woman who was demanding she undress but part of it meant for herself, then reached awkwardly behind her back to release the fastener. Her blushes had been deep before but now they burnt like coals against her cheeks. As she allowed the lacy bra to fall to the floor, she heard the stranger sigh with avaricious approval.

'Now those truly are beautiful.'

It was unmistakably a woman's voice, vaguely familiar and unnervingly close. Justine racked her brains to put a face or name to the voice but it was difficult to think beyond the piercing embarrassment of standing topless in front of an unknown stranger.

'I can't believe you've been hiding these little treasures from me all this time. They are so magnificent.'

A pair of hands reached out for her.

Justine stiffened when she realised fingers were cupping each breast and she could have fainted with embarrassment when a pair of thumbs stroked softly over the thrust of her nipples. The sensations were horribly exquisite: more arousing than she could have expected and twice as deplorable because of that glimmer of pleasure. Trying to remain unmoved,

6

keeping her voice neutral and free from any taint of arousal, Justine said, 'You were going to turn the light on.'

'I will.'

Both hands remained at her breasts, squeezing and kneading the orbs while the thumbs constantly scratched back and forth over the stiff nipples. Justine ached to slap the stranger away, bark a bitter refusal and distance herself from the woman who was assaulting her, but she knew it would be safest to wait until the lights were on before she showed that much defiance.

'Aren't they just perfect?' the stranger whispered.

Justine felt the tickle of hair against her breast, and then lips were brushing against her nipple. The torment of being fondled had been horribly exciting but this made her torture infinitely more unbearable. A cool mouth graced her bare flesh, then the slick warm wetness of a tongue pressed over one nipple. The bud of flesh grew quickly under the stimulation and then trilled with a rush of pleasure when it was playfully nibbled. Fighting to contain her responses, Justine pushed a fist into her mouth so she didn't groan with enjoyment.

'Aren't they truly perfect?' the stranger repeated.

Justine drew a deep breath before trusting herself to speak. Measuring each word, not wanting her statement to sound like a ruse, she said, 'You'll see them much better when you turn on the light.'

'That's right,' the voice agreed. 'I will see them better, won't I?'

Mercifully the mouth moved away from Justine's breast and the hands stopped tormenting her with their vile caresses. As promised the light came on but, rather than the illumination Justine had expected, she realised the bulb had been replaced. The room was turned black and scarlet from the glow of the dim, coloured bulb that now hung in the centre of the room. For the first time

7

she got a chance to glimpse the person who had been assailing her with unwanted intimacies, vulgarities and depraved suggestions, yet the view didn't help much. Too many shadows continued to hold reign and all Justine could see was the outline of a feminine shape. She noticed the narrow waist, buxom hips and full breasts of a womanly figure – she even observed the disquieting detail of the stranger's nudity – but none of that helped her to place the woman's identify.

'Who are you?' she demanded. Trying to sound confident, trying not to show that she was mortified to be displaying her bare breasts in this alien situation, she said, 'I know you, don't I?'

'So many questions,' the naked woman laughed. 'And an answer will cost you your skirt. Are you prepared to pay that much?'

Defensively Justine clutched at the button on her skirt.

Light, keys, run. Light, keys, run. Light, keys, run.

Now that she had some illumination, Justine glanced at her feet to see if she could see the keys. The stone floor was frustratingly bare and it was only when she heard their dull metallic jangle that she realised the woman was now holding the bunch. From the set of her trembling silhouette it was almost possible to imagine that she was laughing.

'You wanted to know who I am,' the woman reminded her. 'And I told you the answer would cost you your skirt. Take it off. Take it off and allow me to introduce myself.'

'I don't care who you are,' Justine decided. 'Just give me my keys and let me out of here.'

'That will cost you your skirt and panties.'

The words shocked her with a thrill of black excitement. Justine couldn't explain why she should find the proposition arousing, or why she should contemplate surrendering herself further to the sadistic woman, but she couldn't deny that the idea was tempting. In the aftermath of her terror the surge of excitement seemed like a natural response.

'Strip naked, and then I'll give you your keys and let you go,' the woman assured her. 'You've already shown me your tits, and I think we both got something out of that revelation, so why don't you humour me with this final request? Take your skirt and panties off and I'll give you back your keys.'

Sighing with frustration – hating the woman, the vault and her own weak will – Justine wrenched the skirt open. Hurrying to undress, not allowing herself to consider the consequence of her actions, she snatched her pants down to her ankles and stood naked in front of her tormentor.

'Beautiful,' the woman proclaimed. 'Truly beautiful.'

Justine shivered with a mixture of cold and shame. She ached to put protective hands over herself but suspected that would only delay her escape from the vault. She had never thought exhibitionism could be such an aphrodisiac and she fervently steeled herself from the temptation of pleasure that it offered. Justine knew her body was attractive, she saw testament to that belief in the bathroom mirror each morning, and she wanted to smile with smug satisfaction as the stranger silently ogled her. But, not acknowledging any enjoyment, determined that she wouldn't be swayed by the pleasurable thrill of revealing herself, Justine extended a hand and said, 'I've done as you asked. Now let me have the keys so I can leave here.'

'In good time,' the woman promised.

Her voice had taken on a husky quality that was rich with arousal. The feral scent of womanly musk struck Justine's nostrils and she wondered if she was drinking the perfume of the stranger or that of her own excitement.

'I made a promise, and I intend to honour it, but I want you to turn your back to me first. I want you to face the wall.'

Knowing she had to do as she was told, Justine turned to the wall. She had time to notice that a fresh layer of panelling now stood where she had expected to find the switch, dimly realised that someone had laid careful plans to ensnare her in this situation, and then she was closing her eyes against the shame of being caressed. Cool hands stroked over her back, hips and buttocks. Inquisitive fingers pushed between her thighs and she was chilled when the woman's fingers stroked the wet flesh of her labia. As treacherous as her nipples, the inner muscles of her sex trembled eagerly as though they yearned for more than mere titillation.

'Beautiful,' the woman whispered. 'Truly, truly beautiful.'

For an instant Justine thought she might know who her tormentor was. Something in the woman's phrasing sparked a memory at the back of her mind and she could feel herself on the brink of making the connection. Then, when the fingers returned to her sex and rubbed at the split of her pussy lips, all such trivial considerations were cast aside. She had to swallow down another rush of mounting panic and bite her tongue to prevent a moan of encouragement falling from her lips.

'I was right when I guessed what you wanted before,' the woman breathed. 'You want a damned good thrashing, don't you? That's why you've come down here.'

'No,' Justine said, praying her voice would sound steady. 'I don't want a damned good thrashing. I only want you to give me the keys so I can get out of here.'

The hands stopped stroking her body and for one foolishly optimistic moment, Justine thought the woman was finally going to relent.

Then she heard the whistle of leather breaking air.

Before she could glance back over her shoulder, before she had the opportunity to protest, the sting of a tawse seared through Justine's backside. A blister of agony spiked her rear and she howled at the painful indignity. While she was still acclimatising her body to the discomfort, she heard the hiss of the leather falling again and tried to brace herself for the second punishing shot.

'Tell me you wanted this thrashing.'

'I didn't want this thrashing,' Justine wailed.

'Tell me this is what you've been needing.'

'I only want the keys so I can get out of here.'

'Tell me what I want to hear, then I'll give you the keys.'

The woman delivered a volley of agonising blows, spiking flesh and coming close to stripping the skin away. After less than half a dozen slices of the tawse Justine had stopped squealing and her respiration had turned into a frantic chug for oxygen. Her rear was ablaze with the punishing torment and she felt dizzy and close to collapse.

'Tell me what I want to hear, then I'll give you the keys,' the woman demanded. 'I'm not asking a lot, am I?'

'Very well,' Justine grunted. She didn't want to submit to the woman but she saw her options had been skilfully whittled away. 'If that's what you want to hear, then yes: I've wanted this thrashing.'

'Touch yourself while you say that.'

Justine stiffened and started to shake her head. It had been traumatic enough undressing, and she still couldn't believe she was allowing the woman to brutalise her with the length of leather, but the idea of following this final instruction was more than she could bear. She told herself she had to refuse, and that the submission had gone far enough but, because the command was delivered with another searing blow, Justine couldn't find

11

the will to resist. Sobbing as she revelled in the pain, snaking a hand between her legs and sliding sweaty fingers against the fetid heat of her sex, Justine teased the nub of her clitoris.

The bead pulsed beneath her touch and she was startled by the pleasure that her casual caress inspired. She hadn't expected any joy from touching herself and the rush of delight was enough to make her quiver. Greedily, she rubbed harder.

The tawse slapped down against her rear. 'Say the words while you're touching yourself,' the woman insisted. 'Tell me that you've truly wanted this thrashing.'

For an instant Justine could almost picture the face of the woman. Then that detail was gone as a surge of pleasure flooded her body. The miserable tears she had shed were forgotten as she basked in a haze of euphoria. The release had never been stronger and she realised the orgasm was continuing in a series of glorious waves. Each time the tawse descended against her buttocks a fresh burst of delight flowed through her and she crested a peak of elation that left her weak and helpless.

'Tell me that you've truly wanted this thrashing,' the woman repeated.

'I've truly wanted this thrashing,' Justine agreed.

The tawse bit viciously against her upper thighs.

Justine pressed wet fingers into the folds of her sex and groaned as the escalating pleasure swept through her in a debilitating rush. The feral musk she had caught before was stronger now and much more intoxicating. Its dark flavour added to her excitement and she had no qualms about giving herself to the next surge of delight that took her in its embrace.

'I wanted this thrashing,' Justine screamed. 'I needed this thrashing.'

'Too damned right,' the woman agreed.

12

Justine heard the clatter of the tawse being thrown aside and then she was being pulled away from the wall. She didn't know what was happening until the woman embraced her, and she was being held by a naked stranger. Bare breasts jostled against her own nude frame and the woman's roving hands smoothed against her aching backside and explored the curves and swell of her body. A tongue pushed against her lips as the woman's mouth met hers and, still giddy from her unexpected enjoyment, Justine allowed the kiss to continue. She let the tongue probe her mouth, daringly allowed the woman to writhe against her, before finally stepping back and snatching a breath.

'I've been wanting to do that since you first started working here,' the woman confessed. 'I'm glad we got the opportunity. You truly were satisfying.'

For the first time since she had entered the vault, Justine recognised her tormentor. She didn't know why she hadn't identified the woman before, blaming panic and her own nervousness on the oversight. But, now she knew who it was, she stepped away and pressed her back against the wall. Even when the woman handed her the keys she had promised, while flexing a reassuring grin, Justine could only think of the embarrassment that now held her after surrendering so easily.

'Mrs Weiss!' Justine exclaimed. 'What on earth did you think you were doing?'

'This is my vault,' Mrs Weiss reminded her. 'I can do what I like in here.'

Justine took the keys that were being offered and then began to snatch her clothes from the floor. 'Maybe you think you can do what you like down here,' she agreed haughtily. 'But you're not going to get away with treating me like some sort of sexual toy.'

'I wasn't treating you like a sex toy,' Mrs Weiss corrected. 'I was simply testing your suitability. I have a little job that needs doing and I had thought you might be the ideal candidate.'

Justine shook her head as she retrieved the last of her clothes from the floor. 'I don't do little jobs for sadistic perverts,' she snapped. 'I don't even work for your library any more. I shall forward a letter of resignation through my solicitor.'

'There's a manuscript that's long been missing from my collection.' Mrs Weiss spoke as though Justine hadn't said anything. 'I've heard this precious document is finally being made available. I want you to acquire it for me.'

Still seething, Justine wouldn't allow herself to be won over by the pull of intrigue. 'There are others in your library better suited for acquisitions. Employ one of them. I've just told you: I shall be tendering my resignation.'

'I'll double your salary.'

Justine stiffened her back and sniffed indignantly. 'Do you think I'm a whore? Do you think you can buy me with a measly increase in wages?'

'I think we're all whores,' Mrs Weiss said solemnly. 'We may not all share the same price but I've yet to meet the woman, or man, who puts virtue above personal gain or the realisation of their own ambitions. Such perverse morality goes against the grain of human nature.'

'I'm not a whore,' Justine said with quiet dignity. 'I do put virtue above personal gain and I'll be telling that to a competent lawyer for the industrial tribunal.'

Mrs Weiss laughed. 'Surely, you won't leave today?' she purred. 'You won't throw away your career on the same day you've been given a chance to single-handedly acquire *La Coste*.'

The final two words were delivered like a killing blow.

Justine heard them and reeled as though she had been struck. She stopped walking toward the vault door and turned to see the earnest expression on the older woman's face. A hundred questions rushed to the front of her mind, each more important than the last. If she had found the breath to speak she knew she would have stammered in excitement. But the one thing she would not have done would have been to repeat her intention to leave. The idea of declining Mrs Weiss's offer was no longer an option. Justine wanted to get her hands on *La Coste*.

One

For one brief moment Justine found herself wondering what she was doing.

She sat at the back of the church, innocently admiring the grandiose frescos and architecture, marvelling at the beauty of the stained glass and smiling approval at the ornate carvings on the pulpit and chancel. With the onset of twilight, candles had been lit around the chancel and within recesses in the broad stone pillars, and she was bathed in the warm glow of their guttering light. A memory of incense perfumed the air with a sultry cinnamon tang. The excess of detail around her was more than Justine was used to observing and, as she gazed with awe on a vividly sculpted crucifix above the altar, she tried to understand why she was troubling herself with Mrs Weiss's acquisition. The library's patron had bullied and abused her, subjected her to the most disquieting ordeal in the vault, and only stopped Justine from tendering her resignation by giving her the chance to acquire a mere manuscript.

Yet, going against her better judgement and flying in the face of common sense, instead of telling the library's patron to hand the job to someone else, Justine had eagerly returned home, packed an overnight case with her passport and a few essentials, then set off to attend the rendezvous that Mrs Weiss had organised. There had been a taxi ride, a train journey, the purchase of a pocket-sized phrase book to help surmount the language barrier she anticipated facing, then a short flight out of the country. That had been followed by another train journey, a second taxi ride and a short walk to one of the lesser-known churches in rural Provence. Everything happened so quickly she supposed it was only within the tranquillity of the church that she had found the chance to contemplate her actions. But it still struck her as bizarre that she was willing to do so much after suffering Mrs Weiss's sadistic abuse.

'I'm doing this to get *La Coste*,' Justine told herself. Her whispered voice was like a prayer in the stillness of the church. The reverential tone was replete with pious righteousness. 'That's why I'm doing it. I'm doing it for *La Coste*.' Strangely, she thought, the answer sounded right. Content that she knew her motivations, even if she didn't fully understand them, Justine settled back in her pew and continued to reflect on the church's majestic interior. She told herself it was better to think about anything other than the pleasure she had received beneath Mrs Weiss's cruel tutelage. Memories of the diabolical excitement continued to plague her with a guilty charge that she didn't want to revisit. The black arousal of exposing herself, being touched and then being striped, had left a mark that lingered longer than any of those weals that had been sliced across her backside. Justine shifted uncomfortably on the hard wooden seat of the pew, trying not to acknowledge the discomfort that still lingered in her behind and reminding herself that it was unseemly to be recalling such a licentious episode in the hallowed sanctuary of a church. The internal censure was enough to make her turn her thoughts back to the splendour of the church's decor but not quite enough to stop her nipples from aching with an unfulfilled need.

'You must be Justine.'

She blinked in surprise when the man spoke to her. There was the inflection of a strong French accent in his flawless English but, other than that, he was nothing like what she had expected. Mrs Weiss had said she would be contacted in the church but she had given neither name nor description. Justine hadn't known if she would be approached by someone older or younger, black or white, or even male or female: but she had never expected her contact to be a priest.

Too startled to respond, she simply gaped at him.

'Am I correct? Are you Justine?'

He stood before her wearing brilliant white vestments over his long black cassock. The addition of chasuble, stole and pectoral cross made it look as though he had just finished preparing for the early evening mass and Justine searched his face to be sure he was really her contact. Mature and darkly handsome, he would have, she supposed, the air of a dependable, trustworthy cleric to his congregation. Yet she detected something less attractive in his thin-lipped smile. His black eyes shone with a wicked glint and, if she had been of a paranoid nature, Justine could have believed he was glowering at her with concealed distaste.

'Is Justine your real name?' he began. 'Or just a germane identity to hide behind for the purposes of this transaction?'

She started to reply but he was already shaking his head and taking hold of her wrist. His hands were large, the knuckles brushed with hairs as dark and wiry as those on his head. 'No matter,' he decided. 'I have only one question for you and, as you are in my church, I expect an honest answer.'

Justine nodded. His fingers were warm and strong around her wrist. Despite the comfort that came from seeing a man in ceremonial robes she got the impression of cruel power from his grip. Stifling her nerves, trying hard to disguise her apprehension, she said, 'Ask what you will, Father. I shall answer as honestly as I am able.'

'Are you worthy of acquiring *La Coste*?'

She swallowed.

Mrs Weiss had warned that the manuscript's seller would want to make sure it went to a worthy recipient, sneering her contempt as she complained about this clause in the sale. 'Marais is selling because he needs the money,' she had explained. Unconsciously her tone slipped into a monologue of vitriol. 'So Marais plays these petty games – as though he's giving up a first-born child – yet I could be outbid by a recycling plant if the offer was more lucrative to him. I'm only glad I was the first one to get the money in an escrow account this time, although I had to filter it through half a dozen agents to keep my identity from him. But it's still insulting. If I didn't want this manuscript so badly I wouldn't even demand that you submit to the bastard.'

'I believe I'm worthy of acquiring *La Coste*,' Justine told the priest. 'But you'll want more than that admission from me, won't you?' Remembering the instruction Mrs Weiss had given her, reciting the words as accurately as she could recall, Justine said, 'I believe you'll want me to prove my worthiness.'

The priest sneered. 'You're quite the eager little bitch, aren't you?'

The words stunned her, almost as much as the shock she received when he pulled her out of her pew. Justine had been brought up with a strong faith in religion and an ingrained respect for the clergy. To be called a bitch by a priest was the most cutting condemnation she could imagine. She stumbled after him as he walked down the aisle, her heart pounding as she tried to guess what test he had in mind.

'*La Coste* was written by a great man,' the priest grumbled. 'It's almost unthinkable that it should ever end up in the hands of *an English girl*.'

The disdain in his voice made Justine feel nauseous. If she hadn't been out of breath from trying to maintain her balance and keep up with him she would have protested that his insults were more severe than she deserved.

'You have a lot to prove if you think you'll get my consent for this purchase,' the priest growled. 'And I should warn you before we begin, you're not going to win me over so easily.'

'I'm worthy of acquiring *La Coste*,' Justine said indignantly.

'Then you'll prove that to me,' he snapped.

To the left of the chancel, facing the pulpit, stood a life-size statue of the virgin and child. Their beatific smiles watched blindly as Justine was dragged to the altar. Above her the gaze from the crucified Christ figure stared down as she was forced to her knees. Justine could only feel her shame intensify when the priest pulled his erection from the folds of his vestments. The long length of flesh was hard and obscenely pink. It struck her as being a disgusting and unholy sight in the sanctuary of the church. Unable to contain her response, she sneered with revulsion and tried to back away from him.

He caught her by the shoulder and dragged her closer to his hardness. 'Touch my cock,' he demanded. 'Stroke it. Wank me. Bring me off. Make me come.'

Each word was like a slap across the face and Justine recoiled from the shock of hearing a priest utter such ungodly instructions. She tried silently to implore him for leniency but the hard set of his jaw told her he would show no mercy. His gaze was devoid of compassion and he looked unable to do anything except repeat the more offensive of his instructions.

'Touch my cock. Wank me. Make me come.'

As she noticed the pearl of pre-come that glistened over the eye of his glans, then caught the salty scent of his arousal, Justine realised she wanted to obey his instructions. Although they were in a church, and even though she knew her thoughts were deeply sacrilegious, she was desperate to do as the priest demanded. Tentatively at first, then with growing eagerness, she reached for his erection and circled him with her hand.

'Praise be to Jesus,' he muttered. 'That's what I need.'

His shaft thickened as her cool fingers pressed against his boiling flesh. The bead of pre-come grew distinctly larger and the strong pulse of his arousal beat steadily in her palm. When she stroked her hand along him, pulling the rubbery flesh of his foreskin over his purple glans, the priest sighed. His exclamation of approval turned into a groan when she tugged the skin back and tautly exposed his swollen dome. Holding him firmly, she could feel the desire for climax shivering through his length.

'Go on,' he spluttered. 'In the name of the Father, use both hands and toss me off now.'

She flinched from the way he called on God to watch down, but that didn't stop her from eagerly obeying. Wrapping both fists around his erection she stroked her hands back and forth in unison. He was more than long enough to be contained within her grip. The bulbous end of his shaft poked out from between the curled finger and thumb of her right hand. Her left hand pressed into the dark thatch of curls that poked through the opening in his cassock. The scent of his arousal grew more noticeable and the quickening pulse of his excitement pounded beneath her fingertips.

'Praise be to all the saints,' he growled.

She dared to glance up at his face and saw the manic glint that shone in his eyes. His eyebrows were knitted together with concentration and his jaw looked peculiarly square and manly. It was unnerving to accept that she was doing something so base in the sanctity of a church, but Justine thought the priest's expression was even more disquieting. The idea of refusing him had long since passed and all that was left was her need to submit.

As she snatched a faltering breath, Justine realised that her desire to obey wasn't her only motivation: there was also the quandary of her own swelling excitement. Kneeling before him, squeezing her thighs together as she dryly tried to address her own arousal, Justine came close to sobbing with frustration.

'Praise be to all that is holy,' he glowered.

She could feel him growing inexorably harder. Twisting her wrists lightly, she dared to increase her pace as she pulled his foreskin back and forth. Above her head she saw his pectoral cross keeping tempo as it bounced against his chest. The tassels decorating the ends of his stole swayed to and fro with the same rhythmic motion.

'*Salope!*' he exclaimed. His hands had tightened into fists by his sides and his jaw was clenched with a fury that could have splintered the enamel from his teeth. In a guttural whisper he declared, '*Putain cochonne.*'

Justine didn't know what the words meant but she suspected they wouldn't be included in the pages of the phrase book she had purchased. She didn't doubt he was insulting her and, given the circumstances, believed she was probably worthy of his vilest slurs. But those considerations didn't stop her as she worked diligently toward wringing the climax from his length. The ordeal was proving more exciting than she had anticipated and Justine was overcome by her own need for satisfaction. As her hands worked on him – her biceps aching from the exertion and her palms glistening with a meld of her own sweat and the priest's arousal – she couldn't shake the demands of her pulsing libido. The inner muscles of her sex quivered with greedy need and the urgent pulse of her clitoris throbbed insistently. The folds of her pussy lips were indecently hot and fluid and she could have sobbed with the injustice of trying to satisfy the priest without being allowed to sate her own appetite.

'Harder,' he growled. 'Faster and harder. Make me come.'

She madly wondered if he would allow her to touch herself, then pushed that idea from her mind. Something in the priest's staunch expression told Justine that he was a hard taskmaster and she felt certain he wouldn't give in to her depraved request for release. It only took one glance at the wicked glint in his eyes and she remembered she was there to satisfy his demands and not her own.

Yet that understanding did nothing to alleviate the torment of her arousal. Inside her bra her nipples stood as hard as bullets. Even the slightest movement was enough to send a shock of pleasure rippling through both orbs and she struggled to remain motionless while she worked on his length. Between her legs the viscous heat was sweltering and her longing to be touched was almost a physical ache. The yearning for satisfaction left her weak and miserable and she struggled to put her own needs out of her mind while investing her efforts in bringing him to climax.

'Go on,' he insisted. 'Milk me.'

The eye of his glans was dangerously close to her mouth. The scent of his pre-come was so strong it accompanied every breath. The taste coated her tongue and tainted each nervous swallow. The temptation to dart her lips against him, take him in her mouth and savour his flavour as she tortured him with fellatio, was almost unbearable. It was all too easy to imagine how his pulsing length would feel against the insides of her cheeks and the idea alone was enough to send fresh spasms of hunger buffeting through her sex. Justine was only able to stop herself from giving in to the impulse because she feared there would be repercussions if she dared to use that much initiative in bringing the priest to the climax he had demanded. Diligently, she squeezed harder on his length and worked on him with a fresh burst of speed.

'That's it,' he declared. 'I'm there. I'm there.'

23

Justine hadn't needed to hear the words to know his orgasm was imminent. The flesh in her hand reverberated like steel rope and she could tell that he was on the verge of ejaculating. She worked both hands more briskly along his quivering length, determined to pull the climax from his shaft.

'Go on,' he urged. 'Milk me, you little whore. Milk me.'

She recoiled from his harsh words, despising the way they added moisture to the heat between her legs. Glancing meekly up at him she shivered when she saw the combination of distaste and excitement that lit up his smile.

'Carry on,' he insisted. 'Don't you dare stop now you're so close.' As he spoke he reached over her head to the altar behind her. Justine watched him snatch an ornate chalice from beside a tray of the communion host and she watched in horror as he pushed it into her hand. One glance into its bowl and a glimpse at the stain of red liquid at its base showed her that the chalice was more usually employed for the communion wine.

'Milk me into that,' the priest hissed. 'I'm going to come.'

Unable to refuse – unable to think how she could possibly say no to such an instruction – Justine took the offered chalice from him. All the time she kept one hand around his thickness, working her wrist back and forth. Determined that he wouldn't see her nervousness, she tried to hide the fact that she was trembling as she held the rim of the sacred cup beneath his swollen glans.

'*The acts of the sinful nature are obvious,*' he began ominously.

She cowered from something powerful in his voice but didn't stop rolling her fist along his erection. Not daring to disobey his instructions, she kept her concentration fixed on coaxing the climax from his length.

'*Sexual immorality, impurity and debauchery,*' he continued.

His tone had the maniac zest of an outraged evange-list and Justine realised he was reciting lines from somewhere within Galatians. The combination of his approaching climax and the biblical quotation jux-taposed discordantly and made her believe she was doing something irrevocably wrong. Perversely, the concept of her own immorality only made her feel more daring and she came close to swooning with a fresh flood of arousal.

'*Drunkenness, orgies, and the like,*' he went on. '*I warn you, as I did before, that those who live like this will not inherit the kingdom of God.*'

A tight smile flashed across his features and she could feel the release of tension from within his muscles as the orgasm finally took its hold. His shaft thickened, then pulsed, spurting a viscous dollop into the ornate chalice. As she gently eased her grip on his erection a second jet of semen spattered into the sacred cup. Justine didn't release her hold on his length until the final droplet of his spend had been carefully squeezed into the chalice.

The priest shivered with obvious satisfaction. When he glanced down at her, Justine could see his smile was lascivious. '*But the fruits of the Spirit are love,*' he intoned softly. His demeanour had changed from some-thing vengeful and unsettling to a facade of beneficence. He winked at her with obscene familiarity and said, '*Finish this now and drink the fruits of my spirit.*'

She started to shake her head, then realised that would be no way to win his approval. The certainty that she wouldn't be able to end this ordeal without drinking from the chalice left her sick with unspeakable excite-ment. Glancing nervously around, she saw the only other eyes that rested on her belonged to the virgin and child, and the crucified Christ. Their mute regard made her feel as though she was the most despicable heretic that had ever desecrated a church. The inner muscles of her pussy churned with fresh arousal.

'Drink the fruits of my spirit,' the priest insisted.

Hesitantly, Justine put the chalice up to her lips.

Over the rim she saw the priest conceal his spent length within the folds of his cassock and noticed he was watching her expectantly. Anxious to appease him she pressed the chalice to her lower lip and tilted its base upward. The slimy residue of his ejaculation slid slowly into her mouth and onto her tongue. Its noxious taste filled her with a bilious urge to gag but she quashed that gut reaction, sure it would earn his staunchest disapproval. Pouring the remainder of the spend into her mouth, trying not to taste its thick sickening flavour, she quickly tried to swallow.

'Drink the fruits of my spirit,' he snarled.

She thought it would have been easier to drink the fruits of his spirit if they hadn't been so copious. Her throat wanted to lock reflexively as she tried to force the gelatinous fluid down the back of her mouth. When she had finally finished she gasped and cast the chalice aside. Breathing deeply, studying him with an expression that came from somewhere between arousal and revulsion, she asked, 'Was that what you wanted from me, Father? Did I perform that chore to your satisfaction? Did I prove myself worthy?'

He helped her from the floor then started away from the chancel. 'Come with me,' he decided. 'I want you outside the church while my parishioners get ready for their mass.'

After the exertion of her unsatisfied arousal, Justine felt too weak to move. Every muscle in her body ached and she fought to find some excuse to delay following him. 'Have I met with your approval?' she asked. 'Have I proved myself worthy to acquire *La Coste*?'

He snorted humourless laughter and turned to glare at her. There was no mistaking the contempt in his gaze. 'Come with me,' he repeated. 'I expect you to do as I tell you.'

'I have to know,' Justine insisted. 'Have I proved myself worthy?'

'The decision on your worthiness is not mine to make,' he said stiffly. 'I am only one of three advisors who will be reporting to Marais, the seller.'

The words made her uneasy and she struggled to take some comfort away from her disconcerting experience. She had thought the priest might be the mysterious Marais that Mrs Weiss mentioned. The revelation that she was to be tested by three advisors left her plagued by a fresh series of doubts and reservations. Briefly she wondered if this development was a punishment from God for the blasphemy she had just performed in His house. She quickly dismissed the idea as being puerile, but not before she had genuflected and glanced nervously behind herself at the martyred figure of Christ. 'You're only one of three advisors?' she repeated.

He nodded.

'Then, did I pass your test?' she asked. Because so much rested on her success it was difficult to keep her tone even and free from nerves. 'Did I do all that you wanted and expected? Will you be advising the seller that I'm worthy of acquiring *La Coste*?'

'I don't know,' the priest growled. His smile turned sly as he added, 'I haven't begun to test you yet.'

Two

The depth of darkness that had fallen since she entered the church surprised Justine. As the priest led her outside she was shocked by the speed with which twilight had surrendered to full night. Faraway stars blinked from the inky canopy above and a small and distant moon dusted silver light at their feet. She had noticed the stone monoliths and grave markers when she entered the churchyard earlier. Their silhouettes now loomed from the shadows alongside a gravel path that cut through the night-black grass. Justine wrapped her coat more tightly around her shoulders and hurried to keep pace with the priest.

'Wait!' he called.

She stood still as soon as he gave the command. His stern voice inspired a tremble of arousal and she crushed her thighs closed as she tried to ignore the swell of excitement that flourished in her loins. It was disquieting enough to be subordinate to the priest. Those depravities he had demanded in the church still left her shocked and incredulous. But the prospect of enjoying his vile attention made Justine feel as though she was being treacherous to her own sensibilities.

'You will go and wait at the Dupont tomb,' he said firmly. He had turned to face her and, with one stern finger, he pointed into the shadows of the church's small cemetery. 'It is just over there,' he explained. 'It is the largest stone in the grounds. Stand in front of it. Remove your clothes: all your clothes. And wait for my return.'

It was too much to take in at once and Justine longed to question the orders. She glared at him in the dim light – wondered if she dared refuse – and struggled to find the words that would form a denial. It was one thing to submit to him in the privacy of the church, but the prospect of undressing in somewhere as public as the churchyard made another shiver tremble through her frame. The solemnity of his face, and some ingrained hesitancy that wouldn't allow her to defy a priest, caused the refusal to die before it reached her lips. After they had glared at each other for what seemed like an eternity, she could only ask, 'Where are you going?'

'I have personal business at the presbytery. I need to make a telephone call to a colleague at *The Society*.'

He said the final two words with such grave intonation that Justine was unnerved. Without knowing why, she immediately understood that *The Society* had some bearing on her situation. Curiosity and intrigue made her ask: 'The society? Which society? What society are you talking about?'

'You must know of *The Society*?'

She knew the name was given to a group of villains at the start of de Sade's *The One Hundred and Twenty Days of Sodom*, but she couldn't think how that applied to her personal situation. 'No,' she assured him. 'I don't know of *The Society*. Who are they?'

'*The Society* are a bunch of perverted heathens all damned to hell.' He made the declaration in the same way she imagined he would deliver a fire and brimstone sermon from the pulpit. Once he had glared at her with enough fury to make Justine cower, he graced her with a final look of unconcealed contempt, and then turned away. Letting the words spill over his shoulder he said, 'You have your instructions, Justine. I have to make a telephone call. Do not prove yourself unworthy before we have begun. And do not trouble yourself with things that are of no concern to you. Go to the Dupont stone.

29

Do as you have been told.' Rather than allowing her the opportunity to argue, he continued walking toward the presbytery at the distant end of the church path. As a parting shot he called back, 'One more sign of insurrection and you will never get your hands on *La Coste.*'

Alone, cold and frightened, Justine considered her options and realised she had none. Trudging miserably away from the path, uncomfortable with the mild desecration that was wrought beneath every footstep, she peered into the gloom and tried to read the names that had been chiselled into the headstones.

De Blangis, Curval, Durcet.

They were all timeworn names and each was forgotten before she had started to read the next. Common sense told her that she should take this opportunity to flee from the churchyard, take a taxi back to the airport, and then return home. In the comfort of her own thoughts it was easy to argue that nothing could be worth the sacrifices she was enduring. And then she reminded herself she was on the verge of acquiring *La Coste.* That thought alone was enough to make her move on and read the next gravestone.

Dupont.

She stood in front of the magnificent memorial, dwarfed by its proud stature. The top was adorned with a weeping Madonna, staring blindly down into the darkness that surrounded Justine. The whole monument looked to have been carved from a glossy black marble that shone wetly in the moonlight. The chiselled lettering had been gilded and the golden letters glowed softly and subtly.

Adamant that she would do whatever needed to be done to acquire *La Coste,* Justine shrugged off her coat and started to unfasten the buttons of her blouse.

It seemed more than a little peculiar to be undressing in a churchyard. But, after the unreal developments she had experienced inside the church, she supposed it wasn't the most unusual event that had interrupted her day. She laid her coat on the top of a neighbouring headstone, then folded her blouse and placed it on top of the coat. Her skirt and shoes followed; their absence made her acutely aware of the cemetery's chill as tendrils of wet grass tickled her feet and ankles; and then she hastily stepped out of her bra and pants.

A prickle of disquiet rumbled through her bowel. The inside of her mouth turned dry with anticipation and she didn't dare swallow for fear of choking on the arid taste of dread. As she put the underwear with the rest of her clothes she noticed her hands shaking and knew it had nothing to do with the night's cool breeze.

Her breathing had fallen to a sultry pant.

The wrongness of what she was doing struck her like a slap across the face. Standing naked – her pale body almost glowing in the moonlight, while the rest of the churchyard was held in shadows – made Justine feel like the world's most depraved exhibitionist. She knew her slender figure and modest breasts looked attractive and exciting: the dusky swell of each breast was tipped with a stiff, *café au lait* tip that turned to *mocha* when she was excited. Her waist was narrow, her stomach flat, and she made a point of keeping her sex shaved and shamelessly free from hair. But, although she had previously admired the aesthetic perfection of her nudity in bathroom and bedroom mirrors, she had never expected to be displaying her secretly prized assets in a Provence churchyard.

Rubbing her arms to ward off the prickle of goose-flesh, she ignored the stiffness at her nipples and deliberately didn't notice the darkening hue of her areolae. It was more of a struggle to disregard the smouldering heat at her sex but she wilfully closed it from her mind. Shuffling from one foot to the other she waited with growing trepidation for the priest to return.

Voices on the path made her momentarily breathless with fear.

It sounded like two women were approaching – she was sure neither could be the priest, both tones were too soft and feminine – and they spoke in the fluid indecipherable French of the local villagers. A cold sheet of panic embraced Justine's naked body. She stood rigid, not knowing what to do for the best. In contrast to her immobility, her heart raced and her mind accelerated as she tried to work out the most prudent course of action. The priest had told her to stand by the Dupont stone but she wondered if he expected her to remain there and court the risk of discovery. Her own embarrassment at being seen would be crippling but Justine reasoned she might be jeopardising the priest's reputation if she didn't hide.

Before she could crouch behind the Dupont stone, her quicksilver doubts stung her with the idea that the priest might want her to suffer this impending humiliation. If he did have a reputation in the village, it wasn't one that he had appeared to consider when he was forcing her to pleasure him in the church. The vivid memory of what she had done added shame to her panic and tinged her cheeks with a cerise blush.

Justine wanted to hide; she didn't want to bring embarrassment on either herself or the priest; but she didn't want to disobey him and jeopardise her chance of acquiring *La Coste*. She cursed the man for not explaining what to do, and then cursed herself for not thinking to ask. And, as her thoughts tumbled back and forth between the options of concealing herself behind the Dupont stone, or blatantly braving the attention of innocent passers-by, the voices drew closer.

She could easily imagine the outrage she would cause. The shocked expressions, the sneers of disgust, and the foreign cries of condemnation were all clear in her mind's eye. But those thoughts only added to the wetness between her legs and did nothing to suggest what action she should take. Trying to retain some modesty, she folded one arm across her breasts and placed a demure hand over her cleft.

The footsteps trudged closer.

The voices were loud enough to shout through the stillness of the cemetery and Justine's overactive imagination made her certain the strangers were bearing down on her. So far she had been unable to see who was approaching: the forest of tall stones kept her relatively sheltered from the view of the path. But she believed, as soon as they came alongside the row of graves where she stood, the approaching parishioners wouldn't be able to miss her. The idea of being seen fuelled equal measures of dread and delight. Too frightened to concentrate, Justine couldn't work out whether she was appalled at the prospect of being shamed, or growing wet from anticipation. Her inner thighs were sticky with excess rivulets of her own arousal.

A gloved hand fell on her shoulder.

Justine never understood how she was able to contain the scream. The mounting terror that tightened her chest had brought her to the brink of shrieking. When the priest grabbed her bare shoulder, then turned her so she was facing him, Justine came close to collapsing with a combination of fright, disappointment and relief.

'You followed my instructions,' he grunted. 'I suppose that speaks in your favour.'

His absence of concern was chilling. She was equally unnerved by the lack of expression on his face. His gaze slipped down to appraise her nudity – Justine was appalled to realise her nipples were now standing fully erect – but she couldn't detect any hint of a smile or even mild approval. She wanted to believe that the churchyard's lack of light was making it hard to read his face but she knew it was more likely that he was simply unmoved or unimpressed by the sight of her naked body. He stared at her coldly, his gloved hand still resting on her shoulder, his dark gaze glowering with an unspoken threat of retribution.

It was only in that moment, when the silence between them was solid and uncomfortable, that Justine realised she could hear no one else in the churchyard. With the shock of having the priest surprise her she had forgotten about the parishioners. Listening intently, she could still hear the voices that had incited so much panic but they were now distant whispers, as though both the women had lowered their voices to enter the church. Thankful that she had avoided the crushing embarrassment of being observed, Justine sighed.

'Turn around,' the priest snapped. His crisp voice carried boldly through the night and she immediately understood he wasn't worried about being discovered. That thought didn't bode well. 'Face away from me,' he barked curtly. 'Hold the Madonna's feet. Part your legs.'

The terse instructions filled her with black excitement.

She briefly toyed with the idea of refusing but she knew the situation had gone beyond such an opportunity. Away from her need to acquire *La Coste* she was now driven by those desires he aroused within her. Her inner muscles were instantaneously transformed to a warm and fluid state, her pulse fluttered to match the urgent haste that beat between her legs, and she hurried to obey.

There was no doubt in her mind that what she was doing transcended sacrilege. She was standing naked in a churchyard and making herself sexually available for a depraved priest whom she barely knew. Touching the feet of the Virgin Mother's statue only compounded that crime and she cringed from the deviance of her actions. But Justine couldn't stop herself from doing exactly as the priest demanded. His voice carried instructions that she wanted to obey and his manner was so worldly and confident that disobedience simply wasn't an alternative she wanted to consider.

And, savouring the delicious rush of expectation, growing acutely aware of the chill breeze that toyed with the split of her pussy lips, she knew her subservience was going to be pleasurable. The inner muscles of her sex were already clenching in small tight spasms of anticipation. Her labia were wet from arousal and sensitive to the lightest movement of air. The stiffness of her nipples ached to be released by the attention of a warm and welcoming mouth.

'Bend forward,' the priest demanded.

His gloved hands were on her hips, the soft leather smoothing against the swell of her buttocks. The coarse twill of his cassock brushed her backside and – shocking her with its hardness and heat – the priest's erection nuzzled against her cleft. The breathlessness of her excitement returned with renewed force. The rush of arousal became a torrent and, as he stroked his length against her sex, a surge of animalistic pleasure overwhelmed Justine. His swollen glans slipped easily against her wet flesh. The friction of his broad dome against her glistening pussy was enough to inspire a deeper need inside her sex. Caught up in the heady thrill, she groaned hungrily.

He slapped one gloved hand against her rear. The echo rang loudly in her ears. The muffled burst of pain was enough to make her gasp again but this time without the same giddy rush of pleasure. 'You are doing this for my satisfaction,' he growled. 'Not yours.'

It was sufficient warning to make her bite her lower lip rather than release another sound. Still quivering with her need for him, poignantly aware of her body's desperate longing for orgasm, Justine tried not to squirm against him as he continued to rub his erection back and forth along the split of her sex.

'Are you ready for this?' he asked.

The head of his shaft rested over her hole. Her labia were already kissing a wet welcome to his glans and she contemplated pushing herself back against him. Knowing he would disapprove of such initiative, Justine tightened her grip on the feet of the Madonna and said, 'Yes. I'm ready.'

His thick length easily plundered her sex. The broad shaft forced her pussy muscles wide apart and burrowed deep inside. The heat of his erection – and the delicious girth that filled her so easily – made for an intoxicating blend. Justine arched her back as he pushed deeper, relishing the penetration and marvelling at the sensations he evoked. When he began to slide back, easing out of her so he could penetrate again, she chugged breath as her body tried to deal with the onslaught of satisfying responses.

'*Putain cochonne*,' he grunted.

The words still meant nothing to her and they were the only ones she could properly discern from the vitriolic outburst he hurled at her back. She understood that he wasn't saying anything pleasant. And she wanted to be shocked or horrified that a priest would insult her with what she suspected were crude expletives. But it only added to her excitement that the priest was cursing her while he used her in the boundaries of his hallowed ground.

The slap of his hand against her backside snapped her thoughts back to the moment. He struck with a punishing force which, while it didn't properly hurt, was uncomfortable enough to remind Justine that she was there for his convenience. She could hear him grunting and every other breath was accompanied by another foreign swear word. The sweat of his excitement radiated from him in waves, and she trembled as the exhilarating thrill buffeted her body. When he slapped his hand against her for a third time she realised he had stopped his guttural incantation at some point during her reverie and had been giving her an instruction.

'Pray,' he demanded. 'I want to hear you pray.'

The hand slapped her rear again and this time she understood she must obey without hesitation. For a moment she was weak with confusion, not knowing which prayer to recite, or if she should be committing such a profanation. When he slapped her backside again the abused flesh bristled with discomfort. She glanced down at her hip and saw her buttock was now livid from the repeated punishment. The shape of his gloved hand was repeatedly emblazoned against her wan flesh.

'Pray,' he insisted. 'I will not ask you again.'

He issued his command with a finality that made Justine certain he was on the verge of damning her as unworthy of retrieving *La Coste*. The thought of failing was enough of an impetus and Justine finally found the words for which she had been searching.

'*Our father,*' she began, '*who art in heaven.*'

He rode her so that each sentence of the Lord's Prayer was thrust from her mouth with a small gasp. The sacrilege of what she was doing struck her harder than any of the slaps he had delivered to her rear. Each word she muttered – reminding Justine of all the times she had innocently knelt and prayed in her own church – felt like the vilest affront to God. Yet, for all her fears of eternal damnation, her body responded with a fresh surge of delight each time he pushed into her.

'*Hallowed be thy name,*' she gasped. The thrill of impending orgasm made her legs weak. The quick contractions of her pussy muscles grew faster and made her certain that her climax was only a breath away. '*Thy kingdom come,*' she hissed.

'Say it louder.'

Despite the night's chill air a sheen of sweat lacquered her naked flesh. Tremors of euphoria bristled along her arms and down her shoulders as the priest continued to plough in and out of her hole. The promise of release inched perpetually closer and, throughout the ordeal,

37

Justine heard herself reciting those same words that she had always considered sacred. '*Thy will be done*,' she declared loudly. Raising her voice, trying to make herself heard to comply with the priest's instruction, she called, '*On earth, as it is in heaven. Give us this day our daily bread.*'

The priest's volley of insults had become an endless stream. She couldn't understand what he was saying but she knew he was damning her with every despicable label at his disposal. His vigorous thrusting was equally unrelenting. A barrage of hateful pleasure was bludgeoned from her sex and Justine bit back cries of protest as she struggled to finish the prayer. '*Forgive us our trespasses, as we forgive those who trespass against us,*' she bawled. '*And lead us not into temptation.*'

The irony of mentioning temptation made her feel ill. She squeezed her inner muscles around his shaft and groaned as an electric frisson of excitement tore through her hole. The prospect of orgasm loomed closer than ever and she renewed her grip on the feet of the Madonna.

'*But deliver us from evil, for thine is the kingdom.*'

She hesitated; sure she had heard more footsteps on the gravel path. The idea that she might be seen still worried Justine, even though she believed her sacrilege had now taken her to previously unplumbed depths of degradation. It was only natural to lower her voice, and try to control the grunting cleric behind her.

But the priest was either oblivious to the approaching strangers or unmindful of being discovered. He continued to ride in and out, holding her hips with renewed force and virtually shaking her to and fro as he came close to his own climax. 'Finish it, you little harlot,' he demanded. There was so much force in his words that Justine could feel them trembling along the length of the shaft in her pussy. 'Finish it now!'

'*Amen*,' she gasped.

He ejaculated as soon as she released the last word.

The throbbing of his muscle triggered her own orgasm and she revelled in a multitude of bliss as his shaft pumped urgently into her confines. The hot fluid of his spend thrilled her with its warmth and made her ache from the bombardment of pleasure. She gripped more tightly onto the feet of the Madonna, not sure if she was still praying or merely basking in the aftermath of the most depraved climax she had ever enjoyed. Her heartbeat raced faster than ever and she faltered giddily as she tried to remain standing while the eddies of joy continued to wash through her sex.

The waves of delight only began to recede as the night's cool chill took control of her body. When she thought she had enough strength to control her legs, Justine pulled herself from the Dupont memorial. After all that she had just endured, she thought it would have been impossible to contain the shiver of disgust that wanted to tremble through her frame.

The priest tugged his spent length from her pussy and hid it back inside his cassock. When Justine dared to glance at him he was considering her with an expression that she hadn't seen him wear before. Aside from the contempt, which she guessed might be a permanent attribute to his face, she could see a tinge of something else in his surly smile.

A part of her wanted to believe she was seeing his grudging acceptance but she warned herself against being too optimistic. From the little she had gleaned so far, Justine knew she was expected to have her suitability tested by three representatives of the manuscript's seller. Common sense told her it would be simpler if, rather than trying to pre-guess her tormentors, she just did as she was told. It would certainly make life easier if she stopped trying to find signs of approval in their every facial expression.

The priest shook his head and then snapped his fingers as he turned his back on her. Considering his businesslike attitude and cool demeanour, Justine found it hard to believe the man had just been riding her pussy with such brutal vigour. His indifference inspired another rush of loathsome excitement and she lowered her gaze and blushed.

'Come back to the church,' he demanded. 'Do not bother collecting your clothes. They should still be out here when I have finished with you.'

He said something else but the combination of his thick accent, and the fact that he had his back to her, made Justine uncertain about what he had said. For a bizarre moment, she had thought he was demanding she join him while he listened to the confessions of his parishioners.

Three

'You'll remain silent while you're in here,' the priest whispered.

Justine nodded.

She was still naked, and silently fretting about the clothes she had left in the cemetery, but the idea of disobeying him was no longer an issue. Cramped into the claustrophobic confines of the confessional her body was pressed tight against his. She held herself rigid, trying to keep her breath below a whisper, and perpetually glancing toward the grilled window that separated her and the priest from the penitent's half of the box.

'Make a sound and I'll deem you unworthy,' the priest pressed.

His mouth was over her ear. Every word he muttered was deafening in the silence and thrilled her with his warmth and nearness. Over one breast she could feel the chilly weight of his silver pectoral cross resting against her flesh. Although it was icy cold against the sweat of her skin, she felt sure the crucifix should be burning her for the irreverence she had already shown.

'Speak, groan or sigh and you will never get your hands on *La Coste*,' he growled. 'Do you understand?'

Despising the injustice of that condition, Justine glared at him. But, in the dark confines of the confessional, she felt sure he didn't see. The sound of movement from the penitent's side of the confessional made them both start. The grilled window shifted and its rasp made Justine want to squeal in surprise. The

41

silhouette of a stranger's face loomed behind the grille of the small opening.

'*Père, pardonnez-moi car j'ai péché.*'

Justine swallowed, understanding the sentiment even though she didn't know the words. She supposed it was the same apology spoken by her fellow Catholics throughout the world: *Forgive me, Father, for I have sinned.* Thoughts of her sacrilege turned to guilt and unease as she realised she would be listening to the confession of the man on the other side of the grille. She tried to calm her anxiety with the argument that she couldn't understand what the penitent was saying. But nothing would sway her thoughts from the knowledge that she was somewhere she shouldn't be and doing something she shouldn't do.

It was all too easy to remember the last time she had been to confession. The event had happened so long ago it should have been forgotten, but she supposed the musty scent of the confessional booth and the feelings of guilt and anxiety were enough to bring it back with vivid force.

'Forgive me, Father, for I have sinned.'

The priest on the other side of the booth encouraged her to continue.

Justine pressed her thighs together, despising the guilt and hating the fact that she had to admit to what had happened. She swallowed, straightened her back, and felt sick when she realised her nipples stood erect. The slightest movement made her blouse rub against the sensitive tips. Her cheeks turned crimson in the dark and she momentarily forgot what she had been about to say.

With only the subtlest inflection of impatience, the priest again encouraged her to continue.

'I've been having improper thoughts,' she said quickly. The silence that lingered between them stretched out until Justine expanded on her sin. 'For part of my university

42

course I've been studying the work of the Marquis de Sade. I had to read one of his volumes and I found the words . . .' She blushed deeper – unfastened a button at her collar and then fastened it again – and tried to find the courage to say the word to the priest behind the grille. *'I found the words . . .'*

'Arousing?' the priest suggested.

She considered his suggestion for a moment, sure that it said what she hadn't been able to say but certain it didn't go far enough. The word *arousing* didn't explain the urgent and overwhelming rush of desire that she had suffered while reading. Nor did it impart the sensations of unsatisfied lust that she wanted to fulfil. But, with a shameful heat smouldering between her legs, Justine couldn't think of another word that would suffice. She drew a deep breath, nodded, then said softly, *'Yes, Father. It was arousing.'*

'Have you sinned because of what you read?'

'Yes.'

'With someone else?'

Her thighs were crushed together so hard the muscles began to ache. Even thinking about de Sade's writing was enough to make her sweat with a fresh and hungry need for satisfaction. Talking about the subject, particularly talking about it with a priest, evoked a furiously exciting shame. *'Not with someone else,'* she confided. She had never spoken so quietly in the confessional. *'Just on my own.'* Saying the words conjured up the memory of the hours she had spent teasing her sex, filling herself with dildos and wallowing in the sweated bliss of bitter climaxes. Masturbation was as new a discovery to her as the works of de Sade and the pleasure was a revelation. The mental pictures of how she had satisfied her needs were so clear Justine feared they would glow like a TV screen in the dark and allow the priest to see exactly what she had been doing. The shame of sharing those private moments made her lips burn with fresh wetness.

He began to tell her about the severity of the sins she had committed.

And, while he spoke, Justine had been appalled to discover she was touching herself. It was only a surreptitious contact – the slightest caress of her hand against her crotch – but it was enough to have her teetering on the brink of climax. She struggled to stifle a shiver and bit back the urge to cry out with joy.

The priest told her to pray for guidance. He advised avoiding such unpalatable literature in future and suggested she should never commit the sin of self-pleasure ever again. Justine had continued to touch herself while she listened, aware that she wasn't going to follow any of his advice. She could see no point in praying for guidance because she already knew what she wanted. Her interest in de Sade was still voracious and she vowed to read everything he had ever written. And it would do no good to promise that she would never pleasure herself again because her body was already teetering on the brink of orgasm. Embarrassed, frustrated and confused, Justine had fled from the confessional booth.

Listening to the heavy sigh of the penitent on the other side of the grille, Justine realised this was the first time she had attended confession since that moment.

The priest raised a finger to his lips and fixed Justine with a warning glare that told her to remain silent. In a soft, almost understanding voice, he addressed his parishioner. Justine didn't want to hear what was being said but she knew she had no option except to remain where she was until the priest allowed her to escape. Frightened of being overheard, she held her breath and closed her eyes as the priest encouraged the penitent to continue. She half-expected to be held in a purgatory of stillness and silence until the final confession had been heard, and she braced herself for the prospect of an hour or more of sitting in one place and suffering the priest's invasive nearness.

But, when the priest pushed two fingers into her pussy, she realised she had underestimated the torment he wanted to inflict. The sudden intrusion came without warning and was far more than she had expected. Both digits slipped easily into her wetness and slid up to the knuckle and beyond. His hands were large, the fingers broad, and she didn't think the small hole of her cleft had been designed to accommodate such widths without some sort of preparation.

It took every effort not to shriek in protest.

She clutched her hands against her thighs and tried not to move as he urged his fingers deeper. Rather than give in to the need to make an exclamation, she buried her fingernails into the soft flesh of her inner thighs and grimaced against the pleasurable onslaught of arousal. Her teeth were clenched tight together and her brow was furrowed as she concentrated on remaining silent.

The penitent babbled in a low and understated tone. Justine couldn't catch a decipherable word but it only took one glance at the priest and she knew he understood every syllable. Even without any knowledge of French she could hear the inflection of guilt in the man's tone and, again, she was tormented by the knowledge that she shouldn't be desecrating the privacy of the confessional booth.

The priest wriggled his fingers inside her cleft.

A flurry of delicious sensations bristled through her sex and made her long to cry out in delight. As well as having two thick fingers buried deep in her wetness, the priest had started to rub his thumb against her clitoris. The stimulation wasn't subtle but her body was now beyond the need for mild sensations. Powerful charges of euphoria blistered her with each caress. Justine bit the insides of her cheeks to stop herself from making any sound that might alert the parishioner that the priest was not alone. Sure any sigh she made would become a groan, she deliberately held her breath.

The priest spoke – low guttural French that she knew wasn't addressed to her – and Justine managed to snatch a soft gasp of air beneath the volume of his words. His thumb continued to rub back and forth and she was dizzied by the ease with which he was increasing her excitement. The friction was tantalisingly soft – his touch was far more delicate than she would have imagined from someone so cruel and domineering – and her body hurtled toward a furious peak of orgasm.

The priest and penitent were involved in a mumbled exchange and, at the back of her mind, Justine reasoned that absolution and terms of penance were being given. But she couldn't properly concentrate on anything beyond the swirl of giddy delight that flowered from her pussy. The priest's fingers slid lightly back and forth and the tips stroked softly on a pad of super-sensitive flesh inside her sex. His thumb continued to wring whorls of joy from her clitoris and her inner muscles turned to a syrupy smouldering fluid.

The onset of orgasm struck her with cruel haste and she tried to hold herself rigid in the facile belief that she could contain the explosion. A panicked perspiration drenched her body; her cheeks flushed crimson; and she tensed every muscle in an effort to stave off the bliss of climax.

'*Merci, mon Père,*' the penitent whispered.

The priest grunted a noncommittal sound and Justine listened as the grille was pulled closed. Through the flimsy wall of the confessional she heard the door being opened and knew the parishioner was going out into the church. She still didn't dare to make any sound but, now that he was out of earshot, she allowed herself to breathe and suffer the searing climax that the priest had wrung from her. A wealth of tingling joy tumbled through her frame and the waves of glorious satisfaction shivered from her pussy.

'Dirty bastard,' the priest mumbled.

He was glancing toward the grille and Justine realised he was talking about the parishioner. Curiosity made her want to ask what the man's confession had been but she didn't dare voice that question. There were already sounds coming from behind the grille. The shuffling of feet, and movement of the small grille, alerted them both to the presence of the next penitent.

'*Père, pardonnez-moi car j'ai péché.*'

It was a woman's voice. Justine strained to see the shape of her silhouette but the booth was too dark. Before she could fix her efforts on gleaning something discernible from the woman, the priest had encouraged his parishioner to speak. As she began to babble fluently in a sensuous French dialect, he started to lower his face down Justine's body.

She held herself motionless.

Her breasts ached to be touched but he seemed deliberately to ignore their demands. His tongue traced a snail-trail down her chest, over her stomach, and toward her cleft. The two fingers he had pushed into her pussy remained deep inside and, when his tongue connected with the outer lips of her sex, he wriggled them gently.

Justine opened her eyes wide. She almost choked in her urgency not to make any sound as he lapped daintily at her labia and fired her sex with fresh blisters of bliss. Placing gentle kisses against her pussy, fuelling her with an insatiable need to feel his fingers tickle deep against the neck of her womb, he occasionally interrupted the penitent while rubbing his nose against Justine's clitoris.

'*Le mari de ma soeur,*' the woman mumbled.

Justine thought she understood the words but her attention was more directed toward the delicious havoc being wrought in her sex. The threat of another orgasm blossomed quickly and she writhed subtly along the fingers embedded in her cleft. The priest's tongue remained a warm wet balm against the split of her labia and his penetrative kisses inspired flurries of wicked and wanton responses. Justine struggled to remain silent beneath his tongue and bit back every gratified sob that rose to the back of her throat.

The priest raised his head from between her legs and glared at the grille. Momentarily his fingers stopped squirming in Justine's sex as he lifted his face to hers. He was panting with arousal and, when he placed his mouth against her ear, Justine could feel that the wetness of her sex had dampened his lips, chin and cheek. The intimacy of that sensation made her excitement grow more profound.

'This worthless *putain* is fucking her sister's husband,' he explained.

Justine nodded, realising she had understood that small part of the penitent's confession. Her concern for the woman's sin was barely negligible. In her heightened state of arousal Justine thought the penitent could have fucked her way through the entire village and she would have cared less. She was more focused on having the priest satisfy those needs that lingered in the fetid warmth of her loins. Nevertheless she forced herself to listen to him when he pushed his mouth closer to her ear.

'I do not want to absolve her of her sins,' he breathed. 'There are not enough penances to atone for such deviance. I want to punish this *putain* the way I would punish you. What do you suggest?'

She hesitated before trying to think of a response. It was clear that the priest genuinely did want her input and she surmised this was another aspect of the test she was undergoing. Racking her brains for the right way to reply, trying to think of an answer that would show him she was worthy of acquiring *La Coste*, Justine was delighted when inspiration finally struck.

Pushing her mouth over the priest's ear, cupping a hand against the side of his head so there was no danger of her voice escaping, she whispered, 'Tell her to show you her bare backside.'

The priest pulled away from her for a moment, and then raised an eyebrow.

Justine pushed her mouth over his ear and urgently whispered the remainder of her plan. All the time she was talking she was painfully aware of the priest's body pressing against hers. He still wore his vestments, the pectoral cross continued to stick painfully into one of her breasts, but his nearness was as sexually stimulating as the two fingers he continued to wriggle inside her pussy. His chest was broad and manly and it crushed heavily against her breasts. Stiffness had returned to his length and she could feel the pulse of his eager shaft through the coarse fabric of his cassock. Their half of the confessional booth was sultry with the heat from their passion and the scents of her arousal tinged every breath. Equally exciting was the daring of her plan to punish and subjugate the woman on the other side of the confessional's grille. She didn't know if the priest would follow her suggestions but she couldn't deny that there was a thrill in dictating a penitent's fate.

The priest pulled himself away from Justine's mouth. His dark smile glinted in the confessional's gloom. Turning to the grille, he barked a series of gruff instructions through the small window. Justine could hear shock and incredulity in the woman's responses but she had heard the note of acquiescence in her tone long before she saw the buttocks being pressed against the open grille.

The penitent's backside was bare. The split of her sex was pushed up against the small opening and, when the priest slid the grille aside, Justine was shocked to find herself staring at a stranger's pussy. Although her idea for punishment had been exciting, and seemed appropriate at the time, she hadn't expected the priest to really use one of his parishioners in such a perverted manner.

49

But the thoughts of her own depravity were quickly brushed aside. She inhaled the heady perfume of the woman's musk and peered at the delicate wet labia surrounding her soft undulating hole.

The priest glanced at Justine. He waited until she had nodded approval before stroking a finger against the woman's pussy. In the thickening silence of the confessional booth they both heard the parishioner moan when he touched her. The delicate flesh of her sex flushed to a darker hue and Justine watched the lips grow shinier in the darkness as they were freshly polished with a new lacquer of arousal.

Silently, the priest encouraged Justine to do as he had done. Before she realised she was obeying him, Justine watched her own hand stroke the curly tendrils of hair covering the woman's cleft. Enthralled by the daring of her actions, she slid the tip of her finger along the split of the penitent's pussy lips. When she heard the woman sigh with fresh enthusiasm, Justine dared to push a finger into her cleft.

The arousal inside her was almost too powerful to contain.

The priest's fingers remained inside Justine's pussy and his thumb occasionally rubbed back and forth over her clitoris. She already knew that the stimulation was more than enough to satisfy her burgeoning appetite for depravity, but touching the stranger provided more excitement than she had ever conceived she would enjoy. The perversity of being abused by a priest; the sacrilege of hearing someone else's confession; and the enchanting sensation of warm wet pussy muscles engulfing her finger; all blended to make her feel sick with an overload of arousal. Nevertheless, although she couldn't recall ever experiencing such furious excitement, she fought to contain her response and merely teased the gaping cleft that had been pushed at the confessional's grille.

'*Retournez à votre soeur,*' the priest growled.

Justine quivered when she heard him speaking. She didn't know what he was saying but the music of his gruff voice trembled through the fingers in her sex. The prospect of another climax loomed closer and she slid a second finger alongside the one she already held in the penitent's pussy. The parishioner sobbed with delight and Justine briefly envied the woman her freedom to voice her responses. She quietly yearned to cry out in gratitude for the ecstasy she was enjoying and could have screamed from the combination of injustice and frustration.

The priest traced his tongue against the labia at the grille, then barked another instruction to the penitent. Justine heard him use the word *putain*, and she guessed he was following the exact plan she had suggested. A fresh flutter of arousal churned through her sex. Her pleasure was exacerbated by the priest's fingers tickling deeper. In the tense silence of the confessional she could hear her labia slurping wetly around his hand.

The penitent moaned, her cries coming from somewhere between arousal and mortification. Justine had suggested she should be made to go home and confess her sins to her sister. She had then said the woman should beg her sister to stripe her backside as punishment for her infidelity. It had seemed like a cruel punishment, and she thought the priest would appreciate her innovation. But, because he had now been speaking for so long, Justine guessed he was saying something more and she wondered if he was elaborating on her idea.

'*Alors, reviens ici si je peux voir qu'il a été fait.*'

He pushed his mouth over Justine's ear and whispered, 'I have told her to come back here once her backside has been striped, so I can see that the punishment has been meted.'

The image was too much for Justine. She could easily picture red weals emblazoned across the woman's buttocks and that thought pushed her excitement beyond being bearable. She squeezed her sex hungrily around the priest's fingers, pushed her hand deeper into the penitent's pussy and allowed the thrill of another release to quiver through her body.

She snatched her hand away and forced herself to remain still while the priest repeated his instructions, and listened as the penitent mumbled mortified agreement. The last thing she heard, before the grille was snapped closed, was the woman whispering, '*Oui, mon Père. Merci, mon Père.*'

'That was nicely vindictive,' the priest chuckled.

Once again, his mouth was over Justine's ear and his breath heated each word. She trembled against him, not sure why he triggered such a lecherous response and not wanting to rationalise her feelings. It was more satisfying simply to press into his embrace and relish the myriad delights he tormented from her body.

'I think I might abuse her fully when the *putain* returns to show me her punished arse,' the priest confided. 'You really are a deviant.'

Justine wouldn't let herself dwell on the picture of the priest forcing the penitent to submit to his will. It was heady enough surrendering herself to the man. The idea of him tormenting another innocent victim was too arousing for her to entertain without suffering another thrill of satisfaction. She wanted to deny the priest's accusation that she was a deviant, but there was already the sound of someone else entering the confessional and she bit her lower lip in an attempt to stay silent.

'*Père, pardonnez-moi car j'ai péché.*'

The priest pushed his mouth close to Justine's ear. She could detect the musk of her pussy on his breath when he spoke and the scent was maddeningly intoxicating. 'What do you suggest I do with this one?' he asked.

'You don't know what's he's done yet,' she returned.

'Does it matter?'

She caught her breath, enthralled by the idea of punishment without motive. Glancing toward the grille, intending to turn her thoughts to something truly twisted, she gasped when she saw the small window had been opened and a face was leering in at her.

The priest above her grinned and Justine instantly understood that he had been expecting this particular man. She glanced again at the newcomer's porcine features and shrank from the lechery in his expression. He drew a dark pink tongue across thick over-ripe lips while appraising her heavily shadowed nudity. Without glancing in the direction of the priest he asked, 'When can I use her?'

Justine shook her head and thought about protesting but she knew it would do no good. Squirming at the thought of what she might be expected to endure, she glanced helplessly at the priest and silently implored him to show mercy.

'If you clear the church for me, Bishop, I shall bring the little slut out.'

Justine glanced from one to the other.

'Consider it done,' the bishop mumbled.

He broadened his grin as he appraised her body for a final time, and then drew his face away from the window. And, still cramped in the confines of the confessional, and growing more frightened than ever, Justine wondered what the pair would plan to do with her once they had her alone.

Four

The bishop opened the door to the confessional and pulled Justine into the church. He wasn't dressed as she had expected: instead of wearing full ceremonial attire he simply wore a white collar, slacks and a sports jacket. His face was fat and piggish with beady eyes and a snout-like nose. The jacket was open to reveal a potbelly straining against the waist of his burgundy shirt. The lechery in his smile was disquieting.

'Very good, Father.' He flashed his grin at the priest behind Justine. 'What do you want to do with her?'

The priest stepped out of the confessional and, dwarfed between the pair of them, Justine found herself growing more and more uneasy. They made a foreboding team and, because she was naked and standing in their church, she realised they had her at a definite disadvantage. Her hands began to tremble with fresh disquiet.

'She wants to acquire *La Coste*,' the priest explained to his colleague. 'Shall we see what she is prepared to sacrifice to make that acquisition?'

Before Justine could think of trying to escape they had each grabbed a wrist. She struggled to pull herself free but they seemed united in their goal of leading her toward the front of the church. Her bare feet had no hope of gaining any traction on the cold stone floor and, as they dragged her past the rows of empty pews, she realised she was at their mercy. Genuine terror began to chill the heat of her arousal and she stared from one unsympathetic face to the other.

The bishop reached for one of her breasts. He squeezed and tugged brutally at the flesh. His plump fingers burrowed into the skin and the calloused pads rasped against her like sandpaper. Moments earlier she had been yearning for the priest to satisfy the unaddressed ache in her nipples. Her breasts had been throbbing with their plaintive need for attention. But, now that the repulsive bishop was toying with her, she simply wanted both men to leave her alone. There was something degrading in the way the bishop touched her and, although her body remained oily with the sweat from her most recent orgasm, she could no longer think beyond the notions of revulsion and sacrilege.

'She's looking for *La Coste*?' the bishop asked incredulously. 'She doesn't stand a chance of getting her hands on it, does she?'

The priest's shrug was indifferent. 'She is on her way to acquiring it.'

The bishop looked surprised. One of the hands that held Justine's wrist momentarily loosened. The fingers that kneaded at her breast were briefly held still. 'You're joking with me, aren't you?'

The priest shook his head. 'So far, she has deemed herself worthy. I have not yet seen a reason to refuse my blessing.'

The bishop looked aghast. 'But she's an *English girl*. Marais would never allow the manuscript to go to an *English girl*.'

'Marais is selling *La Coste*. He is not giving it away to a worthy cause.'

'But still . . .' The revulsion in the bishop's voice was obvious and he seemed at a loss for how to express his dismay. '. . . an *English girl*,' he floundered.

The journey to the front of the church was swift but mortifying. Justine felt as though she was suffering the sneers of contempt from the surrounding statues and stained-glass frescoes. When she was dragged onto the altar, then laid on her back to stare up at the beams on the church's ceiling, she began to fret about what the pair might be planning. Her hands were tied to an invisible point above her head. Her legs were spread open and her ankles secured on either side of the altar. The priest disappeared from Justine's limited line of vision but the bishop continued to hover over her. He constantly licked his lips as his abrasive fingers scurried over her breasts. His caresses scratched against her sides and bare stomach before his hands slipped down to explore her cleft.

She stiffened.

If there had been any way for Justine to show her distaste for the man she would have pulled away from the altar at the first opportunity. Because the bindings at her wrists and ankles were inordinately tight, she could only lay where she was bound and suffer his unwanted exploration. Dry clumsy fingers plundered her sex. Whereas the priest's touch had been sensitive and exciting, the bishop's was coarse and hateful. His hands became dewy with the remnants of her wetness, and she could feel the greasy residue of her passion being used as a lubricant as he prodded the sensitive rim of her anus.

She almost choked on her sudden need to exclaim and tell him not to touch such an intimate place. But – remembering the silence that was expected from her, and the acquiescence the priest had demanded – Justine told herself there were no parts of her body that the bishop wasn't allowed to explore.

The liturgical chant of a Latin prayer interrupted her thoughts. She could hear the priest's mellifluous tones enunciating each word so it rang from the faraway beams in the ceiling. The tang of something different on the air made her sniff and she realised a dusky incense was now perfuming the church. Raising her head, looking beyond her own body as the bishop pawed at her cleft and breasts, she saw the priest was walking toward her with a swinging censer at his hip.

It was a horrible sight to behold: something she knew she shouldn't have been seeing while she was naked and in the clutches of a black arousal. Guilt and self-loathing tormented her, all the time exacerbating her dark need for satisfaction. She started to lie back down and then noticed that, while he had been touching and stroking with one hand, the bishop had also been busy preparing Justine's immediate surroundings. Votive candles, their soft flames guttering gently by her sides, stood precariously close to her bound body. She stared at the bishop with mounting panic and found no reassurance in his lascivious grin.

'What are you prepared to sacrifice?' he asked.

As he spoke, his hand slipped against her sex. The fingers moved easily over her sodden cleft and then returned to the tight ring of her anus. She stiffened at his touch, despising the bristle of pleasure that struck her. When he pushed hard against her forbidden hole, forcing his finger to break past the barrier of muscle, she almost squealed.

The priest continued to chant his Latin prayer, the words adding a mysticism and air of religious authority that Justine felt shamed to be desecrating. She lay on an altar, beneath sorrowful figures of the Madonna and child and a crucified Christ, while a bishop fingered her anus. All those acts that she had done before – drinking the priest's semen from the communion chalice, fucking over the consecrated ground of the Dupont grave, and even tormenting the penitent young woman in the confessional – now seemed like harmless pranks compared to the ungodliness of what she was enduring.

'You want me to initiate her?' the bishop asked the priest.

Justine raised her head so she could watch the exchange between the two men. The priest busied himself with his censer and his chant but he managed to nod consent in the bishop's direction. She glanced at the piggy man looming over her and saw he had already released his erection from his pants.

The sight made her feel dizzy.

The length of pink flesh protruded from the dark trousers. The swollen end was a vicious purple and she could see the eye leaking a clear fluid of arousal. Her breathing quickened and fresh doubts returned as the bishop positioned himself between her legs. Unable to stop herself, Justine shook her head from side to side as though refusing him entry.

'Don't be such a prude,' he growled. 'I can see you want this.'

She swallowed and wondered if the terms she had agreed with the priest would allow her to refuse the bishop. She suspected that any protest would qualify her as unfit to acquire *La Coste* but, still, a part of her was desperate to make her reservations known.

He stood between her spread thighs, the back of one hand stroking absently against the smooth flesh. The contact was maddening: exciting her when she didn't want to be aroused and making her resolve weaken. When he began to push his length closer, nudging the rounded end of his shaft nearer and nearer, she sighed with resignation and told herself she could tolerate whatever the pair planned. It was only when she felt the tip of the bishop's erection touch the centre of her anus that all her doubts returned.

She pulled away from him as far as her bondage would allow.

A brief frowned crossed his face. It disappeared to be replaced by a twisted grin and he didn't need to speak for Justine to understand he was going to take his pleasure from her suffering. Knowing she was in no position to refuse, Justine tried to remain calm and unaffected as he pushed into her forbidden hole.

The ring of muscle resisted at first but the bishop's determination was strong. Within moments of him pressing his shaft against her, Justine felt the length plough into her rear. The muscle was forced open, she willed herself not to be won over by the delicious sensation of being violated. And she wouldn't let her body willingly enjoy the penetration. She held her breath and bit her lower lip as the length pushed further inside.

He was not as broadly built as the priest but he was thick enough to inflict a good deal of discomfort. Admittedly there was a wealth of pleasure flourishing from her anus. The sensations were so intense Justine quickly grew giddy from the effort of trying to fight off the threat of orgasm.

'Bless this godforsaken creature,' the bishop murmured.

He was nestled so deep into her rear she could feel the cloth of his pants pressed against her buttocks. The inner muscles of her rectum bulged from the pressure of his shaft and she choked back the urge to cry out. The bishop's porcine face loomed above hers, his eyelids heavy with bliss and his cheeks flushed with satisfaction. He made the sign of the cross as he spoke, droplets of sweat falling from his fingers like a spattering of Holy Water.

When he began to pull back, sliding his length from her sphincter, Justine wanted to groan. The penetration was painful – his shaft was thicker than anything she had ever dared insert into that particular place – but the experience wasn't just an exercise in discomfort. She chugged breath in an effort to control her responses, resenting the rush of bliss that wanted to erupt from her bowel.

Behind the bishop, the priest continued to idle slowly up and down the empty aisle. He solemnly chanted his prayer and wafted his censer with the same majesty

Justine suspected he would use in front of his congregation. The statues of Christ and the Madonna continued to frown down upon her, the bishop's erection continued to plough in and out of her rear, and Justine couldn't hide from the knowledge that she was desecrating something holy.

The first tremor of an impending orgasm began to tremble through her bound body. The bishop rode her anus with a slow build of speed, his length thickening as the moment of his climax drew closer. The large head of his glans felt infuriatingly divine in her rear and she braced herself for the impact of his eruption.

Her breath had fallen to a series of urgent grunts. Each animalistic cry echoed around the hollow acoustics of the church. Shivers of raw ecstasy made her tug aimlessly on the restraints and she savoured each fresh flourish of pain that was wrung from her ankles and wrists.

And, as the bishop continued to thrust into her, the swelling of pleasure in her bowel grew too large to contain. She clenched her teeth and tried to resist the pull of the orgasm. But the excitement was too intense. The bishop slid easily in and out of her backside, his pace as obvious and urgent as her own growing need. She could feel his length throbbing and knew he was on the verge of a climax, and in that instant the combination of pleasure, pain and degradation proved too much.

With a roar of satisfaction Justine allowed the climax to tear through her.

The bishop held himself still as she shivered and bucked around his shaft. Her anus squeezed and convulsed – she knew her sphincter would have expelled his length if he hadn't been holding himself so deep inside – and another blistering wave of delight scourged her rear. She was madly wondering how he was able to contain his own explosion when his ejaculation pulsed and the hot sticky seed of his climax spurted into her. The combination of warmth and his tremors fuelled another surge of delight and she shrieked as the despicable joy struck again and again.

The fury of her orgasms left Justine's cheeks flushed. Tears streamed from her eyes and she sobbed with a mixture of satisfaction, relief and guilt. Even as the bishop slipped his spent shaft from her anus – his wetness making her feel repulsed and aroused in the same moment – Christ and the Madonna continued to glare down at Justine on the altar. Uneasily, she realised her shame and excitement had blended into one seamless response.

'Continue blessing the church,' the priest decided.

He pushed the bishop aside and placed himself between Justine's legs. His erection, familiar to her now, already protruded from the folds of his cassock. Justine tried to squirm away as he pushed himself toward her but it was a half-hearted attempt at modesty and she didn't try to make it look convincing. Her eagerness to experience more had reached a new level. Even though she felt degraded to have the priest's entry lubricated by the bishop's semen, the desire to have her anus filled was a greater driving force.

His hands went to her thighs and he held her legs apart as he pushed into her.

She gasped happily with delight.

His thick shaft was gloriously wide inside her anus and filled her with a far more satisfying presence than the bishop had managed. The swollen head of his glans felt much too large for her tight confines and she couldn't imagine accommodating anything larger. But he rode her with patient vigour and slid easily in and out of her aching hole. His hands gripped loosely against her thighs, clutching the sensitive flesh and holding her in the position he desired, and he made each forward thrust fill her with his entire length.

This time Justine found the experience more satisfying.

The statues continued to look down on her and, while she could still see disapproval in their stony faces, she no longer found that hampered her ability to enjoy the moment. The priest cursed her with a now familiar vitriol. He emphasised every harsh invective and sprayed her face with accidental droplets of spittle. As he slipped his length back and forth the waves of pleasure flowed through her with furious force.

Voices beyond her range of vision threatened to interrupt the moment but the priest's thrusting quickly tore her attention back to the pleasure between her legs. He reached for her jaw with one hand, held her face so she was forced to stare into his eyes, and muttered something in an indecipherable grunt. Without understanding the words, Justine knew she had been told to ignore distractions and concentrate only on what he was doing for her.

He quickened his pace, hammering into her backside with a force that made her sick with delight. Tremors had begun to pulsate along his shaft and the prospect of his climax was infuriatingly imminent. Justine gritted her teeth, desperate to come again before the priest was spent. Now that she had found the ability to accept the religious paraphernalia around her, the need for orgasm struck her with punishing force. Tensing the muscles of her anus around the priest's shaft, savouring every sordid sensation as he eased himself in and out, she choked back tears when the final eruption coursed through her. The orgasm was made perfect when the priest's explosion filled her hole. The rush of his hot copious spend thrilled her and made her sob with gratitude.

It took her a moment to regain her bearings after the climax.

She expected to recover from a haze of delight while still laying on the altar but the priest quickly unfastened her bondage and dragged her away. She was deposited rudely on the chancel, poignantly aware of her nudity with icy fingers of guilt renewing their grip at her chest. The bishop and the priest loomed over her and, sitting beneath them, Justine saw the penitent young woman had returned to the church. Without the discretion of the confessional booth Justine now felt awkward beneath the woman's sullen frown. The flush of the orgasm, the pleasure and decadence Justine had so recently enjoyed, ebbed away as she realised she remained at the mercy of the priest and his bishop.

'You told this girl to come back when she'd been punished,' the priest reminded Justine. 'What do you want to do with her?'

Justine glanced from the priest to the bishop, then to the penitent village girl.

She suspected that the priest wanted her to issue another punishment, possibly as a further test to prove herself worthy of acquiring *La Coste*. But after all that she had endured so far this evening, Justine couldn't bring herself to inflict any more suffering on the young woman. She was tired and drained and beyond caring about any of those things that had seemed so vital earlier. Not bothered if it affected her chances of attaining the damned manuscript, too weary to think of anything beyond her need for sleep and a shower, she said, 'Absolve her. She's suffered enough abuse for our entertainment.'

The priest and the bishop exchanged a glance that Justine couldn't read.

Too weary to trouble herself with what they might be thinking, Justine levered herself away from the floor and started to stagger past the trio. The priest grabbed her by one arm and stopped her. In a stiff tone, he said, 'Wait here.'

With her shoulders slumped, Justine did as he instructed.

The priest turned to the bishop. 'Do as she says,' he decided. 'Absolve the *putain*. Then tell her, as penance, she will accompany Justine on the next leg of her journey.'

'You're going to recommend her as a worthy recipient of *La Coste*?'

Justine listened attentively, desperate to hear the answer to that question, but the priest turned his back on the bishop without giving a reply. His grin was menacing as he forced her down to her knees. Stepping over her, brandishing his erection in her face, he pushed the sodden end against her mouth. The tip was slick with saliva, semen and the spent musk of bowel. But, even though he had only just climaxed inside her anus, Justine could see he was already growing hard. The length of wet flesh glistened in the church's candlelight.

'You've been obedient so far this evening,' he growled. 'Suck this again and I shall deem you worthy of having met with my approval.'

Her momentary weariness was banished by the instruction. The knowledge that she was on the verge of achieving her goal made Justine eager to do anything he asked. Unable to resist that instruction, she forced her mouth around his erection and sucked. She was delighted to feel him thicken and knew it would not take long to coax the climax from him. And, with her optimism rising, she knew that as soon as she started to swallow the priest's seed, she would be one step closer to acquiring *La Coste*.

Five

Justine awoke to the sound of her mobile phone ringing.

It would have been the perfect morning to be disoriented; she didn't recognise the bedroom; couldn't recall the name of the woman lying by her side; and would have been hard pushed to remember how she had travelled from the church to wherever it was she now resided. The name Sartine nagged at her memory but she couldn't recall why or whether it was in a good context or a bad one. The insistent trill of the phone wouldn't allow her the luxury of lazily recollecting any of those details. She hastily snatched the mobile from her purse and glanced at the display.

PRIVATE NUMBER

She frowned, contemplated not accepting the call, and then decided there would be no harm in pressing the green key.

'Hello?'

'Justine?'

She recognised Mrs Weiss's austere tone and breathed a sigh of relief. Since arriving in France the previous day her employer's was the first familiar voice she had heard. Even though she cared little for the woman, and felt sure her antipathy was reciprocated, Justine surrendered to a wave of gratitude for the call. 'Yes?' She lowered her voice to a whisper and hunched her shoulders conspiratorially. 'It's me,' she hissed. 'I've already seen the first contact and now I'm –'

'You haven't told anyone you're working for me, have you?'

Justine frowned and racked her brains, trying to think if she had let that small detail escape at any point. From what she remembered of the previous evening neither the priest nor the bishop had troubled her with too many questions and Justine felt sure it wasn't a piece of information she would have volunteered without prompting. She felt confident she was telling the truth when she carefully replied, 'No. You told me not to, didn't you?'

'Keep it that way,' Mrs Weiss growled. 'No matter what happens: you don't admit to knowing me. My involvement in this acquisition cannot be made public under any circumstances.'

She spoke with a characteristic brusqueness that reminded Justine why she had wanted to leave the woman's employment. 'Of course,' she began. 'I had no intentions of telling anyone that I'm –'

'And be on your guard when you meet Sartine,' Mrs Weiss broke in. 'The slippery French bastard has a truly sly way about him.'

Justine wanted to ask who Sartine was, and what he might want from her, but her employer was clearly in no mood for elaborating. In a crisp and businesslike voice, she snapped, 'Don't let me down on this. Present a plausible front to Sartine, go on and satisfy the third representative from *The Society*, and you'll receive the bonus I promised.'

'Who are *The Society*?' she broke in.

Mrs Weiss snorted with disgust. 'You'll get a different answer to that question depending on who you ask. The priest will tell you *The Society* are a bunch of perverted heathens all damned to hell. Sartine will say *The Society* are a collective of hedonists and libertines. Marais would undoubtedly come up with some bullshit about them being the living embodiment of de Sade's legacy.

66

Pick the answer you prefer. They've all got their own ring of truth.'

'What would you tell me?' Justine pressed.

Again, Mrs Weiss snorted with disgust. It was frustrating to find herself involved in a conversation over hundreds of miles where she didn't understand much except for the exclamations of contempt. It was also depressing to find the first friendly voice she had encountered since arriving in France was treating her with obvious and upsetting disdain. 'If you asked me,' Mrs Weiss growled, 'I'd say *The Society* was nothing more than a lending library. And if you kept asking me, I'd want to know why you're interrogating me when I'm the one who called you.' Her voice had risen and was suddenly near to screeching with anger. 'I phoned you to make a point, Justine. If anyone asks you, if anyone tries to prise the information from you: you don't know me. Do you understand?'

'Of course I understand,' Justine agreed. 'That was our arrangement.'

Mrs Weiss continued as though she hadn't heard Justine's side of the conversation. 'No matter what else happens, that's the most important thing you must remember: *you do not know me.*'

Justine was about to assure the woman that she had remembered – and say the incessant repetition of the instruction was making her feel stupid and inadequate – but the mobile was already dead in her hand. She continued to frown as she slipped the phone back into her purse, puzzling over all that had been said and trying to make sense of those parts she had understood. It was more than she wanted to think about and, rather than taxing herself with problems she had no hope of solving, Justine took a moment to glance at the room where she had awoken.

It looked like a hotel room – a little plusher than she was used to – but a hotel room all the same. A mini-bar lurked in one corner; identical robust doorways stood on adjacent walls; and a laminated sheet by the dressing mirror showed instructions for what to do in the event of a fire. The furnishings, fixtures and fittings had the tired look she had seen in many hotels previously with everything washed and cleaned to a lacklustre beige. Sunlight filtering through the drawn curtains added a pall of mystical charm to the scene. The light was hazy enough for Justine to imagine that she might still be asleep and dreaming. In that context she could better understand her baffling conversation with Mrs Weiss.

A whispered sigh snatched her attention back to the bed.

The curiosity of the hotel room and the mystery of how she had arrived there were instantly forgotten. Her heart started to race and a warm arousal spread through her loins. She was distantly aware of her nipples growing rigid, the skin stretching as it pulled itself taut. The cleft between her legs was suddenly slick with fetid perspiration.

A naked blonde lay in the same bed that Justine had vacated. She looked pretty, her corn-coloured hair tousled and her pale blue eyes beginning to flutter open as she started to wake. While climbing out of the bed Justine realised she had inadvertently pulled the sheet from the blonde's body and exposed a flat stomach and a pair of deliciously pert breasts. The woman's nipples stood hard, as though she had been revelling in an exciting dream, and Justine shivered sympathetically. Surreptitiously, she stole a hand against her own chest and trembled as her flesh responded to the caress.

Foggy recollection told her this was the penitent she had met at the church. She remembered the priest had said the woman would be instructed to accompany her but Justine hadn't expected to find the blonde sleeping naked by her side. Unaware she was doing it, Justine traced her tongue across her lips. Salacious thoughts began to wend their way through her mind and she was unnerved to find each one slightly more appealing.

For the first time she noticed her own nudity.

Her body bore distinctive marks from the abuse she had suffered in the church. Reddened skin on her breasts – a parting gift from the bishop, she recalled – blazed obviously against her wan flesh. The dry residue of the priest's semen – pungent and sickening – lingered between her breasts and at the tops of her thighs. She couldn't honestly say she was proud of the reminders but she was in no mood for hiding herself from the penitent either. Rather than trying to conceal or cover herself Justine thought it felt more natural to go and sit by the woman's side.

The light weave of the bed's top sheet was cool against her bare buttocks. Her awareness seemed suddenly heightened and she could feel the weft of the fabric grazing against her pussy lips. The caress was invigorating and thrilled her with a sense of dull anticipation. Amazed by her own daring, and excited by the ideas that twisted and formed in the back of her mind, Justine stroked the back of her hand against the penitent's soft cheek.

The woman's eyes fluttered open.

A soft smile stole across her lips.

And she made no objection as Justine's hand trailed lower. The only change in her expression came as her smile grew wide with unspoken encouragement.

Justine watched herself as though viewing the scene through someone else's eyes. Her hand inched downwards: along the length of the penitent's neck and brushing the blonde tresses aside. Her fingertips tingled as though they were charged with electricity. Justine hesitated and drew a short breath before finding the courage to touch the woman's bare breast. The skin was exquisitely soft and, as she drew her fingers over the thrust of the blonde's nipple, Justine was amazed to feel the taut bud of flesh grow fat with arousal.

Together, they both drew eager breaths.

Justine considered saying something and then decided it would be counterproductive and likely to spoil the mood. She didn't speak the penitent's language – it had always been a source of her bitterest frustration that she could never grasp the nuances of French – and Justine suspected that any conversation they could manage would be stilted and inconclusive. Having to go through the rigmarole of establishing a communication system seemed particularly facile when it was clear they had no need for words.

Allowing her confidence to soar in the silence, she lowered her head until her lips hovered over the blonde's nipple.

They maintained eye contact with the penitent's expression spurring Justine's excitement to fresh heights. Even without a common language she readily understood so many things that the blonde wanted to say. There was encouragement in her gaze. The eagerness was muted by wariness and doubt but her desire was clear and obvious. The woman's smile broadened when Justine touched the tip of her tongue against the fat bud of her nipple.

'*Merci*,' she began.

Justine placed her finger over the woman's lips to silence her.

Rather than merely accepting the instruction, the penitent took Justine's finger into her mouth. She encircled the flesh with her ripe lips and sucked lightly on the end. The tip of her tongue trilled against Justine's finger, inspiring a liquid thrill of arousal. Her eyes were wide and her cheeks dimpled as she sucked with sultry vigour.

Startled by the woman's response, Justine pulled her hand away.

She and the penitent regarded each other in a stilted silence while Justine wondered if she should make some attempt to try and find a way for them to communicate. The prospect of rummaging through her case to find the phrase book held little appeal. Even if she found it, Justine didn't think there would be any use in them exchanging *bonjours*, *au revoirs*, or even a *comment allez-vous*. Although the book she had purchased was advertised as comprehensive, she suspected it wouldn't contain translations for the questions she most wanted answering.

'*Has your parish priest always been a perverted bastard?*' and '*How much control do I have over your body?*' or '*Do you truly want all those pleasures I can see in your eyes?*' were seldom included in phrase books.

It was while the thoughts were tumbling through her mind, and as she tried to grasp the relationship she was supposed to have with the penitent, that their lips met.

Afterward Justine couldn't recall which of them had instigated the kiss. She didn't know if the blonde had leaned up or if she had pushed herself on top of the woman. The only thing she did know was that their bodies fitted snugly together in a passionate embrace. The flimsy sheet was pushed aside as they struggled to touch bare flesh against bare flesh. The pert breasts crushed against Justine's chest and she was delighted to feel the scrub of pubic hairs scratching at her thigh. As their arms and legs intertwined she grew delirious with a rush of arousal that tortured her responses.

But it was the kiss that stayed with her as being the most memorable aspect of that morning in the hotel room. Even though they were hugging and touching each other with animalistic ferocity; even though they were scratching thighs, breasts and legs with their nails, squeezing, cupping and clawing with their fervency to experience each other, it was the softness of the penitent's kiss that fixed itself in Justine's memory.

Their tongues touched, explored and tasted. The penitent's lips slipped easily against Justine's mouth. The only time their kiss broke was when each moved her head slightly back to gasp with satisfaction. But those moments were quickly ended as they hungrily returned to tasting each other.

It was an exchange that left Justine crippled with anticipation.

She didn't know why that aspect of the intimacy struck her as being the most rewarding. The penitent had already introduced two fingers into the slippery folds of Justine's pussy and was idly sliding them in and out of the dank confines. The pulse of Justine's clitoris throbbed with an unsatisfied ache and that pace quickened each time the blonde stroked her thumb across the trembling nub of flesh.

The prospect of orgasm loomed ever closer.

Anxious to experience the woman, Justine fondled the blonde's breasts, savouring their size and firmness. The sensation of stroking another woman was something she hadn't enjoyed before. Admittedly, it was a fantasy she had entertained in the seclusion of her own bed but she had never taken it any further than a thrilling image designed to add to her personal pleasure. The subsequent joy of touching the blonde was more gratifying than she had ever expected.

But still, it was the kiss that struck her as being the most erotic aspect of the encounter.

The blonde squeezed a third finger into the wetness of Justine's hole.

She worked her wrist back and forth, never using force, but all the time urging Justine to a higher plane of pleasure. The slurping squelch of her sex lips reverberated through the stillness of the room and the sound made itself heard above the pounding of adrenaline in Justine's temples. Escalating waves promised to drown her in a sea of swelling euphoria and she couldn't decide whether to surrender to the climax or steel herself against its tempestuous strength.

A knock on the door threatened to disturb her mood.

Like startled conspirators, she and the penitent immediately turned to stare at the door. Justine had the time to realise they both looked shocked and guilty and then she was closing her eyes against the rush of ecstasy being wrung from her sex. Continuing to enjoy each other, unmindful of whoever was trying to intrude, they carried on basking in each other's embrace as their climaxes stole closer.

The blonde gasped beneath Justine, her pleasure evident in the depth of each breath and the sultry pout of her kiss. From the familiar tingling in the pit of her womb Justine knew her own orgasm was building to its peak. She squeezed her inner muscles around the fingers, pushed herself hard against the penitent's hand, and waited for the surge of elation to sweep through her body.

Another knock resounded on the door.

'Madame Justine? Are you awake? May I enter?'

The voice was heavily accented, female and young. Although it came from the other side of a closed door, Justine could picture that it belonged to a dark-haired beauty dressed in a servant's uniform of some description. She didn't know where the mental image came from and, before it could settle in her thoughts, she had dismissed it as she concentrated on the woman in her arms.

The penitent pressed her naked body closer. One arm was wrapped around Justine's waist, the hand clutching Justine's backside. Her other was between their writhing bodies with the fingers briskly plundering Justine's cleft. Employing a delicious skill, the penitent stroked in and out of Justine's wetness. Their kiss continued to excite with tongues touching and gliding easily against each other. Tremors began to wrack through them both, and

Justine sighed as their bodies shuddered violently together.

'Madame Justine?'

This time, rather than hearing the caller knock, Justine was aware of the distinctive sound of a key rattling inside a lock. The panic she had experienced before returned with the same brutal force but she couldn't bring herself to end her exchange with the penitent. Thrusting herself urgently on the hand in her pussy, willing her body to broach the precipice of orgasm that she now needed to enjoy, Justine growled with satisfaction as the first rush of pleasure soared through her frame.

She was still shivering through the throes of the orgasm as she tumbled from the bed and rushed to the door to try and prevent the caller from bursting into the room. Her body wanted to languish against the sheets and savour the pleasure but modesty wouldn't allow her to be caught in such an undignified and embarrassing position. After all the humiliation and embarrassment she had suffered the previous evening, Justine didn't think she could endure any more shame and she surprised herself by finding the resolve to rush to the door.

Too late, she saw a maid stood in the open doorway.

Her impassive features revealed nothing. The maid returned a bunch of keys to the pocket of her tabard and studied Justine with measured indifference. 'I am sorry to disturb you,' she began.

Her tone was so bereft of emotion that Justine doubted there was any sincerity in the remark. Not sure she could convincingly pretend to have not heard the maid, and unwilling to offer any other explanation for not answering her call, Justine asked, 'What do you want?'

'Captain Sartine has requested you join him in the dining room. He's expecting you in fifteen minutes.' She

74

cast a cool glance at Justine's naked body and added, 'Clothes have been provided for you in the wardrobe.'

'Who is Captain Sartine?'

'You do not know?'

'No.'

The maid's smile was almost vindictive. 'Captain Sartine is the man you will be seeing in the dining room in fifteen minutes.' Without saying anything further, she left Justine and the penitent alone.

Six

Captain Sartine sat at the head of a long table. Justine could see he was an imposing figure and she guessed he would normally have commanded the attention of the entire room. His neatly styled hair was jet black and cropped so it bristled with military efficiency. Wearing an ice-white shirt that clung to his muscular shoulders and chest, he held himself with a regimented stiffness that made him look like an off-duty soldier. It was easy to picture him in charge of a regiment or a platoon, barking orders and revelling in his authority. Everything about him demanded that he should be considered the centre of attention.

But Justine barely glanced at him.

The room was spacious and brightly lit.

Dominated by a massive dining table beneath a glittering chandelier, the design and decor struck her as typical of contemporary French elegance. The pastel walls were broken by uncurtained windows each framing a majestic view of the Provence valley outside. An azure sky hovered above verdant fields, picturesque copses and a twisting faraway stream. If not for her assignment, Justine knew she would have spent a day admiring every nuance of the view as she sipped endless cafés au lait.

But, this morning, Justine barely blinked in that direction.

She didn't notice the pretty and attentive maids in their black skirts, white blouses and seamed stockings;

or the enthralling selection of framed Impressionists that adorned the walls.

Her attention was fixed on the couple fucking in the centre of the table.

Both of them were naked.

He was a huge man, attractive from what Justine could glimpse, although his face and upper body were hidden beneath the woman straddling him. The definition of each muscle was distinct with tension. Blessed with an athletic build, his flesh was sunbronzed and the fine blond hairs that covered him had been bleached to gold. His large hands stroked and caressed his lover with unhurried urgency.

Justine drew a slow hesitant breath and turned her attention to the slender woman straddling him. Impaled on his length, easing her hips up and down as she rode him, her sighs rose and fell with obvious enjoyment. Her waist looked spectacularly narrow – an optical illusion, Justine guessed, caused by the woman's hips being made large through her ungainly position. Kneeling over her lover, the delicate soles of her small feet were visible beneath her buttocks. Justine could see the woman's toes were curled tight, as though she was held by the same sensation of extreme pleasure that tormented the man she was riding.

Mesmerised by the obscene amount of pink flesh, not sure if she should be shocked, repulsed or delighted, Justine could only gawp as the pair writhed together.

'Good morning, Justine,' Sartine, exclaimed cheerfully. 'Welcome to my hotel.'

She couldn't snatch her gaze away from the couple. The man's erection, glistening with wetness, continued to slide in and out of the woman's sex. She could see the skin was stretched tight from the base of his shaft to the tautly wrinkled sac of his scrotum. The rest of his length was buried deep inside the split of the woman's hole. Her pussy was a lush velvet pink. Glimpses of cerise labia peeped from the dark damp forest of dense pubic curls. Her flushed and glossy lips travelled easily up and down his erection and she moaned with languid enthusiasm.

'The cafetière is still warm,' Sartine said, gesturing to a small table by his side. Justine could see that aside from drinks and crockery there was also a modest selection of croissants. After all that had happened the previous day she knew she should have been hungry but, absorbed by the unexpected intimacy on display, she couldn't bring herself to think about food or drink. She watched the couple on the table as they increased the pace of their lovemaking by a fraction of a beat.

'Don't they make a splendid coupling?'

Sartine could have been speaking the same words that echoed through her mind. After the sordid and unsettling events in the church Justine could only marvel over the beauty of the naked pair on the centre of the table. There was none of the disquiet she had felt as she came to terms with obeying the priest's sacrilegious commands and the participants were perfect specimens of healthy and desirable normality. Admittedly, she could have argued that there was little normality in the pair riding each other on a dining table in the centre of a public room, while staff and guests stood around watching. But, after being used by a priest and bishop beneath statues of Mary and Jesus, Justine couldn't bring herself to condemn the pair for their choice of location.

'They look absolutely splendid,' Justine whispered.

The woman turned to grace her with a warm and welcoming smile. '*Merci*,' she murmured, before turning back to the man beneath her. Her hips didn't once lose their perfect rhythm. As she turned and spoke she continued to glide up and down her lover's long fat erection with perfect practised precision.

'I enjoy watching all my staff,' Sartine explained easily.

He climbed from his chair and chivalrously guided Justine into a seat. With a snap of his fingers he had summoned a maid who set about the chore of organising coffee and a couple of croissants for Justine. She was placed at the foot of the table and had the perfect view of the erection sliding in and out of the beautiful French woman. The sight was so absorbing Justine couldn't drag her gaze away. The food and drink remained forgotten in front of her. The scents of freshly baked bread and delightfully bitter coffee were ignored as she inhaled the perfume of sweat, sex and nudity.

'I don't consider myself a voyeur per se,' Sartine explained as he resumed his seat at the head of the table. He spoke as though they were involved in a hearty discussion, rather than an exchange where Justine had barely managed four coherent words. 'But there's something aesthetically stimulating about the human form during sex. I love to watch the rise and fall of Marie's breasts; the tension in Pierre's body; the beautiful union where their bodies meet; and, of course, the beauty of orgasm. I could watch them for hours, especially when the specimens involved are as stunning as this pair.'

Justine was finally able to drag her gaze away from Pierre and Marie. Even when she wasn't looking she could still catch the scents of their warm bodies and hear the grunts and moans of their pleasure. Although she didn't consider herself to be an expert, she thought it sounded like they were using each other with a forced slowness. The urgency of each gasp, and the wetness easing from Marie's cleft and along Pierre's shaft, made it clear that the couple were close to their inevitable release. Taking a deep breath, and hoping her voice sounded steady, Justine asked, 'Do you have the manuscript, Captain Sartine?'

He laughed. 'That's a very direct question.'

'I'm here to acquire a manuscript.' She finally remembered the coffee and croissants in front of her and busied herself with them. Now that she had finally been able to snatch her gaze from Pierre and Marie she was determined not to be drawn back to the hypnotic pleasure of watching their gorgeous bodies sliding gracefully together. She swallowed a small mouthful of croissant, sipped the coffee and asked, 'Do you have the manuscript that I'm here to acquire?'

'No.' Sartine smiled.

Justine pursed her lips in frustration. 'Then, why am I here?'

'You might be trying to acquire *La Coste*. But that's not why you're in my hotel.'

She raised an eyebrow and studied him guardedly. 'I don't understand.'

'Do you think we make a pretty sight?'

The question came from Marie.

Justine was forced to look away from Sartine and glance up at the woman to meet her gentle gaze. She was a truly beautiful example of femininity. Naked, her bare breasts were visible and the stiff tips of her nipples swayed ever so slightly as she raised and then lowered herself on the erection between her thighs. Her flesh was a swarthy olive tone that complemented her enticing dark hair. The colour of her nipples and areolae was as dark and tempting as the café au lait in Justine's cup.

'I'm sorry?' Justine gasped. She had been caught by Marie's hypnotic gaze and discovered it was almost impossible not to be enthralled by the woman's charm. She had to blink and shake her head to distance herself from the excitement and interest the woman inspired.

'Do you think we make a pretty sight?'

Her voice was heavily accented and she concentrated on each word as though it took an effort to consider and pronounce. There was a husky undercurrent in her tone and Justine didn't think she had ever heard any voice sound so inherently sexy. She squirmed against her seat as she realised an answer was expected of her. Lowering her head, blushing as she nodded, Justine said, 'Yes. I think you make a very pretty sight.'

'Would you like to touch?'

Beyond Marie, lounging idly at the head of his table, Sartine graced Justine with a benevolent smile. His attention seemed relaxed and casual but there was something in the furtive glint of his eyes that made Justine think he was studying her with bright interest. She didn't know if her paranoia came from all that had happened in the church the previous evening, or if some sixth sense was warning that her response to Marie's question would govern her success in acquiring *La Coste*.

Slowly, she extended her hand to Marie.

The French woman grinned and took her fingers. Her touch was warm and moist with a film of perspiration. Holding her hand, Justine was struck by an electric tingle: as though she could feel echoes of Marie's excitement. It was thrilling enough to watch Marie and Pierre as they boldly enjoyed each other in the centre of the table. But the knowledge that she was close to becoming involved in their intimacy made Justine dizzy with arousal.

'I think you would do this much better than me,' Marie confided.

'I doubt it,' Justine said honestly. Bashfully raising her gaze to meet Marie's she added, 'I certainly wouldn't look as attractive.'

Marie's slender fingers encircled Justine's wrist and she guided her to touch the centre of her back. 'Pierre has been ignoring my spine,' she pouted. 'And I adore the sensation of fingers trailing down my back. You can do that for me, no?'

Obligingly, Justine allowed her fingers to glide gently down the centre of Marie's back. The skin beneath her fingers was silky-soft and she shared an echo of the woman's obvious pleasure when Marie shivered and whispered a breathless, '*Merci.*' Delighting in the sensation of touching the woman's bare body, Justine couldn't resist the temptation of stroking her again. Her fingers slipped easily against the curve of her back but, this time, she allowed them to trail lower until they reached the split between Marie's perfect rounded buttocks.

'You want to touch more than my back?' Marie enquired. She was glancing over her shoulder. Her large dark eyes were darkened by the shadows from her fringe.

Before Justine could think how to answer, Marie's fingers had encircled her wrist again. Her hold was firm but not punishing and Justine watched with detached awe as her hand was coaxed toward the union of Pierre and Marie's bodies. Before her fingers connected with the wet flesh she could feel the heat radiating from the pair. Her senses seemed peculiarly attuned to every detail and she sensed herself being won over by the excitement that the couple were obviously enjoying.

And then her fingers were caught up between them.

She found herself stroking the tight sac of Pierre's scrotum. Her touch lingered over the wrinkled flesh, lightly caressing him before moving up to the thick and quivering length of his erection. Justine heard him moan beneath Marie and she was elated to feel his pulse quicken as though he was particularly excited by her caress. Sliding her hand upwards, relishing the wetness that had coated him and now slipped against her palm, she touched the dewy haven of Marie's pussy.

The lips were tight around the thickness invading them. Justine could see the skin was stretched and sensitive. She supposed that was why Marie moaned with such enthusiasm when Justine stole a caress between the inner and outer labia.

The French woman muttered a string of breathy thanks, working herself more quickly against Pierre and clearly approaching her own peak of delight. Beneath her, Pierre's well-defined muscle tone became more rigid and Justine guessed they were both hastening toward their climaxes. Marie's toes were curled impossibly tight and the swarthy complexion of her face had darkened with a rush of heady arousal.

Not sure if she was meant to carry on touching them, or if she had now fulfilled her usefulness to the pair, Justine allowed her hand to trail away. Her fingers were sticky with their wetness and, while the temptation was to inhale their perfume and maybe savour its taste, she wouldn't let herself rise to that impulse while Sartine was watching.

Not that there was a great danger of Sartine noticing her, she thought dourly. His attention was riveted on Marie and Pierre as they rode each other with greater ferocity. The table trembled as they moved against each other with increasing force. Justine watched concentric circles shiver through the surface of her coffee and she was struck by the notion that each one represented a quiver of delicious pleasure.

Struck by a sudden impulse to be involved in the climax, she reached out to touch between Pierre's legs. Her fingers discovered his sac and she found his flesh was virtually pulsing with the tension of an unreleased climax. Circling her hand back around the base of his shaft and squeezing lightly she felt Marie's sex repeatedly kiss her fingers. She knew the orgasm was almost on the pair and when Pierre groaned and Marie sighed she realised she had chosen to touch them at exactly the right moment.

Pierre's shaft pulsed beneath her fingers. The muscle of his erection grew thick and then repeatedly shivered as he shuddered through his climax. Justine had intended to remove her hand but Marie chose that moment to squirm down hard against Pierre's throbbing release.

When Sartine had mentioned the pleasure he got from watching Marie's orgasm, Justine had dismissed the comment. But now, hearing the woman's dramatic sighs and feeling her wet flesh tremble, she understood exactly what he had meant. Marie stiffened as the climax gripped her body; her face flushed; her muscles strained; and she gave herself over to the moment with blatant abandon.

Justine's fingers were trapped between Marie and Pierre and she could only savour the tremors that shook through both bodies. He grunted and writhed against the table while she threw her head back and babbled her gratitude. When Justine was able to draw her hand away the fingers were greasy with the combination of the couple's spent juices. The ends throbbed as though they had experienced their own miniature version of Pierre and Marie's orgasm.

'Didn't I say they were a pleasure to watch?' Sartine murmured.

She glanced up and saw his gaze was now fixed on her. Justine remembered that Mrs Weiss had described Sartine as a 'slippery bastard' and she considered her response with appropriate caution. Waiting until Marie and Pierre had climbed from the table, catching her first glimpse of Pierre's face and surprised by his handsome good looks, she regarded Sartine carefully before giving her reply. 'Why have I been brought here? If you don't possess the manuscript I wish to acquire, what reason is there for me being here?'

He sipped his drink before replying, reminding Justine that she was also thirsty. When she raised the cup to her lips she could detect the scent of Marie and Pierre from where it lingered on her fingers. The musky fragrance was intrusive and threatened to lead her thoughts back to the decadent display she had just enjoyed. Annoyed by her own inability to concentrate, Justine wiped the back of her hand against her skirt and glared at Sartine.

'You aren't here to acquire the manuscript,' he explained patiently. '*The Society* asked me to consider whether or not you are suitable material for acquiring *La Coste*. That is why you are here.'

She frowned. 'I thought that the priest was considering my suitability.'

'He was,' Sartine agreed. 'The priest you met with yesterday assures me you were able to meet his standards on the subject of sacrilege. But you have to pass through two more tests before you can be deemed worthy.'

Justine was amazed to hear the events of yesterday evening being summarised in one clinical sentence. The inner turmoil she had suffered, and all of the loathsome pleasures, had seemed like a lot more than simply meeting someone's standards on the subject of sacrilege. 'If the priest was testing my aptitude for sacrilege,' she began warily, 'what will you be testing?'

Sartine's grin was seductive. 'That's a very perceptive question,' he acknowledged. '*The Society* have asked me to test you, and I've put my hotel staff at your disposal. I'm sure you're aware that the Marquis was renowned for his indulgence in sacrilege and sadism but people forget the strongest of his motives. That's what we'll be testing.'

Justine could feel her heartbeat racing as she finally noticed the army of maids that lined the walls. A pair of them had helped Marie and Pierre out of the room but those that remained were now staring at her with avaricious interest. Each one was as beautiful as Marie and, dressed in their skimpy costumes of black skirts, white blouses and dark stockings, each looked exciting and inviting. Certain that her mind and body needed some time to recover from the excesses she had so far endured, she quickly racked her brains to find a way to distance herself from the giddy indulgences that were apparent all around. Forcing her voice to remain steady, and dragging her gaze back to meet Sartine's, she asked, 'What do you define as the Marquis's strongest motive?'

'Pleasure. Nothing but endless hedonistic pleasure.'

She opened her mouth, not sure if she was going to argue or ask him how he intended to test her. Taking the moment to think and finish the remainder of a croissant, she finally saw a way to give herself the necessary break from Sartine and the demands of *The Society*'s tests. She met his gaze and said, 'I won't be submitting to any further tests until I've seen proof that the manuscript exists.'

He shook his head and laughed. 'I really don't think you are in a position –'

'No,' Justine said firmly. 'I am happy to undergo any relevant tests that the seller deems necessary. I think I proved myself in that regard last night. But there will be no more tests until I've seen proof that your Society really does possess *La Coste*.' She rose from the table, intending to storm majestically back to her bedroom: but Sartine was fast.

His hand fell to her shoulder and, when she turned, she was overwhelmed by his broad bulk. His mouth continued to smile at her but his eyes remained perversely unreadable. She saw he was holding three pages of plain copier paper in one hand, almost as though he had expected this particular demand. A cursory glance at the quality of the print and the distinctive lettering at the bottom of each page told her she was looking at documents that had been faxed to his hotel.

'Here,' he said, pushing the pages against her chest.

Justine took the three sheets of paper and tried not to show her confusion. She had been hoping merely to allow herself a day to recover from the ordeal at the church and prepare herself for whatever it was that Sartine demanded from her. Staring at the clumsy scrawl of foreign writing, struggling to make sense of a language she didn't understand in a handwriting she couldn't properly cipher, she heard herself thank him.

'Take them to your room,' Sartine encouraged her. 'Study them for the next hour.' He glanced at his wristwatch and added, 'At twelve o'clock I'll have two of my staff collect you once you've ascertained the authenticity of those pages.'

His words echoed through her mind like the sound of an escape door clanging shut. She was now in possession of papers that were virtually worthless. And, not sure how she had managed to do it, Justine realised she had committed herself to submitting to the man in exactly one hour. The thought made her feel ill with a blend of dread and arousal.

Seven

Marie and a maid collected Justine from her room as soon as the clock struck twelve. Leading her toward their destination the two women plucked fussily at Justine's clothes and hair. The band was removed from Justine's ponytail, forcing her chestnut tresses to spill down her back and over her shoulders. A single button was first released from her throat; then one at the side of her pencil skirt; and then another at the front of her blouse. The modifications to her outfit were only subtle – nothing so grand that Justine thought she ought to protest – but they had the cumulative effect of making her feel as though she was being prepared for something bold, outrageous and decadent. She glanced from one pretty feminine face to the other and asked, 'Where are we going?'

'Captain Sartine would like you to enjoy the facilities in the penthouse.'

'What does he have planned for me?'

'Nothing you won't enjoy.' Marie whispered this declaration as she opened a door and ushered Justine inside. The room was vast and made light by picture windows on every wall. As in the dining room, Justine was able to see majestic views that would have kept her entertained for hour after hour under other circumstances. But it was the suggestion of hedonism within the room that caught her attention. The opulence of the furnishings – a four-poster bed draped with swags of voile; an array of cushioned couches and padded chairs – suggested a boudoir elegance that made Justine think

88

of perfumes, passion and pleasure. She could see the semi-naked figures she had expected to encounter – a maid with her dark skirt hitched up to show the lacy tops of her black stockings and the white triangle of her panties; Pierre lounging in an open robe that revealed his lean athletic body – but she wouldn't let herself dwell on any one of those figures. She kept her gaze fixed on Sartine as he walked over to greet her. His arms were extended to deliver a welcoming embrace and Justine remained stiff as he caught her with a hug. She struggled not to show any of the natural reservations that made her want to distance herself from the comparative stranger and his intrusive clinch.

'It is a pleasure to have you here,' Sartine mumbled.

'I'm sure it will be a pleasure to be here,' she replied carefully.

She could feel the weight of his erection through his pants. Its forceful length nuzzled against the flat of her stomach with a lurid intimacy that made her think 'too much and too soon'. Behind Sartine, Pierre lounged on the four-poster while the exposed maid languished idly on a nearby chaise longue. It was unnerving to realise that every eye was fixed on her and Justine could feel her stomach tightening as she tried to work out what they would be expecting from her. She didn't doubt they would want sex but she also understood this would be a different experience to the one she had endured in the church. Her heart began to race from the combined effects of panic, trepidation and eagerness.

'Have a seat,' Sartine suggested, encouraging her toward a chair beside one window. He snapped his fingers with a brisk click. His two maids came rushing to his side as Justine made herself comfortable in the chair. They regarded their employer with expressions of expectant servility that were both exciting and demeaning. Still not sure what would be expected from her, Justine paid careful attention to everything the man said. 'This lady is our special guest,' Sartine told the maids. 'Make sure she is treated with appropriate reverence. It is your duty to make today memorable for her.'

Justine didn't know what to make of the phrase 'appropriate reverence' but she tried to contain her surprise when the pair of women threw themselves at her feet. One of them immediately began to place subtle kisses against her left foot while the other stroked her fingers lovingly against Justine's right thigh. The stimulation was disturbingly intimate but she vowed that she wouldn't give in to the animal thrill that stirred in her loins. Nevertheless, her chest was tightening and each breath was arduous with exertion.

'Marie,' Sartine called, 'I'm sure our guest would appreciate a glass of wine. Pierre! Stop idling on the bed, you lazy fuck, and come and introduce yourself to Justine.'

Suddenly the centre of attention, Justine could only squirm in her chair and try not to be crushed by embarrassment. The pliant maids continued to stroke her legs and place kisses against her feet, calves and thighs. While Marie handed her a glass of claret, Pierre knelt by her side and pressed his nose against Justine's ear. She had been interested in him before because of his good looks. Now that he was so close to her, she could feel herself swelling from the arousal he generated.

'You have a very delicate hand,' Pierre murmured.

The comment made her blush as she remembered how she had touched him in the dining room. Hearing his words tickle against the nape of her neck was almost like revisiting the exact moment when she had cupped his sac in one hand and lightly caressed his erection. If she had closed her eyes, she knew she would have been able to revisit the sensation of having his thick length pulsing against her palm.

Hurriedly, Justine sipped at her claret.

When she glanced up she discovered Marie was naked before her.

Sartine held the woman in a loose embrace: one hand on her bare breast, his leg between her coltish thighs. The pair regarded each other with passion and Justine guessed they were frequent lovers. Considering the way their gazes sparkled with unconcealed desire she found it easy to imagine Sartine and Marie entangled together in a dissolute and torrid relationship.

Sartine turned to face Justine and asked, 'Is this all to your liking?'

She blinked herself from the mental image of Sartine and Marie intertwined together and asked him to repeat what he had said. The maids at her feet were inspiring magical thrills that left her breathless and unsure of her responses. Pierre was telling her why he had found her touch to be so stimulating and his every word made her neck exquisitely sensitive. Now, watching Sartine as he fondled Marie, Justine wondered why she had ever had any reservations about surrendering to the man or his entourage. The atmosphere of the room was uncommonly liberating and, rather than resist the temptations they presented, Justine found herself wanting to indulge her lewdest appetites.

'Is this all to your liking?' Sartine repeated dutifully.

She didn't know if the claret was working with exceptional speed, or if there was something about the ambience of his penthouse that had allowed her inhibitions to melt away. Whatever the reason, Justine could feel her inner muscles growing fluid as her excitement built. 'You've made me very welcome,' she assured him. 'This is a greater hospitality than I ever expected. Thank you.'

He shrugged away her gratitude. 'Were those pages sufficient to prove that we are in possession of *La Coste*?'

'They seem authentic,' she conceded warily.

It was a guarded answer because, in truth, she wasn't sure if the pages were authentic or not and the matter was a source of bitter personal frustration.

The three pages that Sartine had given her looked like genuine copies of an eighteenth-century manuscript: but Justine had no way of verifying the content. Her ignorance of the French language had never been more galling and she cursed herself for never having made the extra effort to learn. It was particularly annoying in these circumstances because she thought she could see something in the handwriting that reminded her of de Sade's penmanship. She wasn't sure if it was the slope of the microscopic handwriting, or something characteristic in the meticulous shaping of the tiny accents above the vowels. But there was some detail in the faxed pages that made her want to believe they were genuine copies of pages from *La Coste*.

If she had simply been able to speak French to ask her, Justine knew the penitent could have translated the pages for her. It was horribly easy to imagine them locked in a conversation where she could have learnt whether or not the writing was in de Sade's familiar style. But, because they didn't share a way to communicate, other than kissing, Justine knew that particular avenue was closed to her.

She had briefly considered phoning Mrs Weiss, and possibly reading the text aloud so her employer could translate. But she was repulsed by the idea of exposing her clumsy French pronunciation to the woman and suffering inevitable ridicule. Also, she knew that Mrs Weiss was currently away from the library and, as had been proved that morning by her call from a line with a withheld number, Justine's employer was doing her best to remain incommunicado.

'I'm pleased we managed to satisfy your curiosity,' Sartine smiled. He eased himself from Marie's embrace and stepped closer. Idly plucking open two buttons from Justine's blouse, exposing the lacy fabric of her bra and the swell of her breasts, he added, 'Perhaps you can now satisfy something for me?'

She glanced from his winning smile to the thrust of the erection at the front of his pants. It had been so easy to be lulled into a lascivious mood that she was willing to throw herself into whatever Sartine wanted. The sensation of the maids' lips and fingers against her legs was inspiring a vicious thrill. The pair were constantly growing bolder, stealing their caresses higher up her legs and creating a deep and penetrating arousal. Each time Justine glanced at them she was rewarded by a seductive pout or a glimpse of smouldering eye contact.

Pierre eased the blouse away from her neck, murmuring that she was an exciting and beautiful woman. He drew his lips millimetres above the surface of her skin and she could feel his threatened kisses as they brushed over the microscopic hairs on her shoulders. It was a caress that came without the pressure of being touched and left her giddy from growing need.

She raised her gaze to meet Sartine's. Daringly, she asked, 'How would you like me to satisfy you?'

He chuckled softly and stroked his fingers against her cheek. 'I have one or two questions to ask before we continue,' he explained. 'That won't trouble you, will it?'

'You've made this morning so comfortable I can't imagine anything troubling me,' she returned. Despite her words, Justine could feel a spike of unease pierce her stomach. Mrs Weiss had warned her that Sartine was a slippery bastard. She felt comfortable and relaxed in the penthouse; the prospect of an enjoyable afternoon lay before her; the thrill of arousal was building in her loins; and she was suddenly worried that she might let some secret detail slip that would spoil her chances of acquiring *La Coste*. Nevertheless, knowing she had to present a façade of honesty and openness, Justine held his gaze and said, 'Ask whatever questions you will of me.'

He made a gesture to the two maids and Justine was disturbed to feel the women's fingers slip beneath the hem of her skirt. They went from casually caressing her thighs to easing under her skirt and beneath the sides of her panties. Every inquisitive caress they had made before was invested with a wealth of delicious excitement. But this new intimacy created a heat Justine hadn't expected. She could feel the feminine fingertips stroking the flesh at the tops of her thighs. Her pubic curls were lightly tugged and teased as the two women made their exploration more daring.

Justine snatched a faltering breath and then raised her gaze back to meet Sartine's. From the corner of her eye she watched Marie replenish her half-drained glass of claret. After thanking the woman, she took a hefty swig of the drink and savoured its tart sweetness. An expectant hush had fallen over the room as everyone waited for Sartine to speak.

'Why do you want to possess *La Coste*?'

'Why? Because it's *La Coste*. It was written by the Marquis. What other reason could I need?'

He grinned as though he understood that motive. 'Of course,' he agreed. 'And are you making this purchase for yourself or for another?'

'For myself. I want *La Coste* to take pride of place in my private library.'

'Do you intend publishing it?'

She snorted with disdain. 'Of course not!'

They were questions and answers she had rehearsed with Mrs Weiss. Her employer had refused to say why so many questions would be asked, or why it was necessary to conceal the purchase in a veil of secrecy, but she had made sure Justine understood exactly how to respond to every possible variation. Justine was almost thankful for the training she had endured except,

94

with the constant teasing of Sartine's staff, it wasn't quite the interrogation she had expected.

The maids were now toying boldly with her cleft, their fingers slipping against the wet lips of her labia and occasionally teasing inside. A fingernail grazed against the delicate surface of Justine's clitoris and she snatched deep breaths in an effort to contain her response. Her heartbeat hammered and her forehead grew slick with perspiration. Inside her bra – clearly visible to Sartine, Marie and Pierre she guessed – her nipples stood hard and proud. She glanced briefly down at herself and realised the rigid nubs of flesh were silently begging to be touched.

'Are any of these names familiar to you?' Sartine began. He cleared his throat and said, 'Marais?'

'Marais is the seller, isn't he?'

'Yes. But do you know him?'

She shook her head. 'No.'

'Dupont?'

'No.'

'Weiss?'

'Wait,' she said suddenly. 'Wasn't Dupont the name on one of the headstones I had to hide behind last night outside the church? The name seems vaguely familiar.'

Sartine considered this and then shrugged. 'It might have been,' he allowed. 'It's the family name of the parish priest you met there: the gentleman who was in charge of last night's assessment.'

Justine considered this and thought it was fitting for the depraved priest to take advantage of the opportunity to violate the sanctity of his family's burial plot. Father Dupont had made a deep impression and she knew she would be marvelling at his depravity for years to come. The prospect of ever visiting another church was something she could no longer entertain and, she supposed, each time she saw anything religious in future, it would be an unsettling reminder of her night with the priest.

'I thought the name was familiar,' she murmured. She wondered if Sartine would notice that she hadn't answered his question about the name of Weiss. She didn't know if he would be able to detect the untruth from her tone of voice, or the flicker of some telltale facial expression, but she didn't want to meet his questions with a direct lie unless there was no other option.

'It seems we have been able to satisfy each other,' he confided. Taking the half-drained glass from her hand he stepped back to place it on a dressing table and said, 'I only have one more thing to ask you.'

Her heartbeat raced faster and she wondered if he was going to ask again about Mrs Weiss. He resumed his position before her but this time his face was inches from hers. She could see he was studying her intently and felt as though he would be able to read the truth from her face before she had a chance to murmur a defensive lie. The prospect of failing her employer loomed large enough to make Justine tremble.

'Are you worthy of acquiring *La Coste*?' Sartine whispered.

Justine wanted to heave a sigh of relief. She regarded him coolly and asked, 'Isn't that what you're going to assess?'

He laughed and pulled Marie into his embrace. 'She's quite the eager little bitch, don't you think?' His hands found the woman's chest and his fingers slipped through the loose buttons of her blouse. He freely fondled her as Justine sat breathless in her chair and watched them writhe together.

'I think it is unfair of you to leave her so wanton,' Marie breathed. As she spoke, Sartine released her breast. Exposed, her chocolate-coloured nipple stood bold against her olive flesh. The tiny nub was already hard and Justine was made weak by the tempting idea of standing up and suckling against the woman. She

96

licked her lips, not caring if the action made her look salacious, and silently pleaded with Marie. If Sartine hadn't taken her glass she would have taken another sip of her claret to calm her nervous excitement. The urgent need for satisfaction broiled through her loins and she squirmed restlessly in her chair. Pierre's subtle kisses continued to make her shoulders unduly sensitive and the teasing touches of the maids had fuelled a molten heat between her legs.

'You think I should take pity on her?' Sartine enquired. He rolled Marie's stiff nipple between a finger and thumb as he considered the suggestion. 'You don't think I should satisfy you first, my love?'

'Pierre,' Marie snapped, ignoring Sartine. 'End Justine's frustration.' She glared at the maids and added, 'You can both help him. The poor girl is desperate to come and my sadistic husband is being the cruellest tease.'

Her instructions were delivered in the same stiff tone that Sartine used and Justine was delighted to note they were instantly obeyed. Pierre swept Justine from her seat, lifting her easily and carrying her across to the four-poster bed. The maids moved out of the way but one of them took the opportunity to remove Justine's skirt while the other stripped her pants away. The blouse fell from her shoulders as Pierre carried her across the room and, by the time he had laid her on the silk sheets, she realised her bra had also been removed.

And, amazed by her own attention to detail, all that Justine could think of was the revelation that Sartine and Marie were married. She had watched the woman straddling Pierre in the dining room and Sartine had coolly sat by enjoying the same depraved sideshow. She had suspected the pair were involved in an unusual relationship but she hadn't expected to discover they were husband and wife. The revelation made her sure she had found a new level of decadence and depravity.

'She needs properly pleasuring,' Marie told Pierre sternly. 'Imagine you are taking me.'

Justine shivered as she listened to the command. The decadence of being naked and surrounded by glamorous strangers heightened her arousal and expectation. She was acutely aware of the soft fabric against her back and buttocks and delighted by the way it soothed the heat of her febrile flesh. Pierre placed himself over her while the two maids delivered hungry kisses to Justine's breasts and pussy. The end of his erection brushed against her sex lips and she realised one of the maids was holding his length and teasing its tip against her labia.

'You are here in pursuit of pleasure?' he whispered.

Not trusting herself to speak, Justine could only nod.

'I think you might have come to the right place,' he said and grinned. As he spoke he bucked his hips forward. The maids held Justine's labia apart, stretching the flesh lightly and allowing him to slide easily inside. His thickness was broad enough to make its presence felt against her inner muscles and she groaned happily as he forced himself deeper inside.

The priest had proved to be a capable lover the previous evening but the unnerving element of sacrilege had made it difficult for Justine to enjoy the experience. On this occasion, with two beautiful maids sucking at her nipples and teasing her labia while a gorgeous man slid in and out of her wetness, Justine remembered how easy it was to give in to absolute pleasure. She pushed her hips up to meet Pierre's penetration and was rewarded by feeling his shaft brush against the hard bead of her clitoris. One of the maids gasped noisily and, after casting a brief glance in her direction, Justine was delighted to see the woman had raised her skirt and was eagerly plundering her own pussy.

Traces of self-indulgence were everywhere: from Sartine and Marie kissing and caressing each other by the side of the bed; through to the maid who sucked against Justine's breast as she stroked a loving hand against Pierre's backside. To be a part of their hedonism was intoxicating and Justine gave herself to the moment without a care for the repercussions. She had answered Sartine's questions; convinced him that her intentions for acquiring *La Coste* made her eligible; and now she was able to enjoy every pleasure without fear of being discovered as a fraud.

Pierre rode in and out with a pace that was maddening. While her body cried out for vigorous and demanding haste, he seemed confident that she needed to enjoy a leisurely session of intimacy. Each thrust was just a little less than she wanted, and Justine bucked herself onto him in an attempt to hasten his rhythm.

The maid to her left – fingering herself with urgent bursts of speed – groaned as she started to wring the climax from her sex. Her soft gasps were intermingled with a rush of guttural French words that Justine knew she would never be able to translate. She could see that the woman hadn't gone to the trouble of removing her panties and the shape of her knuckles distended the gusset as she rubbed frantically. When her orgasm finally came, the ice-white crotch of her panties was darkened by the rush of wetness. She raised her gaze to meet Justine's and they exchanged a silent and profound understanding.

The maid to her right, dutifully suckling against Justine's breast, muttered words of indecipherable encouragement. Justine couldn't decide if the enthusiastic rejoinders were directed toward her or the man between her legs. The maid clearly carried a lot of affection for Pierre, a detail that was obvious in her adoring smile and the reverential way she caressed his bare body. But, Justine thought, it was the earthy tone of the maid's exclamations, coupled with the delicious nuance of her accent, that made each mumbled expletive a delightful accoutrement to the uninhibited atmosphere.

'Is this how you take your pleasures at home, Justine?'

The question came from Sartine as he nudged Pierre aside.

Justine was devastated to have the glorious length snatched from her tight confines and she wanted to wail with disappointment. The prospect of orgasm had been looming closer and she was appalled by the injustice of having his shaft stolen from her when she had been on the verge of cresting her own peak of pleasure. Trembling with the need for release, she sighed with contentment when she saw the size of the erection that Sartine wielded. One of the maids grabbed her master's shaft and teased it against the dewy slit of Justine's sex.

Marie climbed on to the bed and positioned herself so her sex hovered over Justine's face. The scent of her wetness was rich and exciting and it was almost more than Justine could abide. The lips of the woman's pussy had separated into a dark pink pout that begged to be kissed. As Justine savoured the raw delight of Sartine's penetration, she began to panic that her body might explode from sensory overload.

Fingertips trailed against her legs and abdomen.

Each light caress added to the stimulation she was savouring through her breasts, sex and mouth. The swell of her orgasm was building with phenomenal speed and Justine knew, when the climax did erupt, it was going to be overwhelming.

'Is this how you take your pleasure at home?' Sartine asked again.

Justine tore her mouth away from the wetness of Marie's hole and shook her head. Her lips and mouth felt sodden with the remnants of the woman's arousal and the urge to savour the taste made a cramp of excitement tighten in her stomach. 'I've never enjoyed myself so much before,' she admitted honestly. It was a struggle to keep her head and not scream with gratitude as she made the confession. A niggling thought at the back of her mind made her wonder if the excess of stimulation was as exciting as the kiss she had shared with the penitent: but Justine felt sure that all the pleasures she was currently enjoying had to be superior.

'This is the most intense stimulation I've ever enjoyed,' she assured him.

'Do you mean that?'

'Yes. Of course. Why?'

He laughed and pushed himself deep inside her. 'I'm simply surprised that you've never enjoyed this degree of satisfaction,' Sartine murmured. 'And, I'm wondering how you will respond when we really begin to work on you this evening.'

With his length buried deep inside her hole, Justine felt the flood of her orgasm begin to rush through her body. She bit her lower lip, struggled to contain a cry, and then decided she couldn't suppress the scream. Her grateful shriek echoed cheerfully around the penthouse.

Her jubilant wail sounded sporadically through the remainder of the afternoon. Sartine rode her until his shaft eventually thickened and pulsed and erupted into her sex in a wet and sticky explosion. He had barely pulled himself away from her before Pierre had returned to slide easily in and out of her sopping hole. After Marie had been licked to a climax she changed places with one of the maids and allowed Justine to tongue a fresh hole while she suckled greedily against a bare breast. The five of them repeatedly changed places, constantly reminding Justine that she was the centre of attention and paying every consideration to her pleasure and satisfaction. Within three hours of beginning Justine ached from the excess of pleasure and was ready to beg Sartine to let her stop and rest from the indulgence. The convulsions of too many orgasms had left her dreading another rush of pleasure. After spending so long swathed in a cowl of perspiration, she felt drained and dehydrated.

As though he sensed she needed a reprieve, Sartine snapped his fingers and commanded that the afternoon's entertainment should be brought to a conclusion. He made some comment about necessary preparations for the forthcoming evening but Justine understood he was really drawing the event to a close so she would have a chance to recover.

Pierre and Marie bade Justine goodbye with delicate kisses to her lips and brow. The subtlety of their farewells made Justine believe she had earned the affection of two genuine friends during their afternoon of unbridled passion. The pair of maids regarded Justine with surprisingly bashful expressions and gave the puzzling reassurance that they would look out for her later. Sartine gallantly draped a robe over Justine's shoulders and led her back to her room and the penitent.

Dizzy from the wine, and still reeling after enjoying excesses in so many pleasures, Justine almost stumbled into the woman's arms as she staggered toward the bed and prepared to sleep.

'Justine?' the penitent began.

'No,' Justine said, pushing the woman away. She struggled to think of the French word for sleep, but that only served to remind her of how little she knew about the language. Exhausted from the thrill of more orgasms than she could remember enjoying, Justine tried to wave the penitent away as she stumbled toward the bed. 'Avec tired,' she mumbled as she fell on the bed and wrestled herself beneath the blankets.

'I have read the pages you left behind,' the penitent pressed.

It took a moment for Justine to realise what the woman had said.

Her wearied thoughts briefly pondered over the puzzle of how she could understand the penitent. Her mind flitted briefly on the idea that she had listened to so many exclamations of French pleasure that she had developed some previously untapped understanding of the tongue. And then she realised she was listening to English. She opened her eyes wide, the need for sleep suddenly gone. Snatching the pages from the penitent's hand, unable to suppress the elated grin that stretched across her features, she gasped, 'You've read these?'

'Yes.'

'You can translate them for me? You can tell me what they say in English?'

'If you want me to do that I can try,' the penitent replied hesitantly. 'But . . .'

Justine didn't allow her to finish. Sitting up on the bed, thrusting the pages back into the penitent's hands, she waited expectantly to hear what was contained within the sample pages from the manuscript.

Eight

'*Escaping from the Bastille was easy. Corrupt guards can be as obliging as well-paid whores when they have been bought. Should I have chosen, I could have implored the chief gaoler to swallow my cock before he escorted me from the prison.*'

'Go on,' Justine encouraged. 'Read more, please.'

The penitent nodded and returned her attention to the first page. She used a finger to follow the scrawl of writing and her lips were pursed with concentration as she studied each word before reading and then translating.

'*"You can't escape the Bastille through blackmail," the gaoler tried to tell me. I assured him I wasn't trying to escape the Bastille and I was not using blackmail. I had paid two whores to fuck him each night for a week. Now they were no longer receiving their money, they wanted to tell the gaoler's wife what had been happening. I explained to the gaoler that I was merely being allowed from the restrictions of the prison so I could find the whores and stop them from disrupting his marriage.*

"Don't think of it as blackmail," I encouraged him. "Think of it as my doing you a personal favour that you don't really deserve."'

The penitent paused for breath, turned the page, and then continued.

'*Fresh air has never tasted so sweet. Liberty's freedom has never held me in such an ecstatic thrall. As the carriage drove me toward my revered La Coste, I vowed I would celebrate my freedom in the lewdest manner*

befitting. The long journey sped quickly past as I enter-
tained a hundred score deviant pleasures that would be
mine for the taking. As soon as I returned home, I would
immerse myself in history's greatest orgy of excess.'

'My God!' Justine breathed.

The penitent glanced uneasily at her. Her finger
remained on the page, holding the spot she had reached,
and Justine could see the woman's hand was trembling.
Seeing her shiver made Justine realise that they were
sharing the excitement of this experience and she
suddenly wanted her more than ever.

'It really is *La Coste*,' Justine whispered.

'It is very old,' the penitent replied doubtfully. 'The
language is . . .' her voice trailed off as she struggled to
find an appropriate word. 'It is not of this time,' she said
eventually. 'I am rephrasing the words so they make
sense to my ear. Is that acceptable?' Her smile was
apologetic and crestfallen.

Her full ripe lips – tightening and stretching as she
shaped each word – became too great a temptation for
Justine to resist. Unable to contain the impulse she leant
across the bed and kissed the penitent.

She could feel the woman's initial surprise but
realised it was quickly banished by a fevered and
welcoming warmth. The blonde's hands went to her
waist and the pair embraced with animalistic hunger.
The faxed pages were forgotten, the penitent's place was
lost, and their copy of *La Coste*'s opening fluttered
unimportantly to the floor. The bed beneath them
creaked on ancient springs as Justine pushed the penitent down and straddled her. They were both naked and
she took a moment to admire her lover's glorious
physique – the perfectly flat abdomen, modest breasts
and freshly shaved pussy – and then her arousal dictated
that she had to act.

Biting kisses at the woman's breasts she briefly
snatched a nipple into her mouth and sucked hard.

After nibbling lightly she moved on to the other and delivered another string of tender punishing kisses. The penitent's sighs of encouragement were enough to fuel Justine's excitement to fresh heights. Hearing the woman gasp and mutter a stream of foreign words, she eagerly moved her face to the split of the penitent's sex. The flushed labia glistened with dewy wetness and Justine traced her tongue tentatively against the fragrant lips. The gently scented flavour of her sex was only subtle but no less exciting because of that.

'Justine!' the penitent gasped. She sat up on the bed, her expression torn between desire and concern. 'Are you sure you want this?' she breathed. 'I thought you had spent the afternoon –'

Justine silenced her with another kiss and pushed her back to the bed. She was moved by the woman's consideration but, regardless of how she had spent her afternoon, or the toll it had taken on her body, she now wanted to have the penitent and nothing was going to distract her from that goal. Their tongues touched as they each savoured the taste of the other. Both driven by the same ferocious desire, neither was able to resist the opportunity to touch, stroke and caress. Justine could feel her breasts being fondled by the penitent's gifted fingers and she bit back a satisfied moan as her nipples were teased to full hardness. Revelling in the adoration, she eventually pulled herself away and whispered, 'I'm sure I want this. I spent the afternoon with Sartine and his harem. It was fun, but not as much fun as I'm going to have with you.'

Throwing herself into the passion with renewed vigour, Justine realised she had spoken an absolute truth. Comparing her experience in the penthouse to the revelation she was enjoying with the penitent she thought it was like the difference between believing a copy of *La Coste* might be available, and finally hearing those first few words from the faxed pages.

The pleasures that had been visited on her by Sartine and his followers were extreme and overwhelming but they had only been physical pleasures of the flesh. Even in the parish church Justine remembered there had been an emotional content that had left an impact greater than any of the delights enjoyed in the penthouse. She didn't want to accept that some remainder of her religious beliefs had compounded her feelings of guilt on that occasion, but she did know the experience had been far more profound.

She also knew that the genuine adoration she found in the penitent's embrace added a greater dimension to the passion than all the skills of those gifted lovers from Sartine's penthouse. Quietly, she hoped the naked hunger in her expression conveyed as much.

'If you are sure,' the penitent conceded. She released the words in a throaty drawl. 'If you are not too tired.'

Justine chuckled and said she could never be too tired. They were the last words she spoke before burying her face between the blonde's legs. The sultry flavour of musk and sweat was a powerful aphrodisiac. As Justine traced her tongue against the velvet pussy lips, her own arousal grew against a background of the penitent's escalating sighs. The blonde bucked her hips up to meet Justine's tongue and, together, they each begged the other to continue.

The blonde shifted position on the bed, never snatching her sex away from Justine's kisses but sliding around so that she was able to return the favour. Their bare bodies slipped together with a friction that was maddeningly exciting. In the moment that the penitent began to lap at her pussy, Justine caught her breath and wasn't sure if she wanted to sigh or scream. The gentle kisses being brushed against her labia were soft, sweet and powerfully exciting. Climbing quickly to a higher plateau of satisfaction, she nuzzled the throbbing nub of the blonde's clitoris and slipped her tongue between the pouting labia.

Simultaneously overwhelmed, they clutched each other and trembled through an explosion of shared bliss. Justine was reminded of every glorious ache in her body but it only served to show her that the penitent had given something more than she could ever have enjoyed in the penthouse. Shivering from the pleasure, and not sure her body could endure any more, she wrenched herself away and retrieved the fallen pages from the floor. The room around her seemed to swim as though she had been drinking. Her hand trembled enough to make the sheets of paper flutter as she pushed them toward the penitent's chest and whispered, 'Please, read me some more. I want to hear the rest of it.'

Nodding, clearly happy to do anything that was asked of her, the blonde pulled herself from the bed and sat up. After scouring the pages, one elegant finger trailing lightly over the scribbled lines of text, she quickly picked up from where she had last read.

'My Renée welcomed me with a long and intimate embrace. I took her in the doorway, while the carriage porter waited for his tip. The insolent bastard watched as we rutted like dogs in heat. Her hot pussy engulfed my cock and she climaxed as soon as I pumped myself into her. I could tell from her stench that she had been waiting for this since my incarceration and the thought of her fidelity made me feel both honoured and unworthy. The smell was ripe with unperfumed need but free from the pungent odour of any other man. If our positions had been reversed, and she had been the one forced to spend time in a gaol, I know I would have been fucking the second of our maids before they locked Renée's cell. Her chaste nobility made me marvel at the treasure that I had in her.

'Renée was flustered, but clearly glad to see me away from that hellhole. After we had finished rutting, and dismissed the carriage porter with his tip, she asked: "What will you want to do now that you are home?" I didn't hesitate to give my response because it had been all

I could think about through the journey back to her arms. "I shall have a massive orgy," I declared. "La Coste will play host to an indulgence that should shame the Roman Empire." '

A tremor tickled down Justine's spine as she listened.

She knew part of her response was due to being near the blonde: she inspired a constant thrill of excitement that Justine found impossible to resist. And she accepted that a part of her arousal was due to the vulgar and exciting detail of the story. Hearing fresh words from de Sade, and anticipating where the story would go, filled her with a sense of excitement and wonder.

But she believed a greater part of her excitement came from the enormity of finally discovering *La Coste*. So many things had been written about de Sade, volumes that dissected his personality and categorised his perversions, that the truth of who he was seemed to blend with the fiction he had created. Most biographers chose to emphasise his failings and dwelt on the fact that he did have excessive and somewhat nefarious sexual interests. Justine had read some dry materials that acknowledged de Sade was nothing more than a man of his time, and pointed out that many of his years behind bars were attributable to the vagaries of the revolution. But she had never found anything that properly balanced the man, the myth and his writing. It was her most fervent hope that this diary – and she wanted to believe it was a genuine diary – might reveal an aspect of his character that had been previously overlooked. From what the penitent had already translated, Justine was forming a picture of a man who admired and adored his wife. That attitude alone seemed to run contrary to the image of a womanising villain that was usually associated with the Marquis.

'Preparations were easy to make. Renée had employed a host of obliging servants and knew enough peasants from the village who would sink to the blackest depths for a single denier. She was as enthused as I at the prospect

of organising such debauchery and we set about making
our plans while her thighs were still dripping from our
welcome home fuck. I wanted to indulge myself in every
possible vice and I catalogued them all to my beloved. She
surprised me with her imagination adding some sugges-
tions that made my tastes seem almost puritanical in
comparison. The collection of whips and scourges she had
assembled in readiness for my return home was sufficient
to make my erection stand instantly hard again. Needing
further gratification, I had one of the maids swallow my
cock while Renée and I continued to add to our list.
Freedom has never felt so good.'

Justine couldn't resist the urge to touch the penitent
as the woman read. She sucked briefly against her breast
and then toyed with the slick wet lips of her pussy.
Listening to the woman's accent she wanted to ask a
thousand questions and knew that every one of them
would break the spell of the moment. The woman's real
name, the cause of her obedience to Father Dupont, and
the reasons why she hadn't revealed that she was
bilingual earlier were details that Justine needed to
know. But, instead of asking anything, she simply
listened to her read from the page and idly fingered the
silken folds of her pussy lips.

'The grounds of La Coste provided enough bounty for
the feast I wanted and I gave the cooks direct instructions
on what to prepare. I was pleased to see that Renée had
employed comely wenches in the kitchen and I took one of
them over the table where she was peeling potatoes. Her
backside was large and soft and inviting. She welcomed
me with a hot hole that was slippery with excitement.
Renée stood watching and wielded a crop while I enjoyed
the cook. I don't know if her unspoken threat was intended
to make the cook obedient or to excite me at the prospect
of what we might do once our celebration had been
organised. Regardless of her reasons, the effect was
enough to make the cook and I come quickly and noisily

110

with our climaxes. I repeatedly slapped her backside to make the wench grip my cock tighter. It hadn't been my intention to hit quite so hard and I was surprised to see the crimson imprint of my hand blossom against the huge cheek of her backside.'

Justine urged the penitent to part her legs. Holding her thighs apart, pushing her tongue close to the centre of the woman's hole, she inhaled the perfume of the blonde's sex and grew dizzy from its intoxicating bouquet. The silky lips were an invitation to kiss. The subtle pout of her clitoris, peeping guardedly from beneath its fleshy hood, made Justine insane with the need to suckle. She pursed her lips against the tiny nub and then rolled her tongue over the quickening pulse. The blonde drew a faltering breath and, when she continued to read, her words stumbled clumsily along.

*'The second cook had watched with conflicting express-
ions of horror and excitement on her face. When I pulled my wet length from the first cook's hole she glared at it as though facing an abomination. "I won't have that in my cunny!" she exclaimed. "You'll have it wherever the Marquis decides," Renée said sternly. She bore down on the second cook, brandishing her crop: but I intervened. "There is no need to beat her into submission. I don't want to use her cunny, yet. I want to watch this one grovel at your lap." The second cook shook her head and looked set to refuse, until I stole the crop from my wife's hand. "You'll lick my wife's cunny while I whip your backside," I said sternly. To my wife I said: "I want to watch you come."'*

'I want to watch you come,' Justine murmured.

The penitent stared down at her. She put the pages aside and spread her legs deliberately wide. 'You have to make me come,' she agreed. 'I have nothing more to read for you. That was the last line of those pages.'

The air between them had been thick before but now it positively bristled with anticipation. Justine rubbed

111

her thighs together and held the penitent's gaze for a moment longer before lowering her head. She darted a gentle tongue against the lips of the blonde's pussy, teased the inner labia lightly apart, and then suckled against the nub of her clitoris. Her fingers had moved to the woman's thighs, holding her open and savouring the contact of bare skin beneath her mouth. She alternated her kisses from languid teasing at her clitoris to penetrative tonguing inside her hole.

The blonde gasped and clutched a fistful of bed linen. Leaning back she tried to squirm away but Justine held her in place. 'I should be doing this for you,' the penitent protested. 'At the church ... the priest said ... I am to do whatever you tell me.'

Breathing heavily, drawing her mouth away from the dripping sex and savouring the wetness that now coated her lips, Justine grinned. 'You're doing whatever I tell you,' she observed. 'I wanted to watch you come, and that's what you're going to do. You're going to come while I watch.'

She could see the penitent was uncomfortable with the instruction but she also knew she would not receive any more protests. Lowering her head back to the bed and relaxing, the blonde spread her thighs further apart as Justine devoured her sex. The flesh was glossy and smooth against her mouth. Justine drew her tongue against the folds of the lips, delighting in the strange textures and flavours of licking another woman. She had not expected her own response to be as powerful but, each time she heard the woman sigh with mounting arousal, Justine could feel her pleasure escalating to the same sultry pinnacle of delight.

She had expected her thoughts to be reeling from the discovery of hearing the opening lines to *La Coste* but, instead, her concentration was fixed on wringing the pleasure from the penitent's sex. Her breathy sighs were a delight to hear. The flavour of her sex – its warmth

112

and viscous wetness – were a positive joy to endure. Teasing her fingers close to the lips, tugging them lightly, spreading them apart so she had easier access to the blonde's clitoris, Justine was enthralled by the whole experience of pleasuring the woman.

'Justine,' the penitent murmured. 'Please. This is not how it should be.'

Justine wasn't listening.

She eased the pussy lips open, stroking her tongue along the lightly stretched flesh, and empathised with every shiver that trembled through her new lover. When she heard the woman above her groan, and felt the afterecho of tremors that bristled through her hole, she knew she had almost taken her to the point of climax. The thought inspired her to lick more urgently until the blonde's cry of release sounded around the room.

Panting heavily, Justine pulled herself away from the penitent's sex and studied her blissful smile. The flush of orgasm had left her cheeks beautifully rouged. The corners of her eyes were wet with grateful tears.

'I want to spend the night with you,' Justine whispered. Suddenly aware of what she needed, she said, 'I want to spend tonight and every night with you: while you read de Sade to me. That's what I want.'

The penitent's smile shone bright with adoration. 'I want that also. I too want every night with you.'

They were on the verge of sealing the arrangement with a kiss when Marie and two maids burst uninvited into the room. Neither Justine nor the penitent responded with embarrassment at the intrusion and the visitors accepted their naked bodies and intimate embrace as though the sight was commonplace.

'Did you want something?' Justine asked stiffly.

'We want you,' Marie smiled.

'And we're going to have you,' one of the maids giggled.

The other joined her in her laughter until Marie silenced them both with a stern frown. Turning back to

Justine, extending a hand, she said, 'Your presence is needed downstairs. Now. You must come with us.'

Justine considered refusing and then thought better of the idea. The expressions of Marie and her maids were bright with determination and none of them looked ready to accept a refusal. Marie's smile was stiff with authority when she said, 'Come along, Justine. You will follow us to the ballroom. We're here to take you to Captain Sartine's party.'

Nine

For the rest of the evening Justine found her thoughts remained with the penitent. Even though the party promised to be a spectacular affair, and she expected she would be offered every physical pleasure she could want, her thoughts constantly returned to the nameless blonde in her hotel room with whom she believed she was falling in love.

Marie and her maids were naked save for the eye-masks they wore. It was a theatrical nod toward anonymity that didn't deceive anyone. Leading a nude Justine through the corridors of the hotel, nodding polite greetings to those similarly masked and undressed guests they encountered, Marie clutched Justine's arm and babbled incessantly about the fun they were going to have. 'Since the Captain discovered he would be assessing your suitability he has been carefully planning this party,' she gushed. 'We have invited our most gifted and talented friends. Several of them travelled for many miles to come here. We also found the most exciting toys and devices that anyone could want to enhance their sexual experience. The Captain and I spent hours calling suitable beautiful partners and trying to organise a party that would rival those of . . .' Her voice trailed off as she struggled to find a suitable comparative. 'A party to rival those of . . .' she began again.

'. . . of the Roman Empire,' Justine suggested.

Marie glanced sharply at her; and then smiled enigmatically. It was difficult to read her expression because of the mask. With her thoughts on the penitent, Justine didn't trouble herself worrying about whether or not she had offended her host's wife and continued to walk calmly by her side. A single doubt began to nag at the back of her thoughts but she couldn't immediately place the reason for her unease. There was some small detail that marked her different to Marie, her staff and the others they met. And, while Justine sensed it was important to notice the nature of the dissimilarity, she could only pinpoint a vague feeling of disparity.

She had to concede that Sartine and Marie had invited a guest list of truly beautiful people. The bare flesh she saw on her way to the ballroom was flawless and exciting. Tanned bodies, all bereft of blemishes or bikini lines, glided by the sides of their muscular well-toned partners. Justine caught glimpses of cleanly shaved clefts, neatly trimmed pubic bushes and an array of breasts that ranged from pert to buxom. She wilfully tried to remain cool and composed: as though attending an orgy was something she did every day of the week. Yet, even after a morning with the penitent and the illuminating day she had spent in the penthouse, Justine found herself torn between extreme responses of dread and daring. The trepidation grew worse as they reached the hotel's ground floor. She could hear the babble of crowded conversation that poured from the ballroom and its drone was almost as loud as the elegant chamber music that accompanied the chatter. Marie squeezed her arm, gently encouraging Justine to step forward and enter the ballroom.

And then she realised the difference between herself and the other guests.

'I don't have a mask!'

It was impossible to make the declaration without feeling absurd by the sound of her own panic. She glanced from her host's wife to the attendant servants and a couple who brushed past them to enter the dining room. Everyone else was nude save for the tiny eye-masks that covered nothing and disguised no one's identity.

'I don't have a mask,' Justine hissed nervously.

'Of course you don't,' Marie agreed. 'But that's because you're here as our guest of honour.' Laughing easily, she didn't allow the conversation to continue and wouldn't hear any further protests or excuses. With the help of her maids they led Justine into the ballroom and were greeted by a rapturous round of welcoming applause.

Too much was happening too quickly and Justine struggled not to be overwhelmed by the experience. The string quartet playing for the party – an elegant trio of dapper men in tuxedos and one beautiful lady in formal wear – brought their piece to a halt. They moved instantly into Khachaturian's *Masquerade Waltz* and, as though everyone expected the development, the crowd moved away from the dance floor. A flutter of flash-bulbs captured the moment for posterity, Justine briefly cringed at the idea that her nudity had been caught on camera, and then that minor worry was pushed to the back of her mind as she found herself alone in the centre of the room with a hundred or more naked strangers admiring her. While she had thought the masks were a lame excuse for a disguise she suddenly realised their presence added a disconcerting edge to the experience. She could no longer recognise Marie or her maids: those people who had nodded courteous greetings to her on her way to the ballroom were now as unfamiliar as those absolute strangers whom she was seeing for the first time.

Since sitting in Dupont's church and being humbled by the frescoes and tranquillity, Justine didn't think she had felt so alone and vulnerable. The memory of the life she had left behind – gloomy libraries and an array of visceral pleasures lived through the pages of dry dusty books – seemed as though it had belonged to someone else. She couldn't equate that existence with the naked pleasure-seeker she had since become and she struggled to understand when the change had occurred. Was it something that had come about when she kissed the penitent that morning? Had it happened during the sacrilege she had enjoyed with the priest? Or did it go back to Mrs Weiss in the private library and her bullying domination? The questions confused Justine and she knew she wasn't going to find answers this evening.

Panic rose in her chest as the drunkenly robust music began to pitch and yaw.

A tall figure stepped from the crowd; she was both relieved and disconcerted to recognise Sartine lurking behind the mask; and then he was leading her around the floor in a fast-paced waltz.

'I wanted the pleasure of the first dance with you,' he murmured as he kissed her neck. 'You look absolutely radiant.'

She released a sigh of relief as they danced together. His body pressed close to hers, exciting her with the intimate contact and making her shiver with a thrill of exhibitionism. Bemused and avaricious smiles glinted from beneath the masks that they passed at the edge of the floor. Justine realised she was still the centre of attention but, with Sartine's hands around her body, and his awakening erection pressing against her stomach, her confidence swelled and she no longer shrank from the interest of the strangers. The worries about when she had been transformed from librarian to libertine were equally easy to set aside.

'You honour me with this party,' she said earnestly. 'Marie tells me that you worked for hours to perfect every detail. Thank you for taking so much time on my behalf.'

The hand on her waist inched slowly downwards as Sartine waltzed Justine around the room. His thickening erection pressed more urgently against her and she could feel the familiar heat of arousal smouldering in her loins. Her bare breasts rubbed against his smooth manly chest and she was stung by a glorious charge of excitement. The music continued to sway at a helter-skelter pace – its majestic melodies soaring and swooping – while Sartine hurried her around the dance floor with meticulous grace.

'You honour our party with your beauty,' Sartine replied. The tips of his fingers teased against her cleft. He was cupping one buttock but he had managed to get his fingers daringly close to her pussy lips. His nails grazed against the dark curls that covered her labia. The tingle of excitement he provoked was sweet enough to make Justine shiver in his embrace. 'Is everything to your satisfaction?'

She thought of assuring him that everything was sensational and then decided to voice the only true reservation that still preyed on her thoughts. 'Why are all your guests, except for me, wearing masks?'

He chuckled. 'There are several reasons for the masks,' he explained carefully. Each step of the waltz made their bodies merge together as though they were involved in a greater intimacy than merely dancing. Justine knew her excitement was in danger of becoming climactic from the teasing steps of the waltz and she forced herself to listen to his response. 'Some of my guests are celebrities,' Sartine explained, 'and they wish to avoid the media attention of being discovered at a party like this. The same applies to many of the respected professionals who would face embarrassment if caught participating in anything so bacchanal as tonight's activities. The masks are also a useful device for identifying you. Everyone here is expected to enjoy themselves with you and treat you to the pleasure of their own particular speciality. If they know you are the only one not wearing a mask, they will have no problems singling you out when they want to inflame your passion.'

She faltered in her steps and glanced at the endless circle of faces surrounding them. The thought that everyone in the room was expected to excite her and enjoy her made Justine suddenly queasy. There were so many people – all of them beautiful and each arousing enough to fulfil at least one of her myriad private fantasies – that she worried she might not be up to the challenge of proving herself worthy of Sartine's standards.

'When this waltz has finished they will have their way with you,' he explained. His fingertips had reached the wet split of her sex and the echo of his words trembled through his touch. As they danced smoothly around the floor Sartine continued to tease the oily lips of her pussy. His touch was light and effortless and made her want to weep from the sudden surge of desire he evoked. The stiffness of his erection was now unbearable against her stomach and she wished he would use it to satisfy the urges he had awoken in her loins. Panting softly and pressing herself more firmly into his embrace, she kissed him as they danced.

Sartine teased her lips with his tongue for a moment before pulling away. Smiling lewdly down at her, still leading her through the waltz as though he had been born for the dance, he sighed, 'I am a little worried that you might not be the right person to own *La Coste*. Is there anything you can say to put my fears at ease?'

The panic his words inspired was almost enough to quell her excitement. Justine's heart quickened and she clutched him more tightly. Her thoughts were no longer fixed on the fingers insinuating themselves between her pussy lips. She swallowed twice as she struggled to find an answer, and then said, 'I'm not sure I could say anything to put your fears at ease. You're assessing how readily I give myself to pleasure, aren't you?'

'That's right.'

'Didn't I give myself wholly to pleasure in your penthouse this afternoon? Aren't I giving myself to this glorious party that you've organised this evening?'

'You proved yourself worthy in the penthouse,' Sartine agreed. 'But you seemed very anxious to leave there at the earliest opportunity. That's hardly the behaviour I would expect from a committed hedonist.'

She nodded, her gaze never leaving his eyes. 'I was anxious to get out of your penthouse,' she agreed. 'I'd experienced all the pleasures I could envision and I wanted to get back to the woman in my room. I spent the remainder of the afternoon listening to her read de Sade while I licked her pussy. If you want to kiss me again, I imagine you'll taste that her wetness is still on my lips.'

He drew a deep breath and his smile was broad with approval. 'That would certainly indicate a degree of worthiness,' he conceded. 'That response might just be enough to help me make my decision, although I'm sure you won't mind if I ask further questions as the evening progresses.'

'Ask whatever you want.'

He nodded and brought the dance to an abrupt halt.

Justine considered him uncertainly, only dimly realising that the music had also been brought to a conclusion. His fingers remained at her cleft and the patter of polite applause rolled around them as the attendant guests showed their approval for the spectacle they had provided with the dance.

'I will be watching you closely for the remainder of this evening,' Sartine explained. 'I will have one or two more questions to help assuage the last of my doubts. But, for now, I want you to enjoy the party.'

He stepped away from her and she suddenly found herself alone and the centre of attention to a room full of masked and naked strangers. The mild arousal she had been enjoying transformed itself into a dire unease and Justine turned from one partially disguised face to the other as she tried to assess the group's mood. So many of the smiles were ambiguous it was difficult to tell whether she was looking at speculative interest or manic appreciation. Stepping back, continually turning, she realised they were inching closer and bearing down on her.

Her nervousness turned to panic.

Hands fell on her arms, shoulders, waist and breasts.

Mouths touched her cheeks and nipples. Fingers stole against her backside, between her buttocks, then against her sex. Tongues lapped at her bare flesh. Beautiful faces and handsome bodies invaded her personal space and pressed intolerably close. The glitter of exquisitely crafted masks caused dizzying sparkles to blind her momentarily. She caught glimpses of hard cocks, splayed pussies and bared breasts – one memorably pierced by a shiny bolt of gold – and then there were too many of them for her to see any one detail. The scent of bare skin; the fragrance of perfume, perspiration and arousal; it was all too much to accept and understand as the crowd descended. With her emotions swaying from dismay to delight Justine felt sure she would swoon from the sensory overload. Every accessible pore of her body was being stroked, touched or caressed. She briefly fretted that she was going to lose her footing, and then that was no longer a consideration as she was swept from the floor by a pair of strong and masculine arms.

A flurry of unknown hands stroked and caressed her body. She was touched in the most intimate places and her excitement rose to the same pitch as her apprehension. Someone kissed her; one nipple was teased between a finger and thumb; something rounded slipped against the lips of her sex; a daring intruder tested the resistance at her anus.

Away from the grunting sighs of those around her, Justine could hear that the string quartet had begun another piece. She couldn't place the melody or the composer but she recognised the music had the same disorienting quality as the Khachaturian waltz to which she had danced with Sartine. Combined with her arousal and excitement, she began to grow dizzy as the crowd carried her around the room.

'. . . see you kiss her pussy . . .'

'. . . I'll have her . . .'

'. . . want to lick every . . .'

'. . . need to taste that . . .'

'. . . fuck her good and hard . . .'

The voices blurred until she couldn't tell if they were male or female; antagonistic or extremely aroused. She realised distantly that her body was now being carried in a specific direction but that observation did little to help her understand the situation or guess how it would now develop. Warm fingers slid easily in and out of her sex while the hands at her breast excited her hard nipples to an unbearable degree. Someone persistent had teased through the tight muscle of her anus and the blossom of expectation left Justine giddy with the need to climax. She tried turning to see who was teasing her with such forbidden intimacy but so many mouths hungered to press against her face that she couldn't differentiate one person from another or see beyond the immediate forest of masked eyes.

'This way.'

Sartine's voice carried over the babble of the crowd.

'I want her over here.'

Justine realised she was being herded toward the sound of the Captain and heard the clatter of furniture being moved and the crowd parting before her. She only understood what was happening when hands went beneath her buttocks, someone pulled the cheeks of her backside apart, and she was eased into a sitting position.

Before she had a chance to think that the guests might have finished having their fun with her bare body, she was deposited on the lap of a stranger.

He was blessed with a deliciously large and hard erection.

The hands that held and positioned her now stretched at the skin of her buttocks until she realised where the erection was going to go. A moment of doubt tightened her stomach – she held her breath and braced herself for the pain – and then the length was sliding into her rear. Justine caught a breath, delighted by the penetration and shocked by the easy way her body was accepting the crude entry. The muscle of her sphincter was stretched to bursting point – a spasm of pain threatened to eclipse the joy of being filled – and then the first burgeoning waves of a climax scorched through her body.

There was no time to savour the glory of the moment. Her heartbeat raced; another pair of strangers kissed her; fingers teased against her buttocks and sex; the shaft ploughed deep into her rear. Someone suckled against her left breast while a crueller mouth nibbled at her right. The constant escalation of pleasure threatened to be more than she could bear. Roughly her thighs were pulled further apart and the weight of a second erection pushed at her cleft.

Justine gasped for air.

She wondered if she should tell the man in front of her that she was already being taken from behind. The etiquette of how to deport oneself at an orgy was something she had never previously encountered but her reservations never made it to her lips. He bucked his hips forward, pushed himself inside, and she was thrilled as his shaft burrowed deep into her pussy. Impaled on two organs, able to feel both of them as they slid inside her and squashed together, Justine knew a scream of delight was building in her chest. The masks continued to hide the identity of those all around her – she had no way of knowing which man was buried in her sex and no desire to see the face of the one pushing into her rear – but their anonymity only added to the exotic mystery of the occasion. Hands and mouths still clawed at her as she grunted her way toward orgasm. With a breathless certainty Justine knew, when the climax did come, it was going to strike her with a furious power. She clenched her jaw and steeled herself in preparation for its impact.

A pair of erections pushed at her mouth.

They came at her from the left and the right and she briefly wondered if the excess of pleasure had inspired double vision. After blinking and shaking her head she understood what was expected of her and wanted to fall on both shafts with animalistic hunger. There was a moment's hesitation as she tried to decide which cock she should accept in her mouth first. But there was never any consideration given to the idea that she could refuse either. The dark dusky purple length and the slender red shaft hovered enticingly in front of her lips. They were both leaking with arousal, a glisten of excitement glossed one glans while the other stared at her from behind a pearl-like bead of semen.

Justine knew she had already given herself to the hedonism of the evening but she was determined to bask in every joy available. That decision hadn't been made so she could meet the criteria of Sartine's standards or maintain a façade that would ultimately benefit Mrs Weiss. She wanted to enjoy every pleasure at her disposal this evening because she knew an opportunity like this would never make itself available ever again. Opening her mouth wide, allowing Sartine's guests to dictate the limitations, she moved herself forward and allowed both erections to punch between her lips. Smiling up at the masked men above her, Justine accepted their cocks onto her tongue.

The taste of pre-come; the scents of sweat and arousal; the sensation of being used by four erections;

the sounds of the crowd hungrily clamouring to be near her; the sight of so much exquisite nudity; all invaded her senses. Justine hadn't known she could climax with such ease and, when the first orgasm was wrung from her body, she was as shocked by its speed and power as the men who were using her.

A spasm started in her groin and then shuddered ripple-like through her body. Its power was phenomenal, jolting through every nerve-ending until she was alive and bright with a glow of pure satisfaction. A groan of elation burst from her lips and she basked in the thrill of release as a second wave of delight tore through her.

The erection in her rear pulsed and her sphincter convulsed around its girth. She could feel the shaft thickening – stretching her anus impossibly wide – and then it quivered and douched her bowel with a scalding rush of ejaculate.

The length in her pussy trembled next. Its pace quickened as it buried deep and bruised the neck of her womb. She gasped, clutched tight at the man above her, and then languished in a roar of responses as he squirted his seed deep into her pussy.

The plateaus of pleasure came so hard they were almost intolerable. Justine hadn't thought her body could suffer so much euphoria, and she began to tense with dread as the first orgasm reached a glorious peak and then threatened to bombard her senses with more cataclysmic bursts of ecstasy. Her heart had raced before: now it pounded like a deafening timpani. She sucked on the two shafts that filled her mouth, throwing every effort into taking them past the point of orgasm, and was rewarded by a pair of united pulses.

Blindingly bright, more flashbulbs exploded. Her earlier worry about being shamed by photographs was now forgotten. The idea that her acts of daring would be recorded forever added a new dimension to the thrill of the evening.

Her tongue was coated with the gelatinous spend from two strangers and she quickly swallowed. The noisome flavour was simultaneously disgusting and delicious. It made her want to gag with revulsion and shriek with delight. Dizzied by the conflicting extremes, she was too busy enjoying the moment to try and rationalise her reactions. Caught up in the mood of the party, she could only swallow and wallow in the joy of being used.

With obscene ease, fresh erections replaced those spent ones that had used her.

The shaft that penetrated her rear slid effortlessly inside, helped by the lubrication of her previous lover's climax. The thicker length that pushed into her pussy was just as easily accommodated, and Justine didn't know whether to feel shocked by her own depravity or giddy from the pleasure of this new extreme. She choked back a scream of animal hunger and accepted the pair of erections that were thrust toward her face. Panting heavily, she sucked on them both and rolled her tongue against their bulbous ends.

She lost track of the number of men who used her and the number of orgasms they inspired. In no mood for playing counting games she simply gave herself over to the delight of being brought to climax after climax. Distantly, she could hear the string quartet shifting from one tune to another, but it was a background music that didn't properly intrude on her concentration. A part of her understood that the evening was rushing quickly past but, with her thoughts fixed only on her personal pleasure, she didn't fret about the details. When the last erection had pulsed into her mouth, the excess spend dribbling over her lower lip to join the creamy beard that soaked her jaw, Justine only wanted to weep with gratitude.

'Are you acquiring *La Coste* for yourself, Justine?'

She blinked at the questioner and realised it was Sartine. After the heady joys of all she had just savoured his question jarred discordantly with the ambience of the evening. Common sense told her he had chosen this moment because he thought her defences would be at their lowest. She didn't know much about the psychology of interviews and interrogation but she reasoned that, when a subject was distracted, they were least likely to remember a lie. And she supposed Sartine was rationalising along the same lines and trying to trick her into giving a truthful response.

'No,' she said softly. 'I'm not acquiring *La Coste* for myself.'

Through the slits of his mask, Justine could see Sartine's eyes widen.

Without hesitating, she added, 'I don't want it *just* for myself. I want it so my new lover can read from its pages while I tongue her pussy. That's what I want it for.'

She didn't know whether it was disappointment or admiration that furrowed his brow but she quietly understood that she had passed another of his tests. There was no time to enjoy any feelings of success from the accomplishment because he chose that moment to hand her to a party of masked females who eagerly crowded around her.

Her legs trembled beneath her and she was aware of aches and stiffnesses that she hadn't expected to suffer. While she had been kept in a sitting position, Justine hadn't thought she was exerting that much effort or energy. But it seemed as though each violent orgasm had taken its toll and her muscles throbbed as though she had come back from an arduous workout. Not allowing the discomfort to spoil her enjoyment of the evening, Justine stumbled eagerly toward the waiting crowd.

A breast was pushed against her mouth.

She had barely begun to suckle against the nipple when a feminine tongue licked at the lustre of semen coating the tops of her thighs. Fingers and lips combined to tease her to a sudden frenzy of arousal. The memory of every ache and pain was suddenly forgotten as the need for more pleasure took hold. At the back of her mind, Justine knew that she hadn't fully recovered from the barrage of climaxes that had already been wrought upon her. But the party's female guests were thrusting her toward a point of no return and she was happy to follow their lead. The inner muscles of her sex throbbed from the repeated spasms and convulsions she had been made to suffer and Justine couldn't bring herself to fight the burden of enduring more.

Delicate mouths moved close to her sex, teasing her clitoris and lapping gently against the sticky labia. Manicured nails and velvet fingers stroked her skin with caresses that were the height of sensitivity. Justine caught her breath, and then released it in a long and tranquil sigh. She stared down at her chest and saw two beautiful masked faces devouring her breasts. Turning from one mischievous smile to the other, shivering as both breasts were teased to an unbearable scream of responsiveness, her arousal spiralled to new heights.

The dynamism of the men was swiftly becoming a memory as the gentle passion of the female guests transported Justine to a dizzying revelation of ecstasy. She groaned as the frustration built in her loins and then sighed as a carefully placed kiss sated the desire for orgasm. Enthralled that so much pleasure could be hers in one evening, she relaxed into the arms of the women around her and allowed her body to be licked, touched and nuzzled.

The climax came more forcefully this time.

Fingers had punctured her sex, sliding easily in and out of her semen-lubricated hole. A gifted hand teased at the nub of her clitoris, squeezing the bead of flesh and treating it to the stimulation it so desperately needed.

Two fingers – possibly belonging to two separate people – penetrated her anus and wriggled easily back and forth. A giddy rush of joy took hold of Justine and hurtled her toward an epiphany of bliss. Her mouth was dry; the tendons in her neck strained from exertion; tremors shook their way through her body. She gasped, grunted and cursed as the welter of delight shook her frame. With a wail of tortured pleasure, she tore herself from all the skilful hands that teased at her bare body and curled into a satisfied ball.

The crowd pulled her back into their embrace and stretched out her limbs.

Whereas before there had been nothing but delicacy to the caresses, Justine could now feel a hard edge to each kiss and nibble. The lights above her provided a glorious halo to every woman who loomed over her and Justine eagerly used her mouth to tongue pussies, breasts and backsides as they were pushed into her face. The stench of sexual excitement was now on every breath and, each time she swallowed, she realised the taste was tainted by the flavour of arousal. Mists of dewy musk erupted over her brow, cheeks and jaw, dousing her with a perfume of raw sex and making her splutter with the need for release. Each time a gifted pair of lips or fingers pushed her past the brink of climax, she wanted to weep with a gratitude so strong it hurt.

It was something of a change to feel masculine hands take her into an embrace. Justine was delighted to have a champagne flute placed in her grasp and she greedily sipped the proffered drink as someone steadied her balance. So much had happened with such intensity that she hadn't realised the thirst that now parched her throat. When she had drained the glass she raised her gaze to see who had been chivalrous enough to hand her the champagne.

Sartine smiled at her from behind his mask. 'Are you working for Dupont or Weiss?'

'You already know who I'm working for,' she sighed. 'Why do you try and tease me with these bothersome questions? Do you think I've been misleading you? Do you suspect me of being duplicitous?'

'Who are you working for?' Sartine pressed. 'I know you're in the employ of one of the senior members. Give me a name so I can know for certain. It won't effect my decision on your suitability. You've already proved yourself to be a hedonist after my own heart.'

She took a deep breath, met his mesmerising brown eyes and said, 'I'm working for *La Coste*. I have no other master except the Marquis's words.'

He smiled.

Justine didn't know where the insight came from but she felt sure she had finally convinced him that her motives met the standard he required. She allowed him to place a tentative kiss on her lips, and then melted against him as his tongue plundered her mouth. She could feel them both becoming swept up by the rising passion and was stunned when he stepped away from her and snapped his fingers.

A dozen men appeared behind him and leered at her with hungry passion. The women who came to their sides wore the same expressions of avarice, lust and determination. With her heartbeat hammering frantically, Justine realised that every pleasure she had so far enjoyed would pale compared to whatever it was she was about to receive.

Ten

'You had a strange telephone call last night.'

Justine brightened when the penitent spoke and she turned quickly to smile. The sudden movement reminded her of all the muscular aches that still pained her following the excesses she had enjoyed at Sartine's party. It was impossible not to grimace. The stone seat and the gloom of their surroundings didn't help to make the discomfort any more bearable. They were sitting in a bleak cellar and the only light came from a barred window high above. The air around them was dank with scents of dirt, dampness and disuse. But those seedier distractions were all forgotten when she heard the cheery lilt of the penitent's voice.

'A telephone call? Who was it?'

'I do not know,' the penitent murmured. 'It was a strange conversation. She was a rather stiff lady. She asked for you. But she would not leave a name. Only a message. And that was rather strange.'

Justine frowned and tried to work her tired thoughts around the puzzle of who could have been calling and why. She could only imagine one potential caller who wouldn't leave her name and might be described as 'a rather stiff lady'. Grimly, she readied herself for the message the penitent had taken from Mrs Weiss. 'Was she rude to you?'

'No ruder than many other English I have met.'

'What was the message?'

'That is the peculiar thing. She did not leave her name. She *would not* leave her name. But she said to remind you that you do not know her.' The penitent shrugged. Smiling uncertainly she asked, 'That is a strange message, yes?'

'Yes,' Justine agreed glumly. 'I guess that's as strange as they come.'

She closed her eyes, annoyed that Mrs Weiss was still pressing on that same point as though it was something she was likely to forget. Justine knew that she wasn't to reveal her knowledge of the woman's identity. She had made a point of pretending she didn't know the name Weiss on each occasion when Sartine had brought it into the conversation. And she didn't understand why her employer was making such a big deal about the issue. The repeated instruction made Justine feel as though Mrs Weiss lacked faith in her abilities to obey a simple instruction.

'Does the message make sense to you?'

Justine nodded. She grinned when the penitent placed a hand on her knee and felt the weight of her dour mood begin to lift. Fingers on bare flesh were always exciting and a prickle of lewd arousal began to shiver through her loins. Justine studied the woman's face to see if they were thinking along the same lascivious line and she was delighted to see the blonde's smile shone with the promise of sultry mischief.

The previous night had ended too soon; exhaustion had left Justine in a state of limp elation; and she had been carried back to her bedroom. The penitent had bathed her, taken her to bed and allowed her to sleep. She had been awake before Justine when the alarm sounded and had carefully helped her dress for the journey to Vincennes Castle. From her studies of de Sade's life Justine knew this was the first place where the Marquis was imprisoned.

Ordinarily she would have been thrilled to enter such an historic building. It was under the control of the French Ministry of Defence, with access limited to those holding appropriate authority. Normally she would have been delighted at having access to such a restricted area and knew her enthusiasm would have bordered on being manic.

But, because she felt weak and tired from the excess of Sartine's party, she hadn't found the enthusiasm to show any interest in her surroundings. Hiding behind a pair of dark sunglasses, she had allowed their limousine to drive through the castle's ornate gates and not noticed any detail as the penitent led her down a series of stone steps into the dungeons of the main keep.

It was only now, when she saw the teasing glint of the penitent's smile, that Justine found her thoughts returning to the arousal that had plagued her since arriving in France. Sartine's driver had given them instructions for where to wait and, now they were alone, Justine wondered if there might be a chance for her to enjoy the penitent's intoxicating charms. The swell of the woman's breast pushed at the front of a tight blouse. Justine could see the shape of a frilly bra: but she could also see the fabric was so flimsy it couldn't contain the stiff nipples swelling inside its confines. The thrust of both buds jutted toward Justine, reminding her of the easy relationship she had formed with the delightful woman by her side. Excited by the prospect of what might develop as they waited, Justine returned the penitent's smile and leaned forward to grace her lips with a delicate kiss.

'NO!'

The whistle of a crop descending followed the exclamation. Justine and the penitent instantly pulled apart and the crop snapped against the stone seat between them. Justine glanced up, ready to splutter with outrage. When she saw the foreboding figure that towered over them the words died in her throat. Beside her the penitent gasped with obvious horror. Justine saw a flurry of movement as the woman put a hand over her mouth to contain a scream.

Tall and broad, the man was swathed in a jet-black robe. A hood concealed his face in a dark grey swirl of shifting shadows. Justine could see he wore black pants and boots beneath the robe, and his bare hands were clean and neatly manicured suggesting a reasonable person was concealed under the disguise. But, because he had crept up on them with a stealth that was almost preternatural, because he wielded a crop and stood in a position of absolute dominion, she didn't dare challenge his authority.

'You will not touch each other in this donjon,' he growled. 'Your movements here will be strictly limited.'

The penitent stared at him with such obvious terror Justine ached to hold the woman in a comforting embrace. She glared at the hooded figure, trying to summon the courage to ask him who he was and on what authority he acted, but she couldn't bring herself to speak. The crop he held looked like a vicious weapon and she didn't doubt he would have no qualms about using it however best suited his needs. The idea made a finger of unease squirm inside her stomach.

'Sit on opposite sides of the room,' he demanded. Using his crop, he pointed at a second stone seat facing the one they shared. 'It will be easier for you both if the temptation to touch is removed.'

'Who are you?' Justine managed.

'I'm the man who is giving you instructions.'

She drew a deep breath, intending to point out that he wasn't giving her instructions because she wasn't going to obey them. Before she could voice her defiance the penitent had scurried to the opposite side of the donjon and placed herself primly on the stone seat. She continued to regard the hooded figure with wide-eyed horror and Justine was pained by the woman's obvious discomfort.

A brilliant white smile gleamed from the shadows of the hooded figure's cowl. She saw a malicious twinkle where she imagined his eyes to be and was unsettled by the thought that she was being lewdly appraised. It was almost as though her fear was being confirmed when he breathed the word: 'Undress.'

Justine stood motionless, determined not to obey.

It was impossible to argue that the idea excited her. She was standing in the donjon of Vincennes – possibly close to the room where de Sade himself had been imprisoned – and a menacing figure was demanding that she undress. It was a sexual fantasy that had played through her thoughts a hundred times before but she was reluctant to surrender so easily. Adamant that she wouldn't prove to be such easy prey, she shook her head from side to side.

'Undress,' the hooded figure demanded. He turned from Justine and glared at the penitent so that she knew his order was meant for both of them. 'Strip. Take your clothes off. I want to see you naked. Both of you naked. Now!'

Clenching her jaw, finally finding a command she could disobey, Justine stood up from her seat and glared at him. 'I'm not following one more instruction until you tell me who you are.' She placed her hands on her hips, determined that she would look like a formidable adversary. Her hopes of defying him began to sink when she saw the penitent was already stepping out of her clothes.

The blonde's skirt and blouse were quickly cast aside. She stepped out of her shoes and then stripped off her bra and pants. The chill of the donjon was enough to make her flesh prickle with goosebumps and Justine found herself torn between the pleasure of admiring the penitent's body and the disappointment of knowing she would now have to follow her friend's lead and strip as they had been commanded. Hesitantly, still trying to think of a way of avoiding the embarrassment if it was possible, she reached for the buttons on her blouse.

'Are you going to strip now?' he enquired. 'Or do you want me to help you?'

Angry, and uncomfortable with the man's anonymity, Justine defiantly pulled her blouse open. After spending an evening being teased by a party of more than a hundred masked strangers she had thought there would be no shame in stripping for anyone. But, as she exposed more and more flesh, and heard the approving rasp that came from within his cowl, Justine was stung by a furious humiliation. Her cheeks flushed crimson, her pulse beat at a faster tempo, and she was appalled to feel a slick heat invade her cleft.

He brushed the tip of his crop against her backside. The curved leather end slipped over the small of her back, across her panties, and then down to her bare thigh. The touch was nothing more than the lightest caress but she flinched as though he had flicked it hard against her rear.

'Remove everything,' he insisted. He briefly turned to glance at the penitent, his hood shifted as though he was nodding approval, and then he was rounding on Justine again. 'You've been told to strip and, if you don't do it faster, I'll stripe your backside and then tear the clothes away myself. Is that what you want?'

Instead of answering, she hurriedly pulled her underwear away. The quick movements reminded her of all the aches and pains she was trying to forget but she didn't allow the discomfort to show on her face. Standing naked before him, holding herself proud and erect she tried not to tremble when he raised the crop. Her bare breasts looked paler this morning, a harsh contrast against the cherry swell of her stiff nipples. She didn't want to accept that the hooded figure's bullying had aroused her and preferred to believe she was still sore from the torment of the previous evening. That explanation didn't cover the bristling hairs at the back of her neck, or the fluid warmth that trembled through the muscles of her sex. But it was preferable to thinking she could be excited by the gruff and menacing figure that threatened her with a crop.

'Is this to your satisfaction?' she asked curtly.

'You've stripped,' he allowed. 'Now turn around and bend over.' Justine was about to voice an indignant refusal when he turned to glance at the penitent and delivered the same instruction to her. 'Turn around and bend over. I'm going to stripe both your backsides in preparation.'

'Who are you?' Justine hissed. 'And on whose authority are you making these demands?'

'Do you want to acquire *La Coste*?'

'Yes. But –'

'Then bend over.'

It was an argument she knew she couldn't win. The penitent was already bent double, her perfect backside exposed, the split down the centre glistening with the same dark arousal that tormented Justine. She held her breath, hoping that the threat of punishment was not serious, and then that idea was banished as the sting of a crop bit across her backside.

'Justine!'

The penitent's concerned cry was a whisper beneath her own hiss of discomfort. A blazing line of pain was branded across both cheeks of Justine's rear and the rush of heat in her loins grew slicker and more furious. She braced herself, ready to suffer another slice of the crop. But, when she heard the whistling descent and the crack of its tip striking bare flesh, she realised it was her blonde lover who had been punished with the second blow.

The penitent released a soft moan.

Justine started to turn, ready to tell the hooded figure that he had no excuse for punishing her companion. He landed a vicious slash against her left buttock and its force was enough to staunch every syllable of complaint

138

she had been about to make. Clutching at herself, trying not to whimper with discomfort, she glared over her shoulder at him as he drove another blow against the penitent's backside. When Justine heard her friend shriek, she could almost feel the woman's pain.

'Six each,' the hooded figure said solemnly. 'More if you insist on moving.'

It was a cruel instruction and Justine toyed with the options of defying him, or allowing the punishment to continue. Common sense told her that she should relent and suffer the torment of the crop but she didn't want to simply submit to four more blows of such brutal force. Some of her reluctance came from a natural sense of self-preservation but a greater part was caused by her knowledge of what would happen once she did give in. As long as she was challenging the hooded figure, Justine knew that she didn't have to acknowledge the arousal that his punishment inspired. As soon as she stopped questioning his authority, she feared that her body would have no reason not to respond to the hateful torment.

The swish of another blow striking the penitent made Justine want to wail at the injustice. She stifled her own sob as the blonde cried out and then braced herself for the slash that she knew was about to strike her own backside.

The hooded figure did not disappoint.

He landed the crop sharply against her buttocks igniting a line of liquid fire across her cheeks. As Justine gasped for air, struggling not to be won over by the surge of white heat that seared the tops of her thighs, she felt the warmth radiate into the moistened lips of her sex. The pain was infuriating and exciting and she quietly cursed her body for taking so much pleasure from the stinging punishment.

The penitent moaned as another lash struck her bottom.

Justine thought it difficult to work out whether she was hurt more from the sting of each blow, or if the cries of the penitent caused more suffering. Listening to the blonde's pitiful sighs – knowing that she was suffering solely because she had accompanied Justine to Vincennes – made for an unbearable sound. When the crop bit against her own backside Justine reasoned that she had the advantage of feeling some pleasure. Hearing the penitent's miserable sobs only made her feel guilty and unhappy.

Another sharp bite from the crop stopped her thoughts from progressing down that avenue. Her tormentor slashed a further blow to the penitent and another across Justine. The force of each shot was despicable and she gasped for air as she tried to make her body accept the pain.

At the back of her mind she could picture her rear striped with crimson lines. The image was as hateful as the pain itself because it fuelled a fresh unwanted arousal. Deliberately, she stared at the timeworn stone seat. She didn't dare to close her eyes for fear of seeing that mental image again and being overwhelmed by its power. From the discomfort she could feel Justine knew her pale cheeks were marked by weals that all but glowed with their heat. She concentrated on the stone seat, scared to look over her shoulder because she knew the sight of the penitent's punished rear would prove as exciting as the mental image of her own behind. Breathing deeply, telling herself the ordeal was almost over, she winced sympathetically when the penitent cried out. A tear trailed down her cheek but Justine couldn't decide if she was crying because of her own discomfort or the suffering that her friend was having to endure.

The crop hissed and spat against her backside.

Justine stiffened and then heard the penitent cry out again.

Her backside was numb from the abuse and she didn't want to believe that she felt the final blow when it struck the tops of her thighs. There was no point in denying the furious arousal that now smouldered in her cleft. When she was allowed to stand up and face the hooded figure she knew the symptoms of her excitement would be as obvious as neon signs. Her nipples were standing stiff and erect, the flush of heat in her loins had made her labia feel sticky with wetness and she knew her colour would be high and obvious.

But she still managed to glare at him when she was told she no longer needed to bend over. 'Who are you and what do you want?' Justine gasped. 'Everyone else I've met throughout this acquisition has had the courtesy to introduce themselves. You are just some coward who hides inside a cowl and bullies my companion and me. Who are you? Why were you punishing me and my friend like that?'

'I am the introduction,' he grinned.

'I don't understand.'

'I'm not the person who will be punishing you. I'm merely an introduction to what you can expect for the next couple of days. I was simply told to come down here and have you both naked and striped in preparation.'

'In preparation for what?' Justine asked warily.

'In preparation for me,' a voice boomed from the stairwell above them.

They all turned to stare at the ominous figure descending upon them. Hooded and cowled, dragging a whip in one hand and a length of chain in the other, the figure was menacing and formidable. 'You've been tested in your responses to sacrilege and found acceptable. You've been treated to an orgy of excessive pleasure at Sartine's hotel and he informs me that you have the nature of a true hedonist. Now comes the true test of your abilities.'

141

Justine glared at the newcomer, sure she knew what would come next and dreading the words she was about to hear. The second hooded figure stepped close to her, tossing the cowl back to expose a familiar face that was twisted with raw rage and anger. Justine's sudden understanding of the situation struck her like a vicious slap across the jaw.

'My name is Mrs Weiss,' the woman thundered. 'And I'm here to see how you respond to pain and punishment.'

Eleven

'You were making things awkward for my assistant,' Mrs Weiss growled. 'Do you have an explanation for your behaviour?'

'I was –' Justine began.

Common sense told her that she should simply state that the assistant had refused to say who he was or explain his authority. She hadn't been trying to make things awkward for anyone: she had only been looking out for her own interests and those of the penitent. It seemed like a reasonable argument to make but the words refused to come and she could only stammer nonsensical replies.

'I'd just . . . I mean . . . he wouldn't say . . .'

'It's a good thing we're not going to be troubled by a language barrier,' Mrs Weiss sneered. Her dismissive sigh indicated that the social niceties of the exchange were ended. 'Shut your mouth,' she snapped. 'Bend over and show me your arse. Let me see if my assistant truly marked you as you deserve.'

Justine paused for the briefest moment.

Mrs Weiss slapped her hard across the jaw.

The blow was not powerful but it was sudden and unexpected. Her head reeled from the force of the palm striking her cheek and she gasped with surprise. Too startled to know how to respond she glared silently at her employer and tried to splutter words that would express her outrage.

'You . . . You hit me!'

'I'll hit you again if you don't do as I tell you.' Mrs Weiss spoke in a bored matter-of-fact tone. 'I won't repeat many of my instructions. I expect you to obey me immediately and I'll treat any hesitation as insurrection. Now shut your mouth and bend over or, truly, I shall slap you again.'

Justine acted with unseemly haste. She turned her back on the woman and assumed the same humiliating position she had been forced to adopt for the assistant. The vulnerability of her situation made her want to cringe but she wilfully pushed that idea from her thoughts. It was bad enough having to submit to Mrs Weiss without dwelling on the depths of shame to which she had now sunk. It would be worse if she was to let the woman know how much upset her domination was causing. Aware of Mrs Weiss's cruel streak, Justine could imagine the woman's delight if she understood the hurt she had inspired.

Cool hands stroked the burning cheeks of her buttocks. Justine could hear her employer draw a deep breath and wondered if the sound was meant to convey excitement, shock or disappointment. She tried not to let her body acknowledge any of the flares of discomfort that came when the woman's nails raked against her punished backside. It was obvious that Mrs Weiss was deliberately touching the marks that had been branded into her rear. She traced each weal with a forceful finger that rekindled every agonising memory of when it had been first inflicted. Cupping a buttock in each hand, pulling the cheeks apart until the flesh of Justine's pussy felt stretched, she sighed again.

'Isn't this fucking typical?' Mrs Weiss growled truculently. 'If you want a job doing properly you have to do it your-fucking-self.'

Justine's buttocks were released from the woman's cold and punitive grip but she suspected that her ordeal was far from over. Breathing deeply, not allowing herself to think about the picture she presented by being naked and bent over, Justine tried to relax in the hope that she would be able to tolerate whatever punishment and abuse Mrs Weiss forced upon her.

'I want a flail.' Without turning, Justine knew the words were being barked at the assistant. The iron in Mrs Weiss's voice was as cold and uncompromising as ever.

'I told you a crop was no fucking good. I said a flail, a cat or some nettles would work best for this job but would you fucking listen, you halfwit?'

Her question was followed by a mumbled apology and the sound of footsteps clattering hurriedly up the stone steps. Staring meekly at the floor, not daring to shift position in case it incurred Mrs Weiss's wrath or punishment, Justine put every effort into remaining still while she fought the tremors that wanted to shake through her body. It was a difficult position to maintain and she came close to spoiling her composure with a shriek when Mrs Weiss pushed a finger inside her pussy.

'I thought as much,' the woman grunted.

Shivering, Justine didn't respond. She stayed absolutely rigid as the slender finger slipped deeper between the lips of her sex. In the stillness she could feel the smoothness of the manicured and polished nail contrasting with the creases on Mrs Weiss's knuckle. The inner walls of her sex felt so acutely sensitive she even believed she could feel the whorls of the woman's fingerprint as they touched her most intimate depths.

'The crop might not have been as punishing as I'd wanted, but it's got you truly fucking horny, hasn't it?'

Justine felt her blush turn deeper.

The finger was snatched from her pussy and a hand slapped sharply across her backside. The pain was unexpected and more severe than she would have imagined. Justine didn't know if Mrs Weiss had flicked her wrist in a specific way, or if she had simply managed to catch a previously punished part of the buttock with chilling accuracy. Whatever the reason, Justine closed her eyes and tried to come to terms with the flare of blistering pain that shrieked from her backside.

'I asked you a question,' Mrs Weiss hissed. She had lowered her voice so she could spit the words into Justine's ear. 'I asked you a question and, whenever I ask you a question, you'll give me an immediate answer. Do you understand?'

'Yes,' Justine gasped. 'Yes. I understand.'

'The crop got you truly fucking horny, didn't it?'

'Yes,' Justine spluttered. The shame of the admission was forgotten as she hurriedly tried to appease the woman behind her. 'Yes, the crop got me horny.'

Two fingers were pushed into her sex this time.

Justine didn't know whether or not she should be appalled by her willingness to surrender to the woman, or if she should be sickened by the ease with which the fingers had slipped into her pussy. The realisation that she had become so intensely aroused by punishment and humiliation left her ill with self-loathing but that only enhanced the fetid heat between her legs. Her shame grew stronger as Mrs Weiss slowly pushed her fingers deep and then began to slide them back out.

'Which aroused you most? Was it the pain or the humiliation?'

'I . . .'

As she hesitated the fingers in her sex stiffened. Justine knew she was a breath away from having the hand snatched from her sex so she could be slapped briskly across her rear. Anxious to avoid that punishment – anxious to avoid any unnecessary punishment – she said quickly, 'I don't know.'

The hand relaxed and resumed the path it had been working before. Mrs Weiss slipped her fingers slowly in and out, exciting a flurry of dark arousal through the muscles of Justine's sex. Although she seemed capable of inflicting a vicious amount of pain when the mood took her, it was apparent that she could also caress with unnerving skill. Justine held her breath, wishing her body wasn't so easily excited, while a stronger tingle of arousal churned through her cleft.

Her nipples hardened. The pulse of her clitoris beat with renewed force. And she knew there was nothing she could do to stop Mrs Weiss from mercilessly dominating her.

'You must have some idea,' Mrs Weiss cajoled. Her tone was deceptively light-hearted and Justine warned herself not to be taken in by the suggestion of playful banter. 'Did you get wet when my assistant told you to undress? Did the humiliation of that instruction make you squirm? Were you excited by the prospect of having to strip for a hooded stranger? Or did you only start to get truly horny when he slapped the crop across your arse? Was it the pain that made you so hot and wet?'

Justine quickly weighed her options before replying. She couldn't recall which part of this torrid episode had inspired her excitement. She wasn't even sure if her arousal had been caused by the assistant's punishment and humiliation, or if she had already been excited from kissing the penitent. The latter option seemed more likely but there was also the possibility that the atmosphere of Vincennes had exerted an effect.

Since her days at university, when she had first discovered her affection for de Sade's prose, Justine had considered Vincennes, the Bastille and La Coste to be spiritual homes. The craving to visit them had never once left her and she didn't think it unreasonable to believe that any of those hallowed locations might have had some influence on her responses. She had certainly entertained countless fantasies about being used and abused in all of those places and she didn't think it unreasonable to suppose that her arousal could have come from the realisation of such a long-held ambition.

147

'Are you going to answer me, Justine?' Mrs Weiss enquired with deceptive sweetness. 'Or do I have to remind you of the rules under which we're operating?'

The fingers in her pussy stiffened and Justine knew she was half a breath away from having them snatched out of her hole so Mrs Weiss could slap a hand across her rear again. The prospect of suffering that humiliation was unthinkable and she rushed to provide a response.

'I think . . .' she began.

The fingers relaxed and stroked in and out.

Justine wanted to heave a sigh of relief. If she had listened intently Justine knew she would have been able to hear the gentle slurp of her labia kissing the fingers as they slid back and forth.

'I think it was . . .'

If she said the humiliation had excited her more, Justine wondered if that would encourage Mrs Weiss to treat her to more physical punishment. Similarly, if she said the pain had made her wet, Justine thought the woman might decide to concentrate her torment on the psychological ordeals of shame and embarrassment. From the little she already knew about Mrs Weiss, Justine was aware that the woman took a lot of pleasure from making people unhappy and uncomfortable. Trying to decide which response was likely to make her own life easier was a frantic game of trying to outthink her tormentor.

The effort made her shiver and sweat with the threat of mounting panic.

'I think . . .'

'You're doing a lot of thinking and no fucking talking,' Mrs Weiss growled. Her hand moved back and forth with unnecessary briskness. The prospect of her mood changing was moments away. 'Answer the damned question, bitch. Which got you wet? Was it the pain or the humiliation? I want the truth and I want it now.'

148

Knowing that the truth wasn't an option – not sure she knew what the truth really was – Justine drew a shuddering breath and said, 'I think it was the pain.' She could feel the muscles of her sex trembling around Mrs Weiss as she made the declaration. 'I'm sure it was the pain,' she decided. 'That's what got me wet.'

Footsteps sounded against the stone steps and the assistant called out an earnest apology as he stumbled to Mrs Weiss's side. Justine was amazed that the man had so easily gone from being a foreboding figure to becoming a mere aide whose presence was so simply forgotten. She marvelled that her employer was so able in her ability to manipulate subordinates.

'Will this suit your purpose, Madame?' he asked.

Justine didn't glance up from her position to watch his approach. She only heard his mumbled apology as he handed something to Mrs Weiss that rustled ominously. The fingers were pulled from her sex leaving Justine to feel wet, empty and frustrated. She tried to take deep breaths – to steady herself and prepare her mood for what was going to come – but she had a mounting suspicion that no amount of preparation would prepare her for whatever it was Mrs Weiss wanted to dole out.

'The pain excited you most?' She sounded almost thoughtful.

Justine dared to glance over her shoulder and saw the woman was idly examining the flail that her assistant had found. It was a horrible-looking instrument, innocent enough with its soft thongs dripping downwards, but Justine suspected it would inflict a lot of pain when it was used against her.

'I'm so glad to hear it was the pain that excited you the most. That means you'll consider me to be very generous when I start to hurt you.' Her pleasant tone of voice vanished and was replaced by the crisp authority with which she had barked instructions before. 'Reach behind yourself bitch. Pull your arse cheeks apart. Now!'

Justine almost hesitated. The instruction came so quickly, and was so appalling and gratuitous, that she almost balked with indignation. Realising that such defiance would only make her suffering worse, Justine reached behind herself, placed a hand on each cheek, and pulled her buttocks apart.

For an instant she didn't think there could be anything worse in the world. The embarrassment of exposing herself in such a position was crippling. The discomfort and humiliation of having to stretch her anus and sex lips for the entertainment of her employer was so intense she couldn't find thoughts to encompass properly the injustice. And then Mrs Weiss struck her and Justine discovered there were far worse things than mere embarrassment.

The flail was an agony.

It crackled through the air – a rush of leather thongs that bristled stiffly together – and then it burnt against her backside like a branding iron. Justine couldn't contain her shriek of protest as the knotted tips of the flail scratched at her cheeks. They stung against the ring of her anus and scourged her pussy lips. The flare of pain was sudden, sharp and excruciating. Her body was instantly drenched with sweat.

Made slippery by the rush of perspiration, her fingers slid from her backside.

'I told you how to hold your-fucking-self,' Mrs Weiss bellowed.

The flail struck twice: once for each cheek.

There wasn't the exquisite agony of being struck on her exposed cleft but the pain was still severe. Justine didn't know if she was experiencing the agony of having her previous crop marks made freshly uncomfortable or if the flail was more punishing an instrument than she had expected. Whatever the reason, she released another grunt of dismay and quickly tried to get her hands onto her backside so she could do Mrs Weiss's bidding and hold herself properly open and exposed. The tips of her nails scratched against the punished flesh and, although she wanted to flinch, she forced herself to stay still in readiness for the woman's abuse.

'That's better. Lose your grip again and I'll whip you like this for the rest of the day.' As though making good with her threat, she lashed the flail hard against Justine's rear.

Justine's scream echoed from the donjon's stone walls. The bitter and panicked cry resounded pitifully but, because Mrs Weiss continued to strike at her as she shrieked, Justine realised that no one was going to come to her assistance. The understanding that all her yelling would prove ultimately useless made the pain of the torture seem even more unbearable and her cries trailed off to sobs.

'Keep on screaming if you like,' Mrs Weiss encouraged. 'It's satisfying to know I'm doing my job properly.'

Justine didn't bother acknowledging the remark. The raging heat at her sex burnt like lava. As the waves of agony rippled through her body the pulse of a black excitement snaked through her stomach. The inner muscles of her pussy trembled with mounting desire and she braced herself for another volley of blows.

'Is this enough punishment for you?' Mrs Weiss demanded.

She thrashed the flail down repeatedly, scourging Justine's flesh and exciting an intolerable heat in the lips of her labia. Her aim was galling and Justine shook her head in a silent refusal of the anguish.

'If you liked suffering punishment so much, is this enough to satisfy you?'

The series of harsh blows followed a pattern that first grazed her right cheek, then her left. A third, downward stroke scoured her exposed cleft wreaking agony against her anus and labia. Shards of raw pleasure were wrung from the hypersensitive skin around her sex. Mrs Weiss repeated the pattern with brisk determination, putting extra emphasis on the final stroke. Panting heavily she asked again, 'Is it enough to satisfy you?'

'More than enough,' Justine gasped.

Each time the multi-thonged whip hissed through the air, Justine thought she was ready to endure the torment. Each time it slapped against her flesh she flinched and released a groan of despair. Admittedly the pain was exciting – a welter of dark responses blossomed in her loins and she could feel herself hurtling toward an unwanted climax – but when she accidentally stretched her fingers as the pleasure took hold, she heard Mrs Weiss grunt with obvious disapproval as Justine lost her grip on the cheeks.

The flail lashed sharply against her buttocks while Mrs Weiss snapped, 'Follow my fucking instructions. Hold your arse cheeks apart until I tell you otherwise.'

Each scratching blow made Justine want to weep from the torment of humiliating pain. The force with which she now administered each slap had gone from cutting to unbearable. Scrabbling to hold herself open again Justine tried to think if there were any words she could use that might get her employer to show some degree of mercy.

'You must stop. You are hurting her.'

The flailing came to an end and Justine realised the penitent had spoken up on her behalf. She glanced over her shoulder and saw the naked blonde stepping out of the shadows and bravely facing Mrs Weiss. Beyond the thundering pulse that beat in her temples she could feel her emotions swing from gratitude to terror. A part of her wanted to warn the penitent to get back in the shadows and remain hidden but a bigger part of her was grateful for the distraction that had brought her torment to an end.

'You are using unnecessary force and you are hurting her,' the penitent said earnestly. 'Can't you hear her cries? Don't you understand that she wants you to stop?'

Mrs Weiss ignored the penitent and turned to her assistant. 'Who the fuck is this?'

Still hiding within the cowls of his robe, he shrugged. 'She was here when I arrived. I don't know who she is. I assumed she was part of the package.'

'That's not an answer.' Mrs Weiss turned to glare at Justine. Using her flail to point at the penitent, she asked, 'Who the fuck is she? What the fuck is she doing here?'

Justin swallowed and tried to think of a way to explain her companion. 'Father Dupont commanded her to come with me.'

'Does she have a name?'

'Possibly. I mean: of course. But I never got round to – I mean I haven't –'

Mrs Weiss raised one eyebrow and her smile lilted with obvious approval. The brief shift in her mood was quickly replaced by her thunderous frown as she said, 'It doesn't matter who she is or what her name might be.' Turning to her assistant she said, 'The bitch has no place here. Get rid of her. I don't want her cluttering up my donjon.'

'No!' Justine cried. She could see her exclamation did not please her employer but she was beyond caring about Mrs Weiss. Standing upright, knowing she was courting the woman's disapproval and almost certainly earning further punishment, she said, 'I want her to stay with me. I've fallen . . .' she faltered before she could say the words she had started and then picked up quickly. 'I've fallen into the habit of having her around.'

'How touching,' Mrs Weiss sneered. 'And how little I fucking care. She has no place here, therefore she goes.' Turning her attention back to her assistant she snapped,

153

'Send the bitch back to her village. Send her to Sartine or Dupont. Send her wherever the fuck you can, I don't care what you do with her, but just get her out of my sight.'

'I don't want her to go,' Justine said defiantly.

The assistant hesitated.

The penitent glanced at Justine with a smile of warming gratitude.

Mrs Weiss stepped between them and glared at Justine. 'Which do you want?' she hissed. 'Do you want *La Coste*? Or do you want this bitch? The choice is yours but, I'll tell you now, you can only have one.'

Justine glared at her. 'Are you serious?'

'Fucking right I am. Which is it to be? The bitch? Or *La Coste*?'

Shocked by the enormity of the decision she was being forced to make, Justine glanced from the helpless face of the penitent to Mrs Weiss's cruel leer. The idea of choosing one over the other was unthinkable and she shook her head as though refusing to make a decision.

'Which is it to be?' Mrs Weiss pressed. 'I can make the decision for you, but I'd like to hear you say the words. The bitch? Or *La Coste*? Choose wisely or your quest for the damned book might just end here and now.'

Justine lowered her gaze and stared at the gloom of the floor. Unable to look at the penitent, not wanting to see the expression of hurt or reproach that would be in the woman's eyes, she released a heavy sigh and whispered, 'I choose *La Coste*.'

Twelve

As soon as the assistant had taken the penitent from the
donjon, Mrs Weiss relaxed. She motioned for Justine to
sit on the stone bench and then removed a pack of
cigarettes from inside her robe. Justine declined the
cigarette and would like to have refused the instruction
to sit on the stone seat. But Mrs Weiss was adamant
and, reluctantly, Justine relented. The gritty surface was
harsh against her punished backside and the coldness of
the stone only served to remind her that her rear was
ablaze with uncomfortable marks. Shifting from one
position to another did nothing except exacerbate the
discomfort and she eventually sat still and accepted the
nuisance of not being at ease.

Mrs Weiss took the seat facing Justine and sat back
as she demurely crossed her ankles. 'You've done well
to get this far,' she said as she lit up. She took a couple
of draws from the cigarette and added, 'I was worried
you might expose me.'

Still thinking of the penitent, Justine said nothing.
The realisation that she would never see the blonde
again was enough to make her spirits sink to a new low.
The humiliation of being naked, and forced to keep her
bare bottom pressed against an abrasive seat, was
almost forgotten as she brooded on the loss of her lover.
If she hadn't thought it might give Mrs Weiss a degree
of pleasure, Justine believed she would have cried.

'I'm surprised you convinced Dupont. He can't stand
English women but I guess that sort of bigotry is typical
for Froggy left-footers like him.' She snorted a chuckle

of dark laughter and added, 'I was worried he might prove to be a stumbling block. Did Sartine make things difficult for you?'

'I passed his inspection, didn't I?'

Mrs Weiss tapped ash from her cigarette onto the floor. She regarded Justine with an expression of narrow disapproval. Her smile twisted into a nasty leer as she asked, 'How long are you going to carry on sulking about your girlfriend?'

The comment hurt and Justine raised her gaze to glare at the woman. Determined to play as cool a hand as Mrs Weiss, she asked, 'What would happen if I told someone you were my employer?'

Mrs Weiss tossed her half-smoked cigarette aside and stood up. Grabbing hold of Justine's hair she pulled her from the stone seat and forced her to kneel on the floor.

Staring down, fearful of the repercussions she had set in motion, Justine found herself swathed in the ominous darkness of the woman's shadow. If there had been any way to retract her question she would have babbled it swiftly but she knew it was too late to recant. All she could do was tremble and try to brace herself for the brunt of Mrs Weiss's wrath.

'That's a fucking good question.' Mrs Weiss's voice was bereft of humour. Her fingernails gouged at the vicious welts that had been tattooed on Justine's rear and it was apparent she was putting every effort into soliciting discomfort. The cheeks of Justine's backside were splayed apart; a palm rasped over the burning flesh of her labia; bony knuckles kneaded the most severe bruises and marks. Struggling to maintain her composure, Justine tolerated the abuse without daring to complain. She repeatedly snatched breaths as she tried to remain immune to the punishment.

'Quite a few things would happen if you revealed that I am your employer,' Mrs Weiss conceded. She pushed one finger against the wetness of Justine's sex. When the easy penetration provoked no response she moved her hand away and then tested the resistance of Justine's anus.

The temptation to shriek and wrench herself free was almost irresistible. But Justine held still as the manicured nail slipped through the muscle of her sphincter. She tried to relax as Mrs Weiss forced the penetration deeper but nerves and apprehension made her rigid. So many things had entered her rear over the past few days that Justine was surprised the muscle continued to put up any show of defiance. At Sartine's party she knew she had been repeatedly used by a dozen or more men, all blessed with erections that had much wider girths than Mrs Weiss's finger. But there was something shameful about the way the woman made the penetration – especially as it was clearly the precursor to a greater punishment – and it caused this entry to seem perverted and wrong.

'If you tell anyone I'm your employer you'll never see another page of *La Coste*,' Mrs Weiss promised.

Justine didn't want to let the woman know that the threat unnerved her. After all she had been through, after all she had endured in her attempt to acquire the legendary manuscript, the prospect of losing that opportunity caused a genuine pain. Those few lines that the penitent had read for her were enough to whet Justine's appetite for much more and she knew her curiosity wouldn't be sated until she knew the contents of every page.

She chugged breath as a second finger slipped alongside the first.

Her sphincter felt full and awkwardly overstretched and the penetration was an obscene joy that she refused to acknowledge. She shrivelled from the sick impulse of taking pleasure from Mrs Weiss's abuse knowing it was wrong: but a part of her craved to bask in the hateful sensations. Her anus was slippery with arousal. Both digits slid easily into her and the sensation of being full inspired a divine warmth.

Mrs Weiss pushed the fingers deep. When she spoke her tone had become brittle with barely concealed anger. 'Tell anyone I'm your employer and you'll lose that bonus I promised you. Your pay rise, promotion, and the cash incentive, will all disappear.'

That much, Justine had expected. She held her breath for a moment longer, trying to concentrate on Mrs Weiss's words rather than her actions. The woman had begun to ease her fingers slowly in and out and Justine could feel her loins wanting to respond with a spasm of pure delight. After going from extremes of pain and humiliation to the ordeal of being blissfully finger-fucked by her employer she wasn't surprised that her treacherous body found the ordeal arousing. But she was loath to let Mrs Weiss know she possessed such an effective control.

'I'll see that your name is publicly blackened,' Mrs Weiss continued. 'I'll start the gossip and the rumours myself if I have to so that everyone knows what a lascivious little tart you are, and I'll have Sartine provide me with photographs if necessary just so I can convince the last of the doubters.'

Justine remembered the flashbulbs exploding at Sartine's party and knew Mrs Weiss could make good on her threat. She remembered being quietly proud of the idea that she was being photographed. For some reason that she could no longer rationalise, she had thought that the prospect of pictures added a lilt of pleasure to the experience she was enjoying then. Now she could only think it had been an act of utter foolishness to let herself get caught on film.

'But the main thing you should keep in mind,' Mrs Weiss growled, 'the point you really should consider before opening your stupid mouth is: you'd earn my displeasure. For every second that I have authority over you – whether it's here in the donjon, tomorrow at *La Coste*, or back home at the library – I'll go out of my way to make your life a constant torment of physical pain and sexual humiliation.'

She said other things but Justine's thoughts focused on one phrase: *tomorrow at La Coste*. The knowledge that she was so close to achieving her goal was enough to let her accept the torment and abuse. The idea gave her such a thrill that, despite her best intentions to appear indifferent, the muscles of her pussy convulsed with a minor shiver.

Mrs Weiss laughed and, with the sound of the woman's nasty cackle, Justine realised she hadn't been concentrating on her words. She drew a deep breath and suppressed a moan as her employer slid a third finger alongside the first two. The stretching at her rear had gone from being delightful to unbearable yet a part of her still savoured the twisted pleasure of being used in such a cruel way. Chugging breath in staggered gasps, Justine tensed her inner muscles for fear they would inadvertently convulse and show Mrs Weiss how much she was really enjoying the humiliation.

'Have you dismissed the idea of exposing me?'

'Yes.'

'Am I assured of your loyalty and obedience?'

'Yes.'

'Are you going to prove your loyalty now?'

Each time Mrs Weiss asked a question she pushed all three fingers deeper. Justine struggled not to cry out but the stretching was so immense she couldn't contain every impulse to protest. Shivering from the embarrassment, and mortified by her own black enjoyment of the punishment, she gritted her teeth around an exclamation. 'Yes,' she whimpered. 'Yes. Whatever you want. Whatever it takes for us to get *La Coste*. I'll do it.'

The fingers were torn from her rear. Justine was left to feel empty and hollow as her inner muscles continued to tingle with the aftermath of a frustrated arousal. Hearing Mrs Weiss's footsteps, and understanding the woman was now standing in front of her, she slowly raised her tear-stained gaze. 'Whatever it takes,' she promised.

Mrs Weiss pulled her robe open. Justine was not surprised to see the woman was naked beneath. She had a lean and slender body that was painfully exciting to look at. Her breasts were ample and inviting, tipped with magenta areolae and thick stiff nipples. With a narrow waist and flat stomach she held herself in a pose that emphasised her silent authority. Lowering her gaze, Justine could see a forest of lush dark curls concealed the woman's cleft. Because her face was on eye-level with Mrs Weiss's pussy, Justine could also see that wetness had darkened the hairs at the centre of her sex. The pink flesh of Mrs Weiss's labia glistened invitingly.

'Prove your loyalty,' Mrs Weiss demanded. 'Prove your loyalty by eating my pussy.'

Justine didn't hesitate. She wasn't sure how close she had come to unfailing obedience but she no longer showed any vacillation when she was given a command. Moving her face forward, extending her tongue to the musky haven of Mrs Weiss's sex, she eagerly lapped the dewy folds of the woman's sex.

The syrupy flavour was cloying and brought tears to her eyes. As well as making her think of the intimacies she had enjoyed with the penitent, it also served to remind her that the pliant blonde was no longer in her life. Sniffing back the notion of crying, concentrating on sliding her tongue against the wet folds of flesh, she heard the woman above her sigh contentedly. The sound encouraged Justine to lap at the woman's clitoris and try to tease her tongue deep into the velvety folds of her hole. Her posture was awkward; the stone floor was harsh against her knees; the position meant her backside was stretched and reminded her of every lingering ache;

and her neck was uncomfortable as she strained to lap at Mrs Weiss's sex. But Justine couldn't deny that the humiliation aroused her.

Her chin was quickly daubed with a lather of the woman's musk. Burying her nose against the labia as she caught her breath, Justine was delighted to hear Mrs Weiss groan with obvious pleasure. She sensed a wave of joy flowing through the woman and then returned her tongue quickly to its chore.

The hand at her hair gripped tighter. Her face was tugged into the woman's cleft as Mrs Weiss thrust her pelvis forward. Guessing that she had to penetrate, not sure why the idea filled her with such a rush of dark need, Justine delivered a long deep kiss to the woman's sex. She pushed her lips close against the inner labia and thrust her tongue into the tight warmth of Mrs Weiss's hole.

The muscle convulsed around her.

As Justine continued to make her kiss as deep as possible, Mrs Weiss pulled harder on her hair and grunted her way through a bitter climax. Her pelvis bucked repeatedly forward, bashing against Justine's face and her groin exploded with a rush of wetness. Justine almost choked on the unexpected flow and made a concerted effort to pull herself free. Miserably, as Mrs Weiss continued to hold her head against her sex, Justine realised there would be no opportunity to escape until her employer decided. She was forced to remain on her knees, still lapping at the dewy labia, until the woman grunted and pushed her head away.

'You were struggling against me,' Mrs Weiss complained.

Justine wiped her mouth with the back of her hand and apologised. From the corner of her eye she noticed Mrs Weiss fasten her robe and then stagger to retrieve her flail from the stone seat. She cringed when she saw the merciless smile that filled Mrs Weiss's face as she clutched the small whip.

'You were struggling against me,' Mrs Weiss repeated. 'And that is unforgivable.'

Justine lowered her head and mumbled an apology. A knot of frustration lingered in her loins but she knew it would not be sated until the prospect either entertained Mrs Weiss or served her purpose. She was appalled to acknowledge the fact that the fury of the woman above her added to her excitement. It came as no surprise when the knotted tips of the flail struck her backside.

Unable to stop herself, Justine sobbed in protest. 'Do you have to go so hard on me?' she moaned. 'I'm doing this for you. Can't you show me a little leniency?'

The six harsh blows that followed seemed to answer her question. They landed in swift succession and scorched a searing heat through the punished flesh of Justine's buttocks. She realised Mrs Weiss wasn't taking the time deliberately to mark the flesh that was already striped but that didn't stop some of the lashes from kissing sharply against the raised weals. By the time the last shot had landed Justine realised she had squeezed tears from the corners of her eyes.

'I have you for the remainder of the day,' Mrs Weiss growled. 'And I have no intention of showing you any leniency.'

Justine said nothing.

Mr Weiss chuckled. 'Admittedly I'm going to give you my approval. But I'm going to make sure you earn it too.' She fell silent for a moment and it wasn't until Justine heard the sound of a lighter sparking a flame that she realised the woman was having another cigarette. The noxious scent of tobacco fumes filled the donjon and reminded Justine that she could still taste the flavour of Mrs Weiss's sex in her mouth and nostrils.

'I'm being harsh with you for two reasons,' Mrs Weiss explained. 'The first is because I don't know how my assistant might report these matters to Marais.' The tobacco smoke thickened her words. 'My second reason is more important though because that's the one that's really driving me to hurt you.'

Justine raised her gaze to study the woman.

'I want to get the full benefits of seeing you suffer underneath me.'

'You're a cruel bitch,' Justine mumbled.

The flail struck hard against her rear.

Justine howled.

'You don't have any idea how cruel I can be,' Mrs Weiss sneered. Her nasty laughter trailed off as she slashed three more blows from the whip across Justine's bare backside. 'You haven't got a clue about how cruel I can be. But, before the day is over, I'm going to make sure you have a better idea.'

Thirteen

They both glanced up when they heard the sound of approaching footsteps.

'That's my assistant coming back,' Mrs Weiss growled. She pushed her face close to Justine's, lowered her voice to a whisper and said, 'When he gets here, I'm going to give you some more rough treatment. If it gets to be more than you can stand: *tell me you want more.*'

'That makes sense,' Justine grunted.

Even as she was saying the words, Justine knew it was a mistake. Mrs Weiss's hand slapped against her cheek and delivered a stinging blow that almost pushed her to the floor. Stunned by the viciousness, Justine glared at her.

'Don't backchat,' Mrs Weiss hissed absently. 'And think sensibly for once in your fucking life: it makes perfect sense.'

Justine continued to glare. Because the woman was now standing and draped in her robe, while she remained naked and cowering at her feet, the feeling of vulnerability was stronger than ever. Justine supposed it was that sensation that made her lower her gaze as though the argument was already lost. She had to bite her lip to stop herself from mumbling a servile apology.

'I'll play the role of the vindictive tormentor,' Mrs Weiss explained. She kept her voice to a hiss and spoke with a quick urgency as the approaching footsteps drew nearer. 'When the torment gets too much for you, *you must ask me to hurt you more*. I'll refuse to give you what you're asking for. That way you won't have to endure any further pain; my assistant will believe you've been left frustrated; but he'll still think you have an appetite for suffering. Does that make sense?'

Still smarting from the blow, but aware the footsteps were almost at the bottom of the donjon stairs, Justine nodded gruff acceptance. She wanted to ask why the assistant's opinion mattered so much but she sensed the answer would involve an elaborate explanation about Mrs Weiss's place within *The Society*. Certain there was no time for such an exchange, and not sure she wanted the details, Justine said, 'I guess it makes sense. But you didn't have to hit me so hard.'

'Don't be so fucking wet,' Mrs Weiss spat. Her lips remained close to Justine's ear. The speed of her words blurred them together. 'Hold out for as long as possible before asking for more. Make it look convincing.'

'I can do that,' Justine admitted.

The flail snapped against her backside. A sharp tang of pain pierced her buttock and rippled through her body. 'Damned right you can do that,' Mrs Weiss agreed loudly.

The tone of her voice, and the way she pulled herself away, made Justine realise that the assistant was now with them. Holding back a squeal of protest she resisted the urge to clutch her punished buttock.

'My assistant's here now,' Mrs Weiss announced. 'Assume the position so he can make use of you before we continue.'

Justine opened her eyes wide: shocked and glaring at Mrs Weiss. The words of protest died on her lips and she realised this was merely another bridge to cross in her journey toward acquiring *La Coste*. And, while the idea of being used so brusquely made her cringe at first, she had to admit that her body craved some satisfaction. Mrs Weiss's brutal torment had left her feeling unfulfilled and the prospect of sating her arousal was an opportunity she didn't want to refuse. But, turning her head warily and assessing the huge figure within the hooded robe, Justine wondered if it was wise to submit to an abusive stranger she hadn't properly seen.

'Hurry it up,' Mrs Weiss demanded. 'We haven't got all fucking day.' As she spoke the flail slashed sharply against Justine's rear.

Another blister of pain skewered her backside. Gasping with surprise, Justine took three deep breaths before trusting her voice to come out without too much anger colouring the tone. 'Which position do you want me to assume?'

Mrs Weiss pointed with the flail and rolled her eyes as though Justine was stupid for not knowing. 'Bend over that stone seat. And do it quickly. You're beginning to piss me off.'

Obedient, not daring to do anything that might incur another display of the woman's wrath, Justine did as she was told. She could see the assistant leering at her from within the shadows of his cowl but wouldn't let herself dwell on what she knew would come next. Moving swiftly, bending over the stone seat and lifting her buttocks high, she tried to empty her mind of all thoughts and fears as she prepared herself for whatever the pair were planning. Her mouth was dry and her heart lurched loudly with every beat.

'Do what you will with her,' Mrs Weiss said sternly. The anger in her voice had mellowed to disinterest and Justine guessed the woman was addressing the assistant. 'The bitch needs to learn her place,' Mrs Weiss continued. 'And I want to have the cigarette she interrupted earlier.'

'She's mine?' the assistant marvelled.

Justine strained to hear an answer from behind her but there was only the crackle of Mrs Weiss sparking her lighter. When she caught the sound of the assistant's malevolent chuckle, Justine guessed the woman must have nodded her consent. Her stomach folded with dreadful anticipation.

Rough, masculine hands clutched her buttocks. The coarse weave of the assistant's robe brushed her rear as he rubbed himself against her. The temptation to scream for him to stop was irresistible but she continued to bite her tongue and willed time to move quickly so the experience would soon be ended and behind her. Unable to control the reflexive response, she stiffened and clenched the muscles of her backside closed.

'Don't start getting all virtuous,' Mrs Weiss growled. Her voice was cloudy with cigarette smoke. Justine could detect the acrid stench of tobacco over the scent of her own arousal. 'I know that you fucked Sartine's entire party last night. You won't shy away from one more cock, will you?'

Justine's cheek flushed crimson. She quietly conceded it was true that she had taken more lovers than she could remember at Sartine's party. But on that occasion there had been the giddy fun of dancing and music as well as champagne and glamour. The crowd had been composed of beautiful bodies and the spirit of the evening had been charged with hedonism, decadence and experimentation. Here there was only the gloom of the donjon, the stench of Mrs Weiss's cigarettes and the lingering pain that had been wrought against her backside. The inept groping of the woman's sinister assistant was like the antithesis of every pleasure she had enjoyed at Sartine's.

She heard the rustling of coarse fabric. Instinct told her the assistant was unleashing his erection and she bit back a moan of apprehension. His fingers had moved from her punished cheeks but, when they returned, she was unnerved to notice he was only holding her with one hand. Swallowing down the lump of unease that filled her throat, Justine steeled herself in anticipation.

The fat dome of his shaft's end brushed against her labia.

She hadn't thought her body would be so responsive but, as soon as he touched himself against her, a shiver

167

of raw need bristled from her sex. She didn't want to acknowledge the heat or the wetness but she knew her inner muscles craved him. Trying not to show her desperation, and still unsure about what else would happen to her while she was under Mrs Weiss's authority, Justine readied herself for the penetration.

The assistant placed the end of his length just inside her sex. He slapped both hands against her hips as he secured his grip and then pushed forcefully inside. His erection was thick, the length seemed to go on forever, and she moaned with a combination of disgust and delight. As he continued to plough into her, his thickness easily spreading her inner muscles, she was tortured by the thrill of being properly used. Since arriving at Vincennes Castle Justine had found herself squirming with frustration. Now that Mrs Weiss's assistant was sliding his meaty erection into her pussy, she didn't think it would take long before her body was allowed the release she needed. Her breath deepened to a laboured pant. She gritted her teeth together, trying to distance herself from every sensation and their twisted black pleasures.

'How does she feel?' Mrs Weiss asked.

'She's more than ready for it.'

The assistant's words shivered through his body and trembled along the shaft he had buried inside Justine. His erection was long enough to bruise the neck of her womb and, because she still couldn't feel his loins brushing against her backside, she suspected there was more of the abominable length to come. The realisation that she was impaled on such a huge erection inspired sensations of joy and horror.

'Don't treat her gently,' Mrs Weiss warned. 'She had enough of that yesterday. Make sure she knows what she's getting into.'

Justine pressed her lips tight together for fear of voicing an objection. The air was pushed out of her when the assistant renewed his grip on her hips and banged the remaining inches of his length into her sex. As though he was little more than Mrs Weiss's puppet he thrust deep on her command and turned the penetration from a fantastic revelation to a punishing encounter. His hold on her hips was vicious and unrelenting. As he began to slide back and forth she realised he was riding her with a brutal vigour. The inner muscles of her sex responded to him with a hunger she hadn't anticipated and Justine knew he would easily force a climax from her sopping hole.

'Make her squeal,' Mrs Weiss laughed. 'I want to hear the bitch scream.'

Her voice was closer and Justine guessed the woman was coming over to get a better view. The idea of someone enjoying her suffering was twisted but she couldn't deny it also sparked another rush of excitement. From the corner of her eye she saw Mrs Weiss's robed figure step into view and she cringed with a blend of shame and exhilaration.

The assistant rode her freely. The force of each penetration pushed hard into her pussy and sent a shiver through her entire body. With her forearms pressed against the stone seat, and her backside raised high in the air, Justine's breasts swayed in rhythm with his thumping tempo. She knew her body was inching closer to orgasm but she balked at the idea of enjoying the release. It was a rigorous exercise in punishing sex and she wondered if it was too early to follow Mrs Weiss's suggestion of how she could end the whole torturous episode.

A hand fell to her hair.

She instantly recognised Mrs Weiss's uncompromising grip and knew what was coming next. It came as no surprise when her head was lifted. Every follicle on her scalp screamed in protest. And then her face was tugged toward the wetness of the woman's sex. Acting on the

unspoken instruction, lapping greedily against the offered pussy lips as the assistant continued to bang into
her from behind, Justine felt the first tremor of orgasm
shudder through her frame.

The explosion happened without pleasure. The satisfying roar that came from her loins was brisk but
joyless. Even though she wanted to relish its delight, a
part of Justine's mind wouldn't let her bask in the
fulfilment that came from such callous treatment. A
cloudy haze blurred her vision, and her nerve-endings
tingled. But, as she regained her breath and returned her
mouth to Mrs Weiss's sex, Justine knew she couldn't
properly call the climax satisfying.

'Make me come, bitch,' Mrs Weiss growled.

She tugged hard on Justine's hair. The assistant
tightened his hold on her hips and pushed forward with
greater force than before. Another surge of responses
was driven through her hole. She began to devour Mrs
Weiss's sex as eddies of despicable delight trembled
along her sex.

'Make me come properly this time,' Mrs Weiss
grunted.

Anxious to obey every instruction, Justine threw
herself into the task of trying to coax another eruption
from the woman's hole. It was difficult to concentrate
on the task as the assistant continued banging into her
sex, but she was desperate to do anything rather than
suffer the woman's displeasure again. Lapping
greedily at the dewy sex lips, hungrily teasing the bud
of her clitoris, Justine struggled to make the woman
come.

'Don't try and tease me,' Mr Weiss warned. 'I want a
proper tonguing.'

Even when she felt the assistant buck hard against
her, Justine was still fixing her efforts on trying to urge
her employer's climax. His shaft pulsed inside her; the
inner muscles of her sex quivered around him; and then

her sex was dripping from the douche of his sticky eruption. But, all the time, she was concentrating on what Mrs Weiss wanted and how best to please her.

The assistant snatched his spent length from her hole, leaving her to feel hollow and empty. Justine barely noticed as she squirmed her lips and tongue awkwardly against Mrs Weiss's sex. He slapped a hefty hand across her rear and mumbled, 'Good pussy. I'll enjoy that again before the day's over.'

Still working hard on tonguing a response from Mrs Weiss, Justine didn't hear the praise. She continued to lap and tease, wishing she could look up at the woman and judge whether or not she was performing the chore properly. Her lips and mouth were lathered with a meld of her own spittle and Mrs Weiss's juices. The flavour of the woman's sex was rich each time she swallowed. The scent of musk filled her nostrils and perfumed every breath. Sure she was close to making the woman's sex burst with pleasure, suddenly desperate to make her groan with delight, Justine threw an extra effort into lapping at the dewy folds of flesh.

Mrs Weiss pulled her head back sharply.

Justine almost screamed with frustration and pain. She was dragged from the stone seat and pushed unceremoniously away.

Ignoring her, calmly studying her assistant, Mrs Weiss said, 'Bind her hands and hang her in the corner. She's more fun when she's suffering.'

Biting back the shocked exclamation she wanted to make, Justine made no move to stop the assistant as he wrapped cord around her wrists in a loose figure eight. She thought of telling him that the bondage was nowhere near tight enough to hold her properly, then realised neither he nor Mrs Weiss wanted to hear her opinions. Tugging her as though she was merely a piece of meat, the assistant led Justine to a corner of the donjon beneath a low hanging hook. He slipped her

171

bound wrists over the aged metal and then turned to Mrs Weiss as though waiting for her approval.

Justine found she had to stand on tiptoe to stop the torment from being a suspended bondage. It was difficult to forget her vulnerability and she despised the realisation that apprehension was adding to her arousal. Having her arms above her head made her feel exposed. The assistant stood in front of her but, with Mrs Weiss lingering behind, Justine didn't know what to expect. A finger of unease tickled down her spine and heightened her sensitivity. She quietly dreaded the woman's reason for having her suspended from the donjon's hook and she wouldn't let her mind speculate about what was going to happen next.

The sting of the flail across her back gave Justine an idea of what the woman was planning. When it was followed by three more lashes – each more punishing than its predecessor – she understood she was going to be thoroughly whipped. The prospect of being flogged was a double-edged barb: one side making her stomach churn with despair, the other heightening her arousal.

'Are you going to help me with this?' Mrs Weiss asked her assistant.

Justine glared at the burly figure, hoping he would say no and knowing there was no chance of that happening. She saw the shaded glint of his smile in the shadows of his cowl, and then watched as he reached for a spare flail that hung from the wall. His large fist encircled the handle; he tested its weight with a short, sharp snap; and then he was slicing the knotted tips against her breasts.

Justine howled with surprise.

Almost as though she was administering the punishment to enforce silence, Mrs Weiss swept her flail sharp against Justine's buttocks. The hiss of leather biting through the air became a constant in the donjon's claustrophobic atmosphere. Interspersed with Justine's pained exclamations, the sound was like something from a medieval torture chamber.

Her breasts were quickly turned raw.

The assistant's punishing blows left a million weals standing stark against her wan flesh. Before any of them had the opportunity to fade, he drove fresh pinpricks of agony against her. Justine was appalled to see her nipples standing hard as the punishment continued and she tried not to think of how that response reflected her appetites.

The flail at her back struck more viciously. Mrs Weiss was clearly trying to scourge every inch of bare skin and alternated her blows from the centre point between Justine's shoulder blades down to the tops of her thighs. Her buttocks were in agony each time the knotted tongs lapped at her punished cheeks. But the pain was no less intolerable when Mrs Weiss inflicted it anywhere else. On those occasions when she struck a hip – causing the lengths of leather to curl around Justine's side and bite at her lower stomach – she could barely contain a cry of protest.

And, acting as though they were ignorant of her suffering, Mrs Weiss and the assistant chatted blithely above her sighs and moans. Because they spoke in French, Justine easily shut out the sounds of their conversation and concentrated on the misery she was enduring. She wondered if it was too early to use Mrs Weiss's suggested ploy to end the punishment early. The prospect of concluding this ordeal before it proved too humiliating was very tempting and she opened her mouth, ready to beg for more. A part of her knew it would be a struggle to say the words – every inch of her body screamed that she should simply beg for it to stop – but she couldn't imagine Mrs Weiss heeding those words.

Drawing a deep breath, telling herself that she could play the role of the submissive for just a little longer,

Justine suddenly realised the pair had started to speak in English. More importantly, she thought she had heard some mention of her beloved penitent.

'Say that again,' the assistant demanded.

'I asked: what did you do with the blonde?' Mrs Weiss repeated.

Justine raised her head, anxious to hear the answer. All thoughts of getting the pair to end the punishment were gone from her mind. Her interest in their conversation was immediate and all consuming. Even though they continued to lash her bare flesh with their flails, the multi-thonged tips scouring her back, sides, buttocks and breasts, she was oblivious to the pain and only aware that they were discussing her blonde lover.

'She'll be on her way back to Dupont in the next half hour,' the assistant told Mrs Weiss. 'Maybe sooner if the car gets back here faster.'

'She's still upstairs?' Mrs Weiss asked.

Justine flicked her gaze between Weiss and the assistant. She wished she could see his face, rather than just the shadows cast by his cowl, and she wondered what Mrs Weiss was considering. A part of her believed it was probably best if she didn't let her thoughts chase too far ahead or try to outguess Mrs Weiss. But, with the prospect of renewing her acquaintance with the penitent, Justine found it impossible to heed her own good advice. She twisted on her suspended bondage and tried silently to implore the woman. The lashes that Mrs Weiss landed now struck her left side. The side of her left breast was repeatedly caught by the woman's flail and, if not for the rising pain, Justine would have marvelled at the woman's accuracy when she repeatedly slashed raw agony through the tip of her nipple.

'Would you want me to bring her back?' Mrs Weiss asked.

There was something in her tone that made Justine think, whatever she wanted, Mrs Weiss would do the opposite. Aware that her spirits were sinking, but unable to give up hope of seeing the penitent again, she said honestly, 'You know that's what I'd want.'

'Is there still time to retrieve her?' Mrs Weiss asked the assistant.

Unable to stop herself, Justine could feel her hopes rising as she waited for the man's answer. Ignoring the discomfort that came from her bondage, putting aside all thoughts of the agony they were whipping from her bare flesh, she turned herself slowly back to face him.

'She's waiting for the car to return. I can't imagine she will have gone yet.'

'What do you think?' Mrs Weiss whispered. She pressed herself close against Justine's naked body. Standing behind her, the woman was able to cup Justine's breasts, squeeze and fondle. The forced intimacy was intrusive and unwanted but, because she was being offered the chance of getting the penitent back, Justine allowed it to continue without a word of complaint. The coarse weave of Mrs Weiss's robe was abrasive against Justine's sensitive buttocks. Her fingernails were long and sharp and delivered scratching caresses.

'Would you want her back?' Mrs Weiss sighed.

'You know I would.'

'Would you be prepared to make a sacrifice to get her back?'

'I'd do anything.'

'Anything?'

Justine could hear the animal hunger in the woman's question but that didn't trouble her. Sure she was on the verge of recapturing the penitent, she nodded eagerly and said, 'Of course. I'll do whatever you ask.'

Her hands were lifted from the hook. The release made her realise her legs were weak and she almost stumbled to her knees. Mrs Weiss helped her to fall completely to the floor and then towered over her.

Frightened, and suddenly uneasy about the blind commitment she had just made, Justine stared up as the woman tore open the front of her robe. Her naked body was exposed in all its magnificent glory as Mrs Weiss stepped closer and pushed her sex in Justine's face.

'If you want her back, then you'll drink my *pipi*,' she growled.

Justine remembered the penitent using the same word at Sartine's and tried to recall the circumstances when it had been used. Horror threatened to overwhelm her when she remembered it was the same word the penitent had used before disappearing to the hotel's en suite. A sickening wave of understanding made her want to shake her head in refusal. But, because she was being offered a chance of recapturing the penitent, Justine wouldn't let herself refuse.

'Of course,' she agreed.

The words almost choked her. She wasn't wholly sure what she was agreeing to, or how bad the ordeal would be, but she pushed her face close to the woman's sex and tilted her head back. Extending her tongue, she lapped tentatively at Mrs Weiss's labia.

'Oh! You good little girl,' Mrs Weiss declared.

Encouraged, but remaining wary, Justine pushed her tongue more firmly against the woman's sex. She slipped the tip between the dewy folds of Mrs Weiss's labia and daringly tasted her wetness. An odour of rich musk and perspiration assaulted her nostrils. A shiver of raw arousal trembled through her bare body.

'That's it,' Mrs Weiss agreed. 'That's just what I wanted.' She grabbed a fistful of Justine's hair and held her head in place. As Justine spluttered for air, she heard Mrs Weiss bark, 'Use her, you fool. Let's both of us use this bitch properly.'

The assistant needed no further encouragement.

Justine sensed movement behind her. She caught the pungent stench of the man's erection and then felt it pressing between her buttocks. His smooth entry into her sex was so easy she felt ashamed. But, all the time, she continued to lap, lick and suck at Mrs Weiss's hole. Even when the assistant began to hammer himself forcefully into her hole, his enormous shaft burrowing perpetually deeper with each thrust, she didn't stop squirming her mouth against the split of the woman's sex. She tried listening for a sigh of pleasure or some other sound that would indicate she was properly satisfying her employer, but Mrs Weiss remained frustratingly silent.

The assistant's hands gripped tight against those punishing weals that had been scratched into her flesh. Justine bit back cries of discomfort as his hold tightened against her aching skin. Each forceful thrust battered raw excitement through her inner muscles but the delight was tempered by the discomfort of his fingers dragging over the sore marks.

The donjon was painfully silent. Justine could hear the vague sounds of the world beyond their closed room; occasional footsteps clipped overhead; a car horn beeped twice; and the faraway strains of birdsong reminded her she was not so far away from the real world. But she suspected there would be a lot more to endure before she got a chance to escape and enjoy any of those banal pleasures.

'Drink me,' Mrs Weiss demanded. The urgency of her voice snatched Justine's thoughts away from her contemplation of the world outside the donjon. 'Drink my *pipi*,' Mrs Weiss hissed.

Her tone was higher than normal: the first indication that she had been affected by Justine's tongue. Although the moment was a blur of confusion as the assistant pounded into her and her body continued to hurt, Justine could sense something was about to happen.

And then Mrs Weiss released a scalding jet of urine.

Justine wanted to gag and rear back but she knew that wasn't what the woman wanted. Reminding herself she was enduring this ordeal for the sake of the penitent, she pushed her face close to the source of the golden shower and allowed the spray to wash her face, nose and lips.

'That's it,' Mrs Weiss exclaimed.

The assistant rode more vigorously.

Justine didn't know if the man was excited by the sight or scent of what was happening, or if he was simply close to his own point of ejaculation. She realised she was suffering from her own blackly excited responses to the ordeal but she couldn't equate those with the despicable pleasures she was enjoying.

Mrs Weiss's *pipi* was a pastel scented douche that burnt on contact and then chilled in an instant. Justine went from suffering the shock of the heat to the shivers of the cold within seconds. Her face streamed with yellow tears, her throat scalded against the shameful taste of Mrs Weiss's release and she felt as though she had reached a new depth of degradation. Her resultant orgasm was strong enough to wrench the climax from the assistant's shaft.

The waves of pleasure were still trembling through her pussy even when she was dragged from her knees and returned to the suspended bondage in a corner of the donjon. There was no opportunity to clean her face or even wipe her hair dry from the wetness that plastered it to her scalp. And, before she had a chance to understand properly what had happened, Mrs Weiss had resumed her cloak and the assistant had begun to slash the flail at her bare and battered body.

'My friend,' she moaned. She twisted on the bondage and glared desperately at Mrs Weiss. 'The blonde girl,' she prompted. As best as she was able, Justine flashed her gaze from her employer to the assistant. 'Are you going to get her back for me?' she gasped.

'It's too late,' the assistant explained. Justine thought she could detect a smirk in his voice. If his face hadn't been concealed by shadows she would have had a better chance of working out if he was laughing at her. 'Didn't you hear the car horn while you were drinking from Mrs Weiss?'

Justine recalled the sound with chilling clarity.

Mrs Weiss landed her flail sharply against one buttock. 'The sound of the car horn was the signal from the driver to say he was leaving,' she explained. Her laughter was short, sharp and callous. 'You should have been faster about pleasuring us,' she snapped. 'Perhaps then you might have been able to save your precious friend.'

It was more than Justine could tolerate. She released a howl as the next flail landed while the following one evoked a sob of despair. Within half an hour she was groaning as each hatefully exciting stroke stung her bare body. Outrage, anger and frustration all vied for control of her responses, but each barb of pain prevented any reaction from winning. It was only when she realised Mrs Weiss had defeated her – and that she had no option except to suffer the cruelty of the woman's discipline – that Justine decided to call an end to the torment.

The assistant used the flail with enough force to make her scream each time his whip descended. Mrs Weiss did not put as much energy into each shot but her accuracy more than made up for that. Every stroke either landed against a breast, a buttock or the tops of Justine's thighs. She rekindled discomfort in every aching red line and evoked a scream with each stroke. The pain was exciting – it inspired a fluid heat between her thighs that was strong and undeniable – but Justine wanted no more of the anguish. Hurting, miserable, and tired of her quest, she thought it was time to end this aspect of the ordeal. Drawing a deep breath, spitting out the air as another stroke of the flail bit cruelly against her left breast, she remembered the instructions she had been given to end the torment and tried to follow them to the letter.

'More,' Justine whimpered.

The pain that held her body was enormous. She didn't know if she was suffering from an excess of ecstasy or anguish but she knew it could not go on any longer. Shivering from the extremes of orgasm, crying from relief, agony and delight, she said, 'I want more. Give me more.'

'More?' Mrs Weiss repeated.

Justine began to relax, thankful that this phase of her ordeal was about to end.

'Did she say she wants more?' Mrs Weiss asked her assistant.

'That's what it sounded like to me.'

A finger of doubt tickled at the back of Justine's thoughts. She could suddenly see the foolishness in trusting Mrs Weiss and she cursed herself for not thinking further ahead.

'If she's asking for more, then we'll give her some more,' Mrs Weiss declared. 'Get yourself hard again,' she told her assistant. 'Let's see if we can satisfy her filthy appetites if we both work together.'

Fourteen

'You're a dirty little bitch, aren't you?'

Justine held herself still when she heard the man's voice. The ruins were pitch black save for a sliver of moon that rent the night sky above. She had never deceived herself that she was alone; the sounds of muted breaths and shuffling feet were all around; there had been several moments, as she staggered through the overgrown ruins of the castle, when Justine could sense a presence so close it was almost as though she was being caressed. But still, coming so abruptly from the darkness, the unexpected voice shocked her. More than that, it reminded her of the words Mrs Weiss had so recently spat from the impenetrable darkness of her private library and she began to wonder if this was some stylised introduction that *The Society* had made their own.

'You're a dirty little bitch, aren't you? You're a dirty little bitch who needs a damned good thrashing. Is that why you've come here? Have you come here to have your backside thrashed?'

'I've come here for *La Coste*,' Justine returned coolly.

Behind her an unseen woman sighed.

She wanted to turn, and try to find out who else shared the darkness with her, but she suspected she was still being judged. Maintaining a defiant pose, not sure she could be seen but unwilling to risk a momentary lapse, Justine stared expectantly into the gloom and waited for him to speak again. Her heartbeat lurched fast within her chest and she struggled not to tremble and show her apprehension.

A metallic click broke the silence. The sound was familiar and Justine experienced no surprise when she heard the ring of a flint wheel striking inside a petrol-lighter. After a flurry of sparks, she saw a broad blue flame dancing before her. The suggestion of a face was illuminated; the flame was applied to a candle; and as the wick flourished to bright yellow life she finally saw the man who was addressing her.

'Good evening, Justine,' he began cordially. 'Welcome to *La Coste*.'

Without any need for an introduction, she knew this was Marais: the book's owner. He extended a gracious smile, gallantly greeting her as she adjusted her eyes to the searing glow of the candle. Rather than looking at him, Justine wanted to admire the crumbling relics of the castle in which they stood.

Being inside *La Coste* – having arrived at her journey's end – was almost more than she could accept. She continued to stare around, noticing for the first time how the ancient stones stood stark against the night sky. Poorly illuminated silhouettes in the night – their uneven edges suggesting forgotten magnificence and encroaching decay – the crumbling ruins added a sense of doom to the night. The atmosphere made Justine believe she was on the verge of meeting her destiny and she caught her breath before it could turn into a sigh of expectant wonder. Her pulse quickened and she was touched by a thrill of adrenaline that inspired a painfully familiar response.

Her stomach folded with dread and arousal.

The sensitive split of her cleft felt suddenly moist and far too warm.

'It's been a long time since anyone got this far,' Marais explained pleasantly.

Justine maintained a polite smile, not sure what the comment meant or how she was expected to respond. The temptation to press her thighs together was almost

182

irresistible but she defied the urge and continued to regard him with forced detachment.

'I've been told you're more than worthy of acquiring *La Coste*,' Marais continued. 'Tonight, before you take this book away, you will have proved that worthiness to me.'

Her eyes shone with anticipation when she realised he was holding the manuscript. The fallen magnificence of the building around them was forgotten as her gaze fixed on the unpublished work. The pages were yellow-brown with age, their contents black, scribbled and smudged to an indecipherable scrawl. Justine realised it was a book written in a language she couldn't understand and she knew she had prostituted herself to obtain it for a woman she didn't particularly like. The incongruities of the situation struck her every time she let her mind consider what she had done or reflect on why she was doing it. But she pushed all those thoughts aside as she reminded herself that she needed to have it. '*La Coste* is mine?' she asked doubtfully. 'I can take it away with me this evening? Tonight? Now?'

Like a skilled magician, Marais made the manuscript disappear from the reach of the candle's glow. He held out an empty hand for her and said, 'You've proved your worthiness to *The Society*. A successful bank transfer has put the necessary funds into an escrow account. I only want to see the evidence of your suitability for myself and then it's yours.' He cocked an eyebrow, tilted his head, and asked, 'Do you think you can prove that worthiness to me?'

She stepped through the overgrown weeds that separated them and, taking the hand he had offered, pressed herself into his embrace. He was the debonair hero she had expected. With his hair swept back from an open and honest face, he looked stylish and attractive. There weren't many verified images of the Marquis de Sade in the pages of any of the history texts she had consumed at university but, if Justine had ever harboured an idea of what he might look like, she suspected he would bear a striking resemblance to the man she now held. His clothes had an antiquated appearance that befitted the splendid decay of the building in which they were meeting. Around him was a subtle cologne that conveyed a sense of clean masculinity but didn't quite conceal an aura of perpetual arousal. He was everything she had hoped he might be and, when he began to kiss her, his passion made the inner muscles of her sex tremble.

While he continued to hold the candle in one hand his other held her tight against his body. A powerful leg pressed between her thighs; her breasts were squashed against his broad chest; his fingers kneaded against her buttocks; and she knew he was going to use her with a cruel and demanding force. The thought filled her with a smouldering excitement.

His fingers crept beneath the hem of her short skirt. Because Mrs Weiss and her assistant had scourged her so severely the previous day, Justine hadn't been able to tolerate the idea of wearing panties for this final part of her journey. Sitting in the back of the limousine had been an arduous chore and she had shifted restlessly throughout the drive as she tried to make her buttocks comfortable against the pressure of the leather seats.

And, although those pains weren't forgotten as Marais's hand smoothed over her bare flesh, they were put aside in favour of more important considerations. She wasn't wearing panties and his fingers were now mere millimetres from touching her uncovered sex. The prospect sent a shiver of anticipation bristling through her pussy. Fired by an urgent need for satisfaction, she pushed hard against him.

Marais laughed. He continued to hold her but seemed to hesitate rather than push his fingers close to the spot where she needed them. Regardless of how much Justine squirmed or wriggled against him, he refused to touch the sensitive lips of her sex. 'You're quite the eager little bitch, aren't you?' he chuckled.

The words shocked her, reminding Justine of the priest she had seen on her first night in France. The temptation to pull away from his embrace came suddenly and she almost acted without thinking about what she was doing. It was only because Marais slipped his fingers against her at that moment, his cool caress sliding over the velvety warmth of her sex, that she was able to stay in his arms. A flutter of electric responses tingled through her hole. She was suddenly swathed in perspiration that defied the cool air of the night. Her heartbeat raced, her mouth turned dry and she responded to him with an eagerness that was almost embarrassing. As he touched more intimately, insinuating the tips of his fingers deeper between her wet and pulsing muscles, she rubbed furiously against him.

'What do you want from me?' she begged.

'Nothing you aren't prepared to give.'

In contrast to his calming words, his fingers pushed further into her cleft. The wetness of her sex easily accommodated his rough entry. The slippery muscles parted eagerly to allow his penetration. And Justine squirmed happily on him. The low-grade fever of excitement that had held her in its thrall for the past three days was now a burning desire. The simple satisfaction of having something inside her was almost enough to inspire a climax. She gripped him tightly, making her embrace inescapable, and then squeezed her inner muscles around his fingers. The ripple of responses that flowed through her body was glorious and intense. Shocked by her easy acceptance of Marais, Justine tried to rationalise her need for him.

It pained her that the penitent was no longer by her side. In the few short days they had been together, the blonde had offered reassurance and perpetually promised a passionate reward. But Justine supposed she had begun this journey alone and it was only right that she finished it in the same solitary state. The thought offered little consolation against the prospect of never seeing her lover again, but she wouldn't allow her mood to be spoilt by brooding on those things she had no hope of changing.

And it was easy to push immaterial thoughts from her mind as Marais slipped the jacket from her shoulders. His fingers were drawn slowly from her cleft, leaving her aching for him and dizzied by her body's responses. In the stilted silence that lingered between them she could hear her pussy lips kissing his fingers farewell as they were snatched away from her sex. She barely had the chance to realise the night was clement when he tugged her blouse away and then changed his embrace.

Rather than holding her with his chest pressed against hers, he was suddenly grabbing her from behind. His candle had been placed on a table and its dim glow showed enough of the polished surface to let Justine know the furniture was not part of the established ruins. But, rather than worrying about such extraneous detail, she found herself concentrating on the way he now pressed against her. The bulge of his erection strained against her and she understood he wanted her with a need that matched her own. Her skirt was hitched up to her waist, no longer a barrier between them, and she could feel the coarse fabric of his pants dragging against her punished buttocks.

Determined to prove that she was worthy, Justine wriggled against him. The movement was uncomfortable because Mrs Weiss and her assistant had left Justine's rear raw and aching. The flesh of her backside felt bruised from the repeated blows of the whip but she was determined the ache wouldn't stop her from pleasing Marais or enjoying what he had to offer. The bulge that rubbed against her felt large and solid and she was surprised by how easily her mind's eye pictured the enticing length of flesh he had to offer. Excited by the thought of squeezing herself around him, Justine reached one hand behind herself and stroked him through the fabric of his pants.

He pushed her hand away, tore her skirt from her hips, and then forced her to bend forward. Now firmly under his control, Justine found herself sprawled across the same table where Marais had rested his candle. The polished surface of the top pressed cold against her breasts. The edge of the table cut into her stomach and, as Marais spread her bare buttocks apart, he slipped a hand firmly against her wetness.

Her heart hammered more quickly when she realised he was going to take her.

Unable to conceal her excitement, Justine released a soft moan.

She remained aware that they weren't alone. From the darkness she could hear murmured breaths, whispered comments and the sounds of muted restlessness. Not for the first time she marvelled that so many people could be involved with *The Society* and she wondered how they had found each other. It sounded as though a hundred or more voices were lurking in the shadows that held *La Coste* and she knew they all shared the same beliefs. Remembering her own private thrill on first discovering de Sade's work, she envied them the confidence that had allowed *The Society*'s members to share their thoughts with fellow libertines.

But, because her audience clearly wanted to remain unseen and anonymous for the moment, she told herself there was no problem fretting about who the voyeurs were or how they had come to form this twisted community. Additionally, with Marais sliding his fingers between the cheeks of her buttocks, teasing her sex lips and then caressing the puckered ring of her anus, she had no urge to think about anything other than the divine sensations his touch inspired.

'Let's start the night with an apéritif,' Marias suggested.

Behind her she heard the familiar sound of a zip being released. The stiff cotton of his shirt rustled as he freed the erection from his pants. And then the warm weight of his shaft was pushing against her. The centre of her sex was touched by the slippery heat of his length. Wet with arousal, either leaking pre-come or lubricated by her own excitement, Marais slipped easily over the split of her pussy lips.

Justine caught the scent of his sweating arousal, felt the pressure of a swollen dome squeezing between the cheeks of her backside, and then he was pressing himself inside. It wasn't until she felt the resistance of her anus, straining in protest at the penetration, that she realised how he intended to use her. By the time that thought had registered properly the first inches of his erection were already ploughing into her rectum.

She shivered and clenched her muscles tight around him. A stiff sigh – not quite a shriek, but close – faltered from her lips.

The sphincter protested at the abuse and she came close to begging him to stop. Then, as the pleasure quickly outweighed the discomfort, she was caught in the thrill of being used. Her body mellowed from its stiffness and her natural response to the pleasure took hold. Won over by her host's brutal introduction, Justine allowed fresh eddies of joy to shiver through her rear.

Marais groaned as he pushed himself deeper. His length was long and thick, sliding forcefully along the narrow channel of her rear.

Lost in the darkness that surrounded them, able to concentrate on every physical sensation rather than being distracted by anything, Justine was able to revel in every glorious sensation. She could feel each millimetre of Marais's erection as it surged deeper into her hole. Her body was so attuned to him that she could follow the rounded shape of his swollen glans as it thrust along her forbidden passage.

Justine curled one hand into a fist while the other clawed helplessly at the table beneath her. Having his shaft fill her bowel was both disquieting and exhilarating. The knowledge that they were little more than casual acquaintances added to her excitement. The freedom of giving herself to this man whom she didn't know was an unexpected enticement to her arousal. As he began to glide back and forth, she wondered when she had turned from being a mere librarian to becoming a woman in touch with her body's needs and responses.

Marais's brutal treatment didn't allow her much scope for reflection. As he battered exquisite sensations through her rear, Justine cried out for him with a mixture of anguish and satisfaction. His pace quickened, the splendid intrusion became even more delightful, and she forgot all about the certainty that strangers were watching from the shadows. Even when unseen fingers brushed against the back of her hand, and hidden voices murmured approval about Marais's technique, she was easily able to think of those voices as belonging to her imagination.

'Go on, you bitch,' he panted. 'Take it all. Take every fucking inch.'

As he hammered each thrust into her anus, he called her a whore, a bitch and a filthy slut. His tone was vulgar and, after beginning in English, he slipped into a guttural French that was clearly more familiar to him. He cursed her with a string of invectives that Justine didn't understand but knew she deserved.

Quietly thrilled by his low opinion, and urging herself ever closer to the climax her body needed, she groaned when he cupped her breasts. His hands were strong, chilled by the night, and they pawed viciously at her flesh. But none of those handicaps stopped the sensations from being delicious. Catching her nipples between his knuckles, squeezing until the pain was nearly unbearable, Marais allowed his fingernails to scourge a litany of anguish against the swollen orbs. With a groan of satisfaction, Marais rode her more vigorously, pounding each thrust forcefully into her backside.

It was a gratuitous experience – devised only for his pleasure – but Justine was elated to be a part of the moment. The inner muscles of her anus were bombarded by the sensations his length inflicted and it did not take long before she shrieked with the joy of release. Her sphincter clenched hungrily around the thick intruder and a spasm of pure delight shook through her frame. Through the all-encompassing darkness she could see explosions of glorious light as the orgasm shivered through her body. Someone groaned with obvious ecstasy and it was only when she felt the cry trembling over her lips that Justine realised she had been listening to her own sigh of contentment. Breathless and elated, she wondered how Marais was managing to resist his own climax.

Behind her, she heard him gasp. There was something in the exclamation that made her realise the cry had come from between clenched teeth and she understood he had been using every effort to stave off his ejaculation. Smiling tightly to herself, eager to show him she was a worthy recipient of *La Coste*, Justine squeezed the muscles of her anus tight. His penetration became harder and more forced. His final thrust was less controlled than his previous movements and, before his groan became a sigh, Marais had exploded inside her.

She had known his orgasm was close but she hadn't expected it to come with such surprising speed or force. He buried himself deep into her rear, exclaiming in a torrent of French expletives that she hoped never to understand. His erection thickened as his shaft released a jet of scalding semen. The douche was enough to inspire a scorching climax inside Justine and, startled by the intensity of her reaction, she cried out into the night. Fresh waves of pleasure washed over her as Marais continued to pulse his seed into her bowel.

The darkness around her took on a mist-like quality and she realised she was on the verge of losing consciousness. Forcing herself to breathe deeply – determined she wouldn't pass out so early on in the evening – Justine lay breathless over the table as Marais dragged his spent length from her backside. Tremors continued to shiver through her body, a testament to the intense delights she had enjoyed. But she wouldn't let herself concentrate on her personal pleasure.

She could hear Marais's breathing was slightly laboured and his words were tinged by a smirk of satisfaction when he finally spoke. 'That was a good beginning to the evening,' he grunted.

Turning round to face him, finally able to discern his features from the darkness, she asked, 'Have I proved my worthiness?'

Marais laughed. She had thought he was too much of a gentleman to appear cruel or unkind but now she could see that idea had been severely misplaced. The malicious undercurrent of his tone evoked a prickle of dread.

'Have you proved your worthiness?' he repeated. 'That was nothing more than foreplay, Justine.' Snatching hold of the candle, raising it high so it fully illuminated his face, he gave a distinct nod.

Justine understood he was passing a signal to someone but she had no idea who it might be. It wasn't until a second candle fluttered into life, and she saw a mature and familiar face, that she realised how the night was going to progress.

A thin-lipped smile beneath hard black eyes appraised her with barely concealed distaste. 'Bonsoir Justine,' he murmured. 'It's good to see you again.'

Her cheeks flushed crimson and Justine swallowed thickly as she mumbled her own greeting to the priest.

Fifteen

'Marais is correct,' the priest mumbled. 'It's been a long time since anyone got this far. You've done better than any of us expected.'

She thought the remark was meant as a compliment but she couldn't bring herself to take it that way. Something about the priest's stiff manner immediately made her feel defensive. Justine subconsciously realised that Marais had stripped her when he used her and she cringed from the idea of being caught in such an embarrassing way in front of the priest. It crossed her mind that this man hadn't simply seen her unclothed before – he had treated her to a humiliating ordeal that left her feeling ill when she recalled the sacrilege she endured – but none of those thoughts stopped her from fretting that she was standing naked and used in front of a minister of God.

'Father,' she said softly. Inadvertently her hands stole to cover her breasts and her exposed sex. The modesty of her actions struck her as being senseless but she couldn't control the impulse to hide her body.

The priest ignored Justine and glanced into the shadows behind her.

Justine briefly marvelled over his ability to see those things in the dark that she couldn't discern. But she got the impression that this was a ritual with which he and the other members of *The Society* were familiar. Two figures loomed close to her and she guessed they were acting on the priest's instruction. They were asexual, and both cloaked in hooded robes that reminded her of

Mrs Weiss's assistant from the previous day. Neither had the commanding bulk that had been possessed by that man but the similarity in their clothes made Justine wonder if this was a dress code for subordinates of *The Society* and another facet that united the members as a group.

Each of the priest's assistants took one of Justine's hands and raised it to shoulder level. She was led backwards until her buttocks touched something solid. Her wrists were swiftly bound to a horizontal plank behind her and she allowed her captors to tie her without protest. It was only when she realised there was no give in the bondage that Justine fully understood she was at the mercy of the priest. Surrounded by unseen strangers – naked, helpless and vulnerable – she was dismayed to think how easily the priest could now abuse her trust. The thought inspired a rush of fresh wetness between her legs and, with that response, she realised her appetites had sunk to a level that was truly depraved.

From the shadows, the assistants lit candles and placed them at her feet.

Justine was able to see that her ankles were touching the base of a stout wooden cross and she shrank from the blasphemy of the pose that the priest had forced her to assume. Struggling against the restraints, suddenly scared that she might be taking the concept of sacrilege too far, she tried to find the strength to pull free. Her stomach folded as she contemplated the irreverence of mocking the crucifixion. A part of her wanted to close her eyes and shrink from the wickedness of what they were doing but she knew Marais would see that as a sign of weakness. She also suspected the priest would be livid if he thought she was not proving herself worthy. But, more important, she found that a part of her longed to be involved in the sacrilege. Breaking so many taboos was a powerful and intoxicating thrill, and Justine found her body now needed that additional excitement that came from doing something so forbidden.

'You've done well to get this far,' the priest assured her. His voice was smooth and controlled: a stark contrast to her mounting panic and unease. 'You've done *very* well to get this far,' he corrected. 'But I want a little extra from you this evening. Do you understand?'

Too frightened to say or do anything, Justine could only nod. She remained uneasy with the thought of suffering this perverse punishment, fearful she was running the risk of damning her soul for all eternity, but the idea of disobeying the priest was equally unappealing. Not only was the fate of *La Coste* at stake but, if there was any chance of getting back her beloved penitent, Justine knew it would come from pleasing the priest. Anxious to do everything he asked as she pursued that particular goal, and telling herself she had no choice because the bondage made her an unwilling participant, Justine watched the priest remove a cat o' nine tails from the folds of his vestment.

The coils of leather unfurled like a nest of snakes. In the stillness of the night, Justine imagined she could hear them hissing as they fell to the floor. Shards of candlelight glistened from their restless bodies as they twitched and writhed ready to make their mark on her. A tremor of wet excitement bristled through the inner muscles of her sex.

'Very nice.'

Marais's approving voice made Justine feel ill. She tried glancing through the shadows to see his face but could only make out a vague silhouette. It was impossible to decide if that made his appeal seem more sinister or more arousing.

The threat of being whipped didn't trouble her. After all she had endured at the hand of Mrs Weiss, Justine felt sure she could tolerate another scourging. Recalling the previous day, she remembered that it had not been without some pleasure, although she couldn't understand how her body could take arousal and satisfaction from such callous torment.

But she still felt queasy about the priest's profane use of sacred imagery and her own involvement in that blasphemy. Drawing a nervous breath, and wishing her body were no longer riddled with the delightful eddies that remained from Marais's heavy-handed use of her, she steeled herself in readiness for the assault.

'In the name of the Father, the Son, and the Holy Ghost,' the priest began. As his voice intoned the words, he slashed the cat hard against Justine's naked frame. The multi-thonged whip cut heavily through the air, tearing the night into shreds. The cruel tips landed against her with shocking force and, unable to stop herself, she screamed.

Each lash was powerful and scratched her with the full and vicious weight she had expected. A part of her had wanted to remain silent through the punishment but the stinging agony was more than her body could tolerate. Stunned by the pain, and disgusted by the excitement her suffering inspired, Justine released a second wail as the priest lashed her again.

The wicked tips of the thongs bit at her breasts and abdomen.

She didn't dare glance down at herself, fearful of putting her face in danger and uneasy at the thought of seeing how severely her body might have been marked. When he struck again it felt as though he was aiming purposefully for her nipples. Both buds of flesh had been grazed by the cat and they stood hard, hot and proud. The stimulation was enormous, thrilling her with an urgent need for satisfaction. Equally powerful was the ache that also held her and Justine squeezed her eyes closed to keep back further tears. Breathing heavily, she tried to prepare herself for the next blow of the cat.

But it didn't land.

When she dared to open her eyes and glance at him, she saw the priest was fixing her with a menacing glower. 'I want to hear your confession.'

She stiffened at the words, as she would have recoiled from another bite of the whip. Shaking her head, not sure who else was there listening from the shadows but appalled at the idea of confessing her sins to them, Justine thought of begging him to reconsider his punishment.

The whip twitched in his hand, as though he was preparing to administer more stinging encouragement. His inscrutable features studied her with the gravest solemnity. 'Your confession, Justine,' he prompted. 'Let me hear it now.'

'Forgive me father, for I have sinned.' She blurted the exclamation before he could hurl the whip at her again. Trembling from a combination of cold, terror and mounting excitement, she fixed him with a steely gaze and said, 'It has been three days since I was last in a confessional box.'

The priest's smile was bitter. He genuflected quickly, the sharp movements of his hand making it look as though he was swatting at flies from the night around him. 'Carry on,' he encouraged her. 'Tell me your sins.'

She could sense an air of expectation around her and wondered briefly where she should begin. The sins she had committed over the past three days had been numerous and embarrassing. To reveal them to the priest in the privacy of a confessional booth would have been mortifying: to expose them to a crowd of peers that she couldn't see was more intimidating than Justine would have believed. There was no question in her mind that she had to keep her association with Mrs Weiss a secret. But she supposed everything else needed to be confessed to the priest for fear of suffering further consequences.

'I eavesdropped on the confessions of members of your parish,' she began.

The whip slashed through the night, its multitude of thongs biting harshly at her thigh. Justine squealed – incensed by the pain – and stung by the arousal that the punishment generated.

'Shocking,' the priest mumbled. 'Have you no respect for the sanctity of the confessional booth?'

She glared at him and knew there was no opportunity for her to remind him she had only been there at his instruction. Gritting her teeth in anticipation of the next blow, Justine said, 'I submitted to the depraved demands of a priest in that confessional.'

This time the whip flicked at her breasts. Her chest was a shriek of raw anguish that came close to blinding her with tears. Both orbs throbbed from the brutal treatment the priest was making her suffer and she began to realise the pounding pulse in her nipples matched the rhythm of her arousal. A wail of despair crossed her lips as she realised her body was enjoying the humiliating torment of being abused.

'Go on,' the priest urged. 'Tell me all of your sins.'

She snatched a breath before continuing. 'I committed sacrilege on the altar of your church. I gave my body to you and your bishop.'

'Despicable sins,' the priest muttered. He slashed the whip back and forth. The first blow caught her across the breasts: the second scoured at the tops of her thighs. A stray thong – agonising and cruel – sliced at the pulse of her clitoris. The extreme pain was more severe than she expected and Justine almost choked on her cry of surprise. She stared at him through a veil of tears and braced herself when he urged her to continue.

'I took an innocent woman from your church,' Justine breathed. 'And I used her as my sexual plaything.'

The whip fell again. It cut viciously through the night before landing against her bare breasts. The pain was phenomenal and, this time, she did risk glancing down at herself. Blinking through the tears she was amazed to see that her nipples were still attached to her body. The punishment had been so severe she would not have been surprised to find the beads of skin had been torn away with the last bite of the cat.

'I allowed myself to be used at Sartine's party,' she gasped.

'Whore!'

She locked her throat, desperate not to let another cry escape into the night. When he snapped the whip this time it branded fiery anguish in the centre of her sex.

'And I enjoyed every second of it,' Justine declared.

'Filthy, unrepentant whore!'

She turned her face away from him, unable to watch the cat leaping out of the dark and then feeling its scratch against her tormented flesh. The night's cool breeze continued to caress her bare body but she was sweating freely from the ordeal.

'There were scores of men and women,' she gasped.

She clenched her jaw so as not to squeal when the next blow struck.

'And I was used by them all.'

'You've got a lot of repenting to do,' the priest growled.

She stared at him through the dark, half-expecting to hear another crack of the whip and not daring to hope that that part of the punishment was ended. Watching him toss the cat aside, then seeing him extend a hand into the darkness, she was puzzled to see someone hand him a rosary.

'I want to hear the paternoster from you and ten Hail Marys.'

She cringed from the idea of reciting more prayers while suffering his sadistic abuse, but didn't dare make her reluctance known. Despite the blasphemy of mimicking the crucifixion, she told herself that the act of penance was to be expected following her confession. And, because the priest was walking toward her with the rosary, she believed he might actually release her from her bondage on the cross. Daring to hope that her ordeal might soon be over, she shivered with relief as he bore down on her.

'The paternoster and ten Hail Marys,' he reminded her.

She nodded.

And then, with sudden horror, she watched the priest fall to his knees. He still held the rosary in one hand and used his other to swat her legs so she spread them further apart. On an intuitive level she understood what he was going to do it before he had pushed the beads against her. The act was depraved and obscene, but she realised that those factors no longer stopped her from indulging in any act if it seemed likely it would satisfy her needs.

He slipped the first bead against the tight ring of her anus.

She bit back a squeal.

Working quickly, slipping them easily inside her bowel, the priest mumbled something in Latin as his fingers gently pushed bead after bead through her sphincter. The weight of the first one made her feel full, its alien presence sitting heavily in her rear. By the time he had completed the first decade Justine thought she had never endured anything more profane or embarrassing.

'You will begin when I tell you,' the priest mumbled.

She stammered in her haste to agree, and parted her legs wider to allow him slowly to ease a second decade inside her rear. The muscle of her rectum felt overfull and bloated. Heightened sensitivity made her acutely aware of each bead inside her bowel. As the priest's large fingers forced another and then another through her sphincter, she recoiled from the blend of discomfort, shame and humiliation. His face was unbearably close to her exposed cleft and she wondered if he could detect the scent of fresh musk that seemed to be flowing from her. Despite the embarrassment of this ordeal Justine could feel the fresh waves of sexual excitement charging through her, and she dreaded the idea that the priest might notice her response and disapprove.

Without warning, he flicked his tongue against the lips of her sex.

After all the attention he had invested in pushing the rosary into her rear, she hadn't realised her pussy was so excited and swollen. The sensation of his mouth against her sex was unexpected and allowed her body to shift to a plateau of unwonted pleasure. As the eddies of delight began to subside she realised he had stopped thrusting the rosary beads into her backside and understood it was time to begin her penance.

'A paternoster,' the priest reminded her. 'And ten Hail Marys.'

She hadn't forgotten the instruction. Even with his breath warming the tops of her thighs, and the sacramental beads filling her bowel, Justine didn't think it would be possible to have forgotten what was expected of her. The crucifix she had seen dangling from the rosary tickled at her buttocks. In her mind's eye she could picture it swinging between the cheeks of her backside and that image alone was enough to make her believe she was committing the ultimate profanity. She shivered from the idea of saying the prayers, and then told herself the alternative wasn't worth considering. Nervously, she took a deep breath and steeled herself to do as he had asked.

'Our father, who art in heaven,' she began.

As she spoke, the priest tugged on the crucifix.

Justine had expected this humiliation, and yet it was still a shock to feel the nauseating pleasure being torn from her anus. Her sphincter clenched tight around the first bead, fighting him for possession, and she fervently wished her body would relent and allow him simply to tear the beads away. Wishing there was time to think about all that was going on, trying to concentrate on the words of the prayer rather than the sordid pleasure she was enjoying from this terrible sacrilege, Justine mumbled her way through the paternoster as the first decade was torn from her.

Her anus reluctantly opened to allow each bead to be pulled free, and then closed tight as though trying to hold on to the remainder of the rosary. The sensation was horribly reminiscent of visiting the lavatory, and she knew those associations were colouring her shame and arousal. The priest applied an unhurried pressure on the crucifix: constantly pulling downward and perpetually making her sphincter feel as though it were fighting him in a tug o' war.

Occasionally, almost as a random treat, he flicked his tongue against the swell of her clitoris. The sudden rush of pleasure, usually coming while she was trying to recover from another burst of shame, invariably made her stumble through the words of her prayer. The priest's growls of displeasure, and her own torment as she was torn between arousal, frustration and embarrassment, threatened to overwhelm her with confusion.

As she mumbled the first 'amen,' he pulled a full decade from her rear.

She groaned.

'Now the Hail Marys,' he demanded.

Sobbing back tears of frustration, she mumbled, 'Hail Mary, full of grace.'

He tore another bead from her backside. His tongue rubbed easily against her clitoris and Justine moaned. If not for the ropes at her wrists, holding her against the cross and forcing her to accept this twisted ritual, she would have doubled over and hidden herself from him. Because he was continuing to pull at the rosary,

202

perpetually threatening to wrench another bead from her anus, she knew she had to continue.

'The lord is with thee, blessed art thou amongst women . . .'

She remembered the words with frightening ease and was appalled that they could come back to her at this particular time. The priest was merciless in demanding that she repeat the prayer again and again, constantly easing one bead and then another from her rear. The discomfort was only minor but the blasphemy of what she was doing struck her with the same force she had suffered when he had been striking her with the cat.

By the time he had wrenched the final bead from her backside, Justine realised she had gone beyond shame. His tongue brushed her clitoris again, inspiring the climax she had known was coming, and she continued to babble the words of the prayer as the unholy orgasm coursed through her body. Sobbing with relief and satisfaction, she barely noticed that the priest had pulled himself from the floor and gone back to the shadows where he conspired with Marais. It was only as the haze of pleasure began to subside that Justine heard their lowered voices.

'I told you she was more than worthy,' the priest grumbled. 'The twisted little bitch has appetites that even I consider depraved.'

Justine flinched on hearing the words, not sure if they should be considered as praise or condemnation. She saw the priest turn his back and wished there had been some chance to shout after him and ask him about her beloved penitent. If there was ever any opportunity of reacquainting herself with the woman, she knew it would only be through the priest. But, before she could call him back, or make her interest in the woman known, he was already disappearing into the shadows. And, as the blackness shrouded him, she saw a host of others bearing down on her, each striking life to their own candles. The number of them surprised her: a dozen at first, and then twice or three times that amount. It wasn't until she recalled Sartine's penchant for group pleasure that she understood what was going to happen.

Unable to stop herself, Justine groaned.

Sixteen

Sartine's women surrounded her.

Sensuous fingers fell against her bare body: stroking, smoothing and exciting. The ravages that had been inflicted by the priest's cruel blows were lovingly caressed. Each vicious mark was kissed, licked and teased until Justine couldn't decide whether she was being tormented through pain or pleasure. The humiliation of the confession and her penance was quickly forgotten as those beautiful people she had first met at Sartine's reacquainted themselves with her body.

'You're so daring, Justine.'

As the woman's lips moved away, Justine realised she had been kissed by Marie. The brunette, so seductive and sultry, allowed her fingertips to trail against Justine's bare breast. She was as naked as the rest of the women who descended on her, the comparative warmth of her body making Justine think the woman had recently shrugged a cowl from her shoulders. Candlelight complemented her skin tones, softening her swarthy complexion and making her look like the embodiment of a living shadow.

'You took that punishment so bravely,' Marie enthused. 'I didn't know whether to envy you, help you, or save my sympathy and come over here to kiss you better.'

Not sure what to say, not sure there was anything she could say, Justine merely smiled and allowed the woman to kiss her again. A tongue slipped between her lips and explored inside her mouth. A cool hand brushed the burning flesh of her breast. And the agony and shame that had epitomised the priest's control of her body were instantaneously banished.

Fingers worked on the ropes at her wrists.

Justine glanced to her sides, vaguely recognising the women who were kindly releasing her from her bondage. There had been so many new people at Sartine's that she had thought their faces would become a forgettable blur. But, remembering the shape of so many smiles, and the mischievous glints that shone in so many eyes, she understood that she knew nearly all of these women.

As one hand came free she found herself embracing a slender brunette. The woman grinned and squirmed until she was able to place a mouth over Justine's nipple. The stiff flesh was suckled, nipped and then gently teased to a state of full and wanton excitement. The memories of being scratched by the priest's cat were pushed from her thoughts and, unable to resist the simple pleasure of being aroused, Justine pushed herself against the brunette.

Her other arm was released and a crowd of bodies helped her away from the obscene cross she had been bound against.

'I want you,' Marie whispered.

The warmth of her words tickled against Justine's earlobe. As she was laid down on the floor of the ruins, she was aware of hands continuing to touch and stroke her. Dewy blades of grass touched her back, buttocks and bare legs, reminding her she was out in the open. She glimpsed the canopy of stars that festooned the night sky above, realised her eyes were becoming used to the candlelit night around her, and then saw a pair of perfect feminine buttocks looming over her face. The shaved split of the women's sex revealed her pussy lips were dewy with excitement and aching to be kissed. As she lowered herself toward Justine's face, the scent of her arousal grew stronger and more appetising. Justine extended her tongue and raised her face to meet the slippery labia.

The taste of the unknown woman was intoxicating.

The sensation of kissing a stranger's pussy was made more exhilarating by the pleasure of feeling another tongue against her own sex. She didn't know if it was Marie or one of the many others who had helped her from the cross and, as the clean and painless arousal soared through her body, Justine understood that she was beyond caring. Her heartbeat raced with a thrill that came from knowing her excitement would soon be sated and she gasped and groaned as the surge of pleasure became quickly unbearable.

Pushing her tongue as deep as she was able, taking time to savour the thrust of a pulsing clitoris against her lower lip, Justine wanted to giggle as all the agonies and embarrassment that had been caused by the priest were washed away by the kisses of Sartine's women.

The grass beneath her quickly warmed.

And, although she could see nothing beyond the buttocks that loomed over her face, she was aware of heavy sighs and passionate groans, as though the ruins were suddenly filled with like-minded souls all enjoying a wealth of carnal pleasures. Without properly registering the fact, she realised the tongue at her sex had changed, but that was a detail she only noticed as an afterthought, when the tongue against her began to slide deep inside rather than simply teasing around the flushed flesh of her outer lips.

The sex at her face was torn away, to be quickly replaced by another one.

Whereas the previous pussy had been rimmed by a scrub of dark downy hairs, this one was shaved smooth. Acknowledging the piquant difference in flavours, and eagerly thrusting her tongue between the perfect hairless lips, Justine was delighted to feel a groan of approval shiver through the woman above.

Another mouth took over at her own sex, greedily tonguing and this time nibbling at her sensitive labia. Her breasts were teased, each nipple sucked and tormented with passion and vigour. Loving hands roamed over her body in silent sensitive appreciation.

'Do you agree that she's worthy?'

Justine heard the question from a distance. She recognised Mrs Weiss's voice and knew the woman was speaking to Marais. Her concentration was fixed on the dewy sex lips that hung over her face but she wondered if *The Society*'s head could hear the desperation in the woman's tone. To Justine, Mrs Weiss sounded almost frantic in her need to hear his acceptance.

'Will you allow her to have the manuscript?'

'She's shown an appetite for sacrilege,' Marais allowed.

'She's giving herself quite freely to Sartine's sluts,' Mrs Weiss observed.

Marais sniffed. 'We've all given ourselves quite freely to Sartine's sluts. That proves nothing.' There was a moment's silence between the pair and, as she found herself lapping against another pussy, and feeling the subtle nuances of a different mouth at her sex, Justine wondered if their conversation had ended. She was mildly surprised when Marais eventually asked, 'Why are you so concerned about her worthiness? Do you have a vested interest in this one?'

The timbre of Mrs Weiss's laughter was rich with denial. 'I don't have a vested interest in anything.' She spoke too quickly, as though she was trying to conceal a truth. 'I was only asking to see if you agreed with the opinions we've all given you. There's nothing more to my curiosity than that.'

Justine wanted to push the woman away from her face and peer into the candlelit darkness to watch the exchange between Marais and Mrs Weiss. After all she had been through over the past three days, and all the efforts she had made to keep her relationship with the employer a secret, Justine found it incredible to think that Mrs Weiss could be foolish enough to jeopardise the secrecy of their plans with such guileless questions. Fretful that the ruse might be exposed, and worried about how she might suffer if that did happen, she could feel her involvement with Sartine's women diminishing in importance.

The mouth at her pussy continued to tongue with the divine kisses it had used before, but her body was no longer responding with the same wanton glee. Those mouths that sucked at her breasts were simply a nuisance and Justine had to struggle against the urge to push them away. Diligently, she continued to lap and suck at the cleft above her nose but the interaction inspired none of the arousal she had enjoyed before.

'She appears worthy,' Marais decided.

Justine breathed a sigh of relief.

'But I'm reserving my final judgement until I've seen her fully tested.'

Those words were enough to make fresh tension tighten each muscle in her body. The machinations of the evening resounded through her thoughts and made it impossible for her to enjoy any of the pleasures that should have been hers. Fearful that Mrs Weiss had exposed their arrangement, and anxious about the repercussions she would face if *The Society* discovered she had been a participant in the duplicity, Justine strained to hear what else Marais was saying.

'I'll have a better idea of her suitability once this evening's concluded,' Marais said. There was a lilt of vicious cruelty in his voice as he added, 'I do trust you'll take her to her limits, Mrs Weiss.'

'I'll take her to her limits and beyond.'

When she heard those words, Justine realised the woman was going to make her suffering unbearable. The thought made her stomach churn with dread. As her thoughts lingered on the inevitable torment she was going to endure, she felt the familiar tingle of arousal surge through her loins.

Someone clapped their hands.

The buttocks above Justine's face moved away and she saw that Sartine was commanding the women to move back. They shifted away with obvious reluctance but no real complaints. Her sex lips received a farewell kiss, one woman pressed her mouth against Justine's ear and whispered, 'Later, lover,' and then she was alone in the centre of the darkened ruins and only able to make out silhouettes standing by the faraway candles.

'Did you enjoy my women?' Sartine asked cheerfully.

She swallowed before replying. The taste of feminine musk lined her throat and added a delicious bouquet to every breath she took. 'Thank you,' she murmured. Trying to make her tone even and dignified, she stared into the darkness where his voice came from and said, 'It's barely been two days, but I'd forgotten how much pleasure they could give.'

He laughed easily, raised his hand, and the shadows around him began to move. Justine stared meekly from her place on the floor as cowled figures surged toward her. It was only as they were disrobing, dropping their hooded robes from their shoulders and revealing themselves naked and aroused, that she understood Sartine had given the instruction for his men to entertain her.

They were no less exciting than the women, and they handled her with the same sensitivity and gentleness. The hands that stroked her breasts – touched her thighs and explored her cleft – were neither rough nor demanding.

But she suspected they wanted more from her.

As soon as that thought was fixed in her mind she realised she was facing two penises. The rounded domes pushed toward her face and she immediately understood what they wanted. In the shadows of the night, she was aware of hands stroking her legs and breasts, exploring her cleft with fingers slipping between the folds of her pussy lips and sliding inside. But the erections that lingered in front of her mouth commanded the most attention.

She grasped one in each hand, and pulled gently on them both. Hungry for the taste of them, she eased herself into a sitting position and tentatively lapped at one, and then the other. The flavours of their pre-come were salty and cloying. After drinking from a variety of wet responsive women, she found herself driven by a hunger to savour the taste the erections properly. Wrapping her lips around one, taking its entire length into her mouth and allowing the flavours of sweat and arousal to bombard her tongue, she moved her face away from him and gasped with satisfaction.

The other length remained in her hand and she devoured it with the same hunger with which she had tasted the first. Both quivered in her grasp, telling her that she was doing her duty to their clear approval. Suddenly desperate to taste their ejaculation, she squeezed both erections together and tried to force them into her mouth at the same time.

'Didn't I tell you she was worthy?'

Justine could still hear the anxiety in Mrs Weiss's tone. Trying to ignore the woman, concentrating on the two thick and swollen domes that she had managed to slip into her mouth, she chased her tongue in a figure eight. One loop circled one glans, then moved easily onto the other. Her mouth grew wet with a rush of pre-come and she had to repeatedly swallow their blended flavours for fear of choking.

'You told me she was worthy,' Marais agreed. 'You keep telling me that she's worthy. It's almost suspicious the way you keep dwelling on the point.'

Unable to contain the sound, Justine groaned. A part of her wanted to scream at Mrs Weiss to shut up and stop jeopardising all that she had so far done. But she knew that such a bold move would immediately draw attention to their scheme. Additionally, because she was so involved with the men surrounding her, she didn't want to break the momentum of what was happening.

Strong hands grabbed her thighs and lifted her in the air.

The movement didn't cause her any worry because she believed herself to be in safe hands. It crossed her mind that the men surrounding her could abuse the trust she had invested in them but she knew there was little danger of that happening. And, even if they decided to take advantage of her, she didn't think there was anything they could do that she wouldn't happily allow.

When they lowered her back down she found there was a male body beneath her. Her buttocks touched his hips. An erection pushed between her buttocks. And she instantly understood what they were planning. A twisted thrill of anticipation soared through her body. She sucked more eagerly on the two erections she was trying to squeeze into her mouth and allowed the stranger beneath her to push himself upward. There was never any doubt in her mind that he was going to penetrate her anus – the prospect was enough to make her arousal reach fresh and fevered heights – and she tried to relax as the huge end pressed against her sphincter. Her legs were parted, she felt clumsy movements happening between her thighs, and then realised there was a second erection pressing at her pussy lips.

Another groan shivered through her. Because her mouth was now filled by two lengths there was no opportunity for the sound to escape. She greedily slurped at the pair of erections and was thrilled to feel them trembling against her tongue.

The men between her legs surged forward in the same fluid motion.

The shaft at her rear tested the resistance of her sphincter, pushing firmly and forcing the muscle to part a little. The length at her sex eased slightly forward, slipping effortlessly into her hole but doing nothing more than parting the lips. The gentleness they used was maddening and Justine simply wanted to urge herself onto them both. But, knowing she needed to leave control in their hands, she could only hold herself still and breathe deeply as they dictated events.

The length at her rear slipped further inside.

Her sphincter protested, battling every millimetre of the penetration before relenting. As Justine was won over by the surge of satisfying response being thrust into her bowel, the length at her sex plunged inside. The sensation of being too full, and overstretched, were easily outweighed by the pleasures she was enjoying.

And then those considerations were brushed from her mind as the pleasure began in earnest. The men between her thighs rode in and out in perfect synchronisation. The last time she had enjoyed this forbidden pleasure, Justine recalled that one man had plunged deep while the other had withdrawn. This time they each pushed in and pulled out at the same time. Rather than being allowed to feel as though she was constantly full, she experienced the delight of being stretched beyond her previous limitations, then left to feel hollow and in need of more. Their timing left her breathless and weak and gasping and she didn't doubt they would easily wring the climax from her body. Anxious to return the pleasure that was being bestowed upon her, she attacked the shafts in her mouth with renewed hunger and sucked greedily against both lengths.

The first orgasm struck her like a slap across the face.

She didn't know if the pleasure had started from one of the erections that penetrated between her legs, or if she was simply overwhelmed by the sensations that had been excited in every part of her body. Mouths were pressed against her breasts, too many pairs of hands touched her thighs and buttocks, and the sensory overload promised to be more than she could withstand. Elated by the pleasure, grimacing from the sheer joy of satisfaction, she held her head back and allowed a scream of delight to ring from her lips.

One of the erections she held spurted as Justine came. The douche of semen spattered against her face, tainting her nostrils with the tart zest of its scent and making her close her eyes against the second pulse it spat at her. She blinked her eyes open, briefly saw the dark world around her through tears of sticky white semen, and then closed her eyes again as another barrage of euphoria battered her body.

Another erection was pushed into her hand before the first was properly spent.

The shafts inside her sex and her pussy ploughed back and forth with a fresh burst of speed. She had little time properly to taste the fresh flavour of the new cock near her mouth before the other one she had been holding was pulling away from her lips and ejaculating against her cheek. The stench of semen was sudden and nauseating but did nothing to lessen her appetite for the erection that replaced the spent one. She accepted it hungrily into her mouth, madly alternating from one to the other. The night became frenzied and centred solely on her and her pleasure and she decided: if this was all that was required from her, she could happily endure several more hours of proving her worthiness to Marais.

The erection in her anus pulsed, the tremors of the man's orgasm adding a marvellous frisson to the sensation of being filled. Justine didn't know whether she enjoyed a climax in response, too consumed by the pleasure being driven through her sex and the satisfaction she was taking from the erections in her mouth. Her face was lathered with a wash of dripping semen, its sticky residue clinging to the corners of her eyes and trailing down her cheeks like tears. She exchanged one shaft for another, taking no time to bother herself with the detail of whose erection she was holding, only concerned with her own rush of satisfaction.

'Enough!'

Marais's clipped voice wasn't raised but it broke through the grunts and groans that now filled the ruins of *La Coste*. Justine released both of the lengths she held, using the back of her hand to wipe a film of semen from her brow, and flitted her gaze through the darkness as she tried to locate him. The shafts that were buried in her bowel and in her sex held themselves perfectly still. She could feel the faint throb of their separate pulses, pounding subtly inside her body, and the intimacy of that sensation inspired another thrill of black desire.

'You've proved your point, Sartine,' Marais said.

Justine saw the pair of them as the two men before her stepped away. Sartine was naked, his erection already coming back to hardness, and she guessed she had either felt or tasted his cock in the previous minutes. His shoulders were thrown back and he stood with quiet confidence before the smartly dressed figure of Marais.

'You were right to say she was worthy.'

'I never doubted that.' Sartine grinned arrogantly.

He turned to his guests, clapping his hands and ushering them back to the shadows. Justine was treated to a handful of kisses and grateful smiles before Sartine and Marie came to help her from the floor. She hadn't realised her body had suffered such tremendous exertion until she tried to stand up. Then, the ground seemed to give way beneath her feet and she knew she would have tumbled gracelessly over if they hadn't been there to provide assistance. Her sphincter felt loose and over-used. The lips of her sex were raw from enduring too much.

'You've done very well, Justine,' Marie confided. 'I've never seen anyone throw themselves into that as whole-heartedly as you did.'

Justine thanked her, and privately wished people would stop telling her that she had done very well. She kept hearing those words, and other similar sentiments, but still the torment refused to come to an end. Stumbling toward the table with Marie at one side and Sartine at the other, she briefly entertained the idea that she might now be allowed something to eat and drink before being told she had finally proved her worthiness.

For the first time she was able to see that most of the seats around the candlelit table were empty. The priest and his bishop sat on either side of the foot; Marais had his place at the head; and she guessed the two empty seats belonged to Captain Sartine and his beautiful Marie. But, rather than concentrating on any of those details, Justine could only think about one thing: Mrs Weiss stood by the side of the table as though it was now her turn to take another shot at abusing Justine's body.

Seventeen

'You're a dirty little bitch, aren't you?' Mrs Weiss growled.

Justine groaned when she heard the words. She immediately understood what was coming and closed her eyes as though that would ward off the dreaded punishment. In the darkness it was like being back in the private library vault where Mrs Weiss had first approached her for this acquisition. She remembered the nervousness, terror and the black arousal and she tried to find the strength within herself to face those emotions again.

'You're a dirty little bitch, aren't you?' Mrs Weiss continued. 'You're a dirty little bitch who needs a damned good thrashing. Is that why you've come here? Have you come here to have your backside thrashed?'

Justine opened her eyes to discover the woman was wielding a stout leather paddle. It was not the most intimidating weapon she had seen over the past three days. Compared to the cat she had suffered this evening, or any of the crops Mrs Weiss had used on her at Vincennes Castle, it looked positively benign. And, in truth, the sight of the paddle stirred a blend of curiosity into her arousal. But she still didn't want to submit to the punishment and she took an involuntary step back.

Mrs Weiss was on her in an instant. Her cowl flapped about her shoulders, she hurled herself at Justine, and then she had driven her to her knees. One hand grabbed a fistful of hair and, tugging back, she made Justine glare up at her. The paddle was raised and the threat of retaliation was obvious and intimidating. 'You're here to prove a point,' she hissed. 'You're here to show Marais that, as I told him, you are more than worthy of acquiring *La Coste*. Do you think you're going to prove that point by cowering away from me? Do you think Marais will see that sort of behaviour as a sign of your worthiness?'

Justine glared at the woman and realised Mrs Weiss no longer scared her. The woman had been an intimidating presence in the library – she had been particularly frightening on the day Justine had encountered her alone and in the dark of the private vault – but that was all in the past. Even her memory of suffering the woman's abuse at Vincennes Castle seemed to validate her sudden belief that Mrs Weiss was not a woman to be feared.

'You can strike me a dozen times,' Justine told her. 'But no more than that. A dozen times should be enough to prove the point you're trying to make.'

'No more than that?' Mrs Weiss growled. 'Are you threatening me?' She pulled hard on Justine's hair until she had forced a squeal of pain. 'I can strike you as many times as I like. You seem to forget which of us is wielding the paddle and which of is trying to prove their worthiness.'

Justine forced herself to remain strong. Glaring firmly at Mrs Weiss, not allowing the woman to see the pain she was inflicting, she said, 'One dozen times.' Lowering her voice, anxious that the others wouldn't hear what she had to say, Justine added, 'If you strike me any more than that, I'll tell Marais that I'm working for you.'

The hand clutching her hair loosened.

Mrs Weiss regarded Justine with a range of expressions that swept from shock to fury and then to outrage. 'He wouldn't believe you,' she hissed.

'Considering all the guileless questions you've besieged him with this evening, I imagine he already

218

suspects we're in collusion,' Justine returned. 'Make my suffering last more than twelve strikes from that paddle and I'll confirm his suspicions.' She considered adding more, and asking Mrs Weiss how such a revelation would affect her position within *The Society*, and then decided there was no reason to press her advantage.

'You vindictive little bitch. Are you trying to blackmail me?'

Justine shook her head and remembered a line from *La Coste* that the penitent had read for her. It felt strange to be using de Sade's words against Mrs Weiss but Justine didn't think there was anything more appropriate that she could say. 'Don't think of it as blackmail,' she encouraged. 'Think of it as my doing you a personal favour that you don't really deserve.'

Mrs Weiss tightened her grip on Justine's hair and yanked hard. Her neck was stretched back and her body was pulled into a fresh and uncomfortable position. The jolt of pain that shook her was swift and harsh and hatefully exciting.

Maintaining her composure, Justine simply glowered. 'Make it ten strikes from the paddle now,' she decided. 'And remember: the number will continue to fall each time you do something I don't like.'

An eternity of silence lingered between them. As she studied the woman's furious features Justine understood that Mrs Weiss was struggling to find a way of imposing her will on the situation and failing with each idea that came to her. 'Very well,' she gasped eventually. 'We'll do this your way.' Her smile turned suddenly bright as she added, 'But we're still doing it on my terms.'

Justine had only a moment to reflect what this might mean before Mrs Weiss had dragged her from the floor. The woman's hand was still in her hair, pulling and tugging so that Justine was forced to follow. She stumbled in the woman's wake, trying not to think of the course of action she had put in progress, and didn't stop walking until Mrs Weiss threw her against the priest's wooden cross.

'Stand against that. Spread your legs, stick your backside out and don't even think about moving.'

Justine did as she was told, her apprehension mounting. She could feel the weight of every gaze was fixed on her. The night had taken on a stillness that could only come from being surrounded by a crowd of unseen strangers who were all holding their breath in anticipation. Justine didn't know if anyone had heard the whispered conversation she had managed with Mrs Weiss and, as the moment of her punishment drew closer, Justine realised she was now beyond caring. She stiffened against the cross, stopped herself from thinking about the vulnerability of her exposed backside, and tried to prepare her body for the harsh impact she knew she was about to suffer.

Mrs Weiss slammed the paddle against her rear.

Justine had quietly vowed that she wouldn't scream, but she came close to breaking that personal promise with the first slap of the paddle. The reverberation shook through her backside, igniting a hateful thrill of arousal and a low gnawing heat in her loins. The sting of agonising pain was accompanied by a slap that sounded like a gunshot in the night. As she chugged each breath in low guttural moans, Justine marvelled that her body could be so resilient as to withstand such torture.

'Count them,' Mrs Weiss insisted. 'I wouldn't want accidentally to do more than ten.'

Justine waited for a moment before replying, not trusting her voice to be steady when she answered. 'One,' she muttered.

She had intended to say more but Mrs Weiss didn't allow her to get any further.

Striking with a brutal force, and landing the paddle hard against Justine's cheeks, she delivered the second blow with more violence than the first.

'Two,' Justine murmured.

Her buttocks were ablaze with agony. The sound of the clap continued to ring in her ears and the warmth from the slap quickly spread through her cheeks to the split of her sex. Her inner muscles relished the warmth, responding with their own tickle of enjoyment. Amazed that her treacherous body could glean pleasure from such brutal abuse, Justine didn't try fighting the enjoyment. Instead, she quietly savoured the effect and pushed her backside further out in readiness for Mrs Weiss's third shot.

The flat blade of the paddle sighed as it broke through the air.

Justine braced herself for the impact and then allowed the pain and ensuing heat to flood through her body. If it had not been for the cross she held, the force would have been enough to push her over. She could feel her knees wanting to buckle and understood that a part of her would be happy to fall down, admit defeat and allow Mrs Weiss the satisfaction of knowing she had broken another helpless victim.

But there was another part of her that wouldn't let the woman win. And she was also desperate to find out if the repeated blows would give her the satisfaction her body now craved. Drawing a deep breath, no longer caring whether she sounded defiant or defeated, Justine called, 'Three.'

'You really do enjoy suffering, don't you?' Mrs Weiss sneered.

The excitement in Justine's voice was obvious when she replied. Overwhelmed by the experience, she felt sure she could taste the arousal on her tongue when she spoke. 'This isn't suffering,' she whispered. Stifling a laugh, sure that would be bound to infuriate her employer, she added, 'Another three blows from that and I think I'll be screaming for a reason that has nothing to do with pain.'

Mrs Weiss slapped the paddle hard against her.

'Four,' Justine groaned. She could feel the woman was increasing the force of her blows with each shot but that was only adding to her enjoyment. Her rear was an inferno of seared flesh and the chill of the night did little to help soothe the burning sensation.

But Justine knew it would soon transport her beyond the pinnacle of orgasm. Her inner muscles throbbed with their own urgent heat, erratically clenching and convulsing as though the first throes of orgasm were already working their way through her body.

She counted off the numbers belonging to each blow, her breathlessness growing more profound each time. After three more she was responding automatically and not sure if the numbers she was saying had any bearing on the torment Mrs Weiss inflicted. Her thoughts were fixed solely on the glorious heat that now smouldered inside her sex and she knew the orgasm was about to tear its way through her.

As she called out the number eight, Mrs Weiss delivered her penultimate blow and Justine screamed with gratitude. The blend of pleasure and pain, heat and excitement, became an absolute arousal. The rush of satisfaction streaked through her and she clutched the arms of the cross for fear of falling to the ground.

Her heartbeat raced furiously and it was only as an afterthought that she realised Mrs Weiss had delivered her final blow while the climax was searing through her body. The woman stepped close, breathing heavily, with a cruel smile tainting her voice. The coarse fabric of her cowl brushed against Justine's bare body as she lowered her voice to a discreet whisper.

'How were those ten?' Mrs Weiss asked.

'They were unbearable,' Justine panted. She raised her head and dared to glance at the woman's menacing scowl. 'But you knew that before you asked, didn't you?'

'Do you still feel in a mood for giving me orders?' Mrs Weiss taunted. She raised the paddle, using its presence as a sly reminder of the power she held. 'Do you still want to tell me how many times I can hit you? I'm always happy to give insubordinates a lesson about which of us is in charge.'

'I'm not giving orders,' Justine said quietly. She glanced at the paddle and then glanced back to the stern-faced woman holding it. The intimidation was no longer there and she felt as though she was speaking to an equal rather than a cruel dominatrix. 'I'm simply stating facts. If you allow me to suffer any more, I'm telling Marais all about our relationship.'

Justine considered repeating the line from *La Coste*, and then stopped herself from pushing Mrs Weiss too far. She could see the impotent venom in the woman's gaze and knew she now had the upper hand. Even when Mrs Weiss backed away, and started barking instructions to anyone close enough to fall under her command, Justine realised the dynamics in their relationship had changed forever.

'Lay her there,' Mrs Weiss instructed. She pointed to the centre of the table and Justine dimly realised she knew the two people who were helping her away from the cross.

Marie delivered short kisses and words of praise and admiration. Sartine had an arm around her waist and took the brunt of her weight. Justine glanced gratefully from one to the other, murmuring her thanks and hoping this was the last time she would find herself between the pair. It wasn't that she hadn't enjoyed her time with either of the couple but it seemed, after each encounter with either of them, Justine found herself suffering an unnecessary amount of pain.

'You've been a triumph,' Marie told her.

'I've never seen better,' Sartine agreed.

Justine thanked them for the kind words, and then sighed with relief as they laid her on the table. It hurt to have her buttocks against any surface but the top of the table was cool enough to be a balm against the blazing flesh of her rear. Once the initial discomfort of the contact was over, she discovered the sensation was almost soothing.

Around her, she heard the shuffle of chairs as the senior members of *The Society* resumed their seats. A murmur of conversation, most of it in French, was bantered above and around her. Although she didn't usually give herself over to paranoia, Justine thought that, on this occasion, it sounded as though the foreign language was being used to keep her from understanding the conversation.

Deciding there was no sense trying to interpret the words, confident she would soon find out what they were saying if it had any bearing on her situation, Justine rested her head back against the table and stared directly up.

From her perspective, Justine could see the canopy of the night stars above her and the faces of her tormentors looming from the periphery of her vision. Mrs Weiss's features were austere but Justine could see that Marais appeared equally stern and resolute.

'She's proved herself worthy,' Mrs Weiss growled. 'Just give her the damned manuscript and let the poor bitch go home.'

'Aren't you going to give me a final show of her abilities?'

Justine could hear the jeer of contempt in his voice as he made the suggestion. She glanced nervously at her employer, wondering if the woman was going to do as Marais asked, or deny him and run the risk of exposing their ruse. Having already suffered under Mrs Weiss's brutal treatment, Justine didn't know how she wanted the woman to respond but she couldn't bear the thought of her efforts of the past three days being for nothing.

'Put your fingers inside her.' This command came from someone standing beyond her range of vision. Justine recognised the voice but couldn't immediately identify it with a face or a name. 'Put your fingers inside her and I'll prove her worthiness for you.'

She remembered the burly cowled figured as soon he stepped into her view. Having spent the previous day suffering beneath him as he and Mrs Weiss administered their cruel punishments, Justine was surprised she hadn't immediately recognised the woman's assistant from her time in the donjon at Vincennes Castle.

Icy fingers touched the lips of her sex.

After being used by so many of Sartine's men she wasn't surprised that her sex was wet and slippery. The digits slid easily inside and their chilliness made her want to shiver. She steeled herself against the unpleasant cold feeling and tried to grip tightly around the three fingers Marais had plunged into her pussy.

'Is she wet?'

'Yes.'

'And warm?'

The fingers wriggled inside her. Justine could feel them exciting a tremor of unwanted pleasure as they touched firmly against those sensitive spots that had been almost neglected so far. She didn't know whether it was coincidence, or some skill on Marais's part, but he caressed the lining of her sex in a way that had her weak and wanting him.

'She's warm,' Marais admitted. He sounded bored and indifferent. 'Is there a point to this demonstration?'

'There's a point. Mrs Weiss proved this one's appetites to me yesterday. I've never encountered a woman so anxious to suffer pain and so responsive to any form of torment. Do you want me to show you how responsive she is?'

'Go on.'

Justine held herself still, not sure what to expect. She saw a movement of light from the corner of her eye and realised the assistant was lifting a candle. She glimpsed the shape of his pleasant manly face, and then saw the glint of his beard. She assumed he was raising the candle so she had a better view of him and it was almost automatic to smile politely as their gazes met.

And then he tipped the candle.

A trail of molten wax spilt from the meniscus of the candle. The flame briefly soared higher as it was allowed a chance to burn against the exposed wick. And a searing heat burnt against the thrust of her right nipple. The pain was infuriating, sudden and unexpected and she felt as though the blazing heat had branded her flesh. As the molten wax trickled over her skin, settling into the creases of her areola and then spilling around the swell of her breast, she wanted to scream.

Instead, her inner muscles clenched around the fingers that penetrated her and a surge of wetness rushed through her sex. The liquid that suddenly surrounded the fingers inside her pussy felt as warm and copious as the molten wax that had gushed over her breast.

'Damn!' Marais exclaimed. 'She is responsive.'

Mrs Weiss's assistant chuckled.

Breathless from the experience, surprised by the easy way her body translated pain into pleasure, Justine wanted to smile and join in their obvious appreciation of her reaction. She glanced from one man to the other, weakly grinning at each, and then watched as the assistant poured a second stream of wax over her left breast.

This time the pain was exquisite.

A shock of bright fire ignited against her sensitive skin. She was sickened by the intensity of the heat, and overwhelmed by the way her body responded. Whereas before she had clenched the muscles of her sex voluntarily, this time the reaction was beyond her control. The muscles gripped tight around Marais's fingers. She held him with so much force she could tell for the first time that he had three fingers inside. The sensitivity inside her muscles was so strong she could feel each of the knuckles trying to flex in response to her punishing hold. And then she lost track of what was happening as paroxysms of pure delight ebbed through her body. Curling her hands into fists, arching her back as the orgasm took hold, she hammered against the table and basked in the glorious climax.

'Didn't I tell you the bitch was insatiable?' Mrs Weiss grumbled.

'She's that and more,' Marais marvelled.

As he spoke, the vibration of his words trembled through his fingers. Justine placed a hand against her mouth to stifle a moan. The familiar threat of a pending orgasm had tightened in her chest and she struggled not to submit to it for fear that they might prolong her ordeal.

'I'll show you again,' the assistant said.

Before anyone could stop him, he had reached for the solidified cap of wax that covered her right breast and peeled it away. Justine thought the sensation was something akin to having her flesh stripped. She glanced down at her body just to make sure he hadn't torn away the nipple and was amazed to see her skin was still intact. The removal of the wax ignited a heat that was every bit as potent as the wax first splashing against her. Her nipple was stung by so much raw heat the hard bead of flesh stood rigid. In the candlelight it was such a vibrant red the colour seemed to throb.

Justine moaned.

The assistant raised his candle and started to tilt it.

She was torn between needing to feel more and desperate not to suffer the anguish. The night had been a constant torment of pleasures and pains she had not anticipated and would never understand. Throughout her ordeal at Vincennes Castle Justine had thought her limits had been exceeded but that endless punishment had not been anything like this. Tears squeezed from the corners of her eyes as she closed them and she silently begged the assistant not to drip more wax onto her.

After a moment of nothing happening, she dared to open one eye.

Mrs Weiss had stayed the assistant's hand. Her authoritative glare was enough for Justine to know which of them wielded the power at the table.

'Justine's worthiness has been proven,' Mrs Weiss said coolly.

Justine shivered with relief on the table.

The assistant glanced toward Marais and, after receiving a nod of approval, slowly lowered his hand.

Justine dared to glance at the other faces and saw the priest was nodding indulgently while Sartine and Marie grinned with almost juvenile appreciation.

Marais slowly drew his fingers from Justine's sex. The slippery egress inspired a final rush of pleasure that could have pushed her past the brink of orgasm, but she refused to let it take her there. Instead, after gathering her thoughts, she pulled herself from the table and staggered to her feet. It was impossible to tell where her clothes had gone in the darkness and she doubted there would be any chance of retrieving them. Deciding she could possibly use one of the discarded cowls that lay in amongst the ruins, she turned to face Marais.

'Well?' she demanded. 'Have I earned *La Coste*?'

Marais considered her solemnly. From out of the darkness he plucked the battered yellow pages and thumbed through them as if they were nothing of any great importance. 'I'm not sure.'

She glared at Marais, shocked at the idea that he might now be trying to cheat her of her prize. Outrage, despair and fury shrieked through her thoughts but she knew better than to give voice to any of them. Trying to rationalise her argument, certain that all would be lost if she responded angrily, Justine asked, 'What does that mean? You've received your money. I've proved myself worthy. What possible barrier could now stand in the way of you giving me *La Coste*?'

'Are you sure you want it?'

'I've spent the last four days surrendering to every depraved whim *The Society* can imagine,' Justine sneered. 'Doesn't that give you a clue?'

Rather than taking offence at her stiff tone, he laughed as though they were sharing a joke. 'You deposited a large sum of money in my account,' he reminded her. 'I could offer you several things instead of these tattered old pages.'

'I only want *La Coste*.'

'I could reimburse you now, here, with double the cash. Wouldn't that be better than gaining the book?'

'Are you backing out of the sale?'

'No. I'm just making sure you get what you want. Would you prefer to make the investment in property? I have several estates, each one with a market value at three or four times the amount you're paying for this book. I'll let you have any one of them if you elect to have that instead of *La Coste*.'

'I only want *La Coste*,' she said firmly.

'Of course you do,' he agreed. 'And I can see now that there's nothing else I could offer you that would sway your decision. You wouldn't even be interested if I could find that blonde girl who was with you at Sartine's. I doubt you'd even want her if I could organise for you take that delectable *putain* in exchange for your investment.'

Her mind raced ahead as she tried to work out what he was offering. It stood to reason that Marais would know about her lover. If the priest, Sartine and Mrs Weiss had told him how she had fared in their respective challenges, Justine didn't doubt they would also have shared the titillating information about her girlfriend. But hearing him use her as a bargaining chip against the book she had been trying to acquire made Justine wonder if she was still proving her worthiness. 'You know how to get hold of the penitent?' Justine gasped. She realised she had said the words without thinking. From the shadows she could almost feel the livid gaze of Mrs Weiss as the woman glared at her furiously.

'Would you prefer that?' Marais asked quickly. 'Would you rather I had her indentured into service for you? I can organise it so easily she'd be back home with you, doing everything you told her, before the ink was dry on our arrangement.'

Justine considered the choice carefully.

At the back of her mind she could almost feel Mrs Weiss silently screaming for her to pick the book. The woman's angst was obvious, even though she remained silent in the dark. But, although Justine wanted to please her and end the ordeal now, she couldn't let her last hope of having the penitent slip through her fingers.

'You can get her for me?'

'Easily. Is that what you want?'

She saw a shadow loom behind Marais and realised Mrs Weiss was there. The threat of retribution Justine had expected to see wasn't on the woman's features. Instead, Mrs Weiss merely looked expectant as she waited for Justine's decision. As her eyes finally grew accustomed to the darkness, Justine noticed the same expression on the face of the priest, Sartine and Marie. A shiver trembled through her bare body and she understood, of all the tests she had so far endured, this was the only one that truly mattered.

That thought was enough to make the decision for her.

'No,' Justine said eventually. 'I don't want the penitent from you. If I have her, it will be through my own enquiries and my own devices.' Glaring at Marais, she said, 'All I want from you is the manuscript I've purchased. Give me that and I'll be on my way.'

Smiling tightly, he handed the pages over to her. And, as Justine acknowledged the thrill of holding the parchment, she heard him say, 'You chose well this time, Mrs Weiss. But I'll choose a better one when it's my turn next month.'

After the Journey

A month later, flicking the switch for the vault, Justine felt a smile stretch across her face. The expression was no longer unusual, even for the chore of crosschecking the contents of the private library. The vault was as gloomy as ever, with glimpses of drab walls visible between the bookcases. But the room no longer filled her with a sense of despondency. The contents were as priceless and inaccessible as they had been before, yet she no longer considered the treasure to be pointless. And, more surprisingly, she realised she was almost happy to be working in the library's private vault.

Not troubling herself with the shift in attitude, accepting the change without needing to analyse its cause, Justine didn't let herself worry about that or her newly found tolerance of her job's day-to-day drudgery. It was easy to brush the smaller matters of boredom aside because the cataloguing was no longer the chore it had once been.

Her new assistant followed her warily into the room.

'These books are so old,' she gasped. Her heavy French accent made the declaration sound both innocent and grand. 'Are they valuable?'

'I've been told they're priceless,' Justine mumbled. She said the words as though she didn't care. Guiding the penitent to the vault's latest acquisition, urging her to take a seat so they could begin another day's work on the translation, Justine brushed away her lover's attempts to kiss and made her concentrate on the illicit task with which they were involved.

'I don't want to translate,' the penitent complained. 'I want to make love to you.'

Her mouth was a hungry pout. The simple dress she wore clung to the contours of her body with such loose ease that Justine instantly knew the woman wasn't wearing underwear. The temptation to surrender to the penitent's desire for intimacy was almost irresistible, but Justine told herself that she had to be strong willed.

'You can kiss me when we get home this evening,' Justine promised. 'Right now I need you to translate this for me while I type. I want it finished by the weekend.'

Pouting, the penitent asked, 'What is the hurry?'

Justine spoke as she set up her laptop and waited for the operating system to load. 'Mrs Weiss informs me that Marais has been approached by another potential buyer. She thinks this one is acting on Sartine's behalf. If the woman proves herself worthy, the manuscript could be in their hands by Monday morning.'

'Do you think that is likely?' the penitent gasped. She placed a protective hand over the yellowed pages of the manuscript as through trying to defend it from being taken by someone else. 'Do you think this woman will prove herself worthy?'

Justine shrugged.

Being alone with the penitent always made her thoughts turn lurid. Rather than continuing with the illicit translation she was making, Justine now wanted to have the woman kneel on the floor, between her legs, and lick the broiling split of her pussy. They had an hour away from the library floor and were not going to be disturbed. The opportunity to enjoy each other was maddeningly tempting, but Justine found the will to resist.

She opened the text document they had started a week earlier and held her fingers over the keyboard ready to transcribe the penitent's translation. As was always the case when the woman was near her, Justine saw that her hands were trembling with excitement.

'You did not answer my question,' the penitent complained. 'This woman that Captain Sartine has found: is she likely to acquire *La Coste*?'

Justine shrugged again. 'I've been told it's unlikely,' she admitted. With a sly grin she added, 'But I guess we'll find out for ourselves. We're going to help Mrs Weiss prove this one's worthiness.' Not allowing the conversation to continue, determined that they would get the translation finished before *La Coste* ended up in the hands of another deserving recipient, she pointed sternly at the yellowed pages and said, 'We need to begin now.' Glancing down at her laptop, trying to locate the last point they had reached, she added, 'The last words you read out to me were: *forbidden reading*.'

nexus

The leading publisher of fetish and adult fiction

TELL US WHAT YOU THINK!

Readers' ideas and opinions matter to us so please take a few minutes to fill in the questionnaire below.

1. Sex: Are you male ☐ female ☐ a couple ☐?

2. Age: Under 21 ☐ 21–30 ☐ 31–40 ☐ 41–50 ☐ 51–60 ☐ over 60 ☐

3. Where do you buy your Nexus books from?
☐ A chain book shop. If so, which one(s)?

_____

☐ An independent book shop. If so, which one(s)?

_____

☐ A used book shop/charity shop
☐ Online book store. If so, which one(s)?

_____

4. How did you find out about Nexus books?
☐ Browsing in a book shop
☐ A review in a magazine
☐ Online
☐ Recommendation
☐ Other _____

5. In terms of settings, which do you prefer? (Tick as many as you like.)
☐ Down to earth and as realistic as possible
☐ Historical settings. If so, which period do you prefer?

_____

☐ Fantasy settings – barbarian worlds

□ Completely escapist/surreal fantasy
□ Institutional or secret academy
□ Futuristic/sci fi
□ Escapist but still believable
□ Any settings you dislike?

_____

□ Where would you like to see an adult novel set?

_____

6. In terms of storylines, would you prefer:

□ Simple stories that concentrate on adult interests?
□ More plot and character-driven stories with less explicit adult activity?
□ We value your ideas, so give us your opinion of this book:

_____

_____

_____

7. In terms of your adult interests, what do you like to read about? (Tick as many as you like.)

□ Traditional corporal punishment (CP)
□ Modern corporal punishment
□ Spanking
□ Restraint/bondage
□ Rope bondage
□ Latex/rubber
□ Leather
□ Female domination and male submission
□ Female domination and female submission
□ Male domination and female submission
□ Willing captivity
□ Uniforms
□ Lingerie/underwear/hosiery/footwear (boots and high heels)
□ Sex rituals
□ Vanilla sex
□ Swinging

☐ Cross-dressing/TV
☐ Enforced feminisation
☐ Others – tell us what you don't see enough of in adult fiction:

_____
_____
_____

8. Would you prefer books with a more specialised approach to your interests, i.e. a novel specifically about uniforms? If so, which subject(s) would you like to read a Nexus novel about?

_____
_____
_____

9. Would you like to read true stories in Nexus books? For instance, the true story of a submissive woman, or a male slave? Tell us which true revelations you would most like to read about:

_____
_____
_____

10. What do you like best about Nexus books?

_____
_____

11. What do you like least about Nexus books?

_____
_____

12. Which are your favourite titles?

_____
_____

13. Who are your favourite authors?

_____
_____

14. Which covers do you prefer? Those featuring:
   (Tick as many as you like.)

☐ Fetish outfits
☐ More nudity
☐ Two models
☐ Unusual models or settings
☐ Classic erotic photography
☐ More contemporary images and poses
☐ A blank/non-erotic cover
☐ What would your ideal cover look like?

_____

15. Describe your ideal Nexus novel in the space provided:

_____

_____

_____

_____

16. Which celebrity would feature in one of your Nexus-style fantasies?
   We'll post the best suggestions on our website – anonymously!

_____

THANKS FOR YOUR TIME

Now simply write the title of this book in the space below and cut out the
questionnaire pages. Post to: Nexus, Marketing Dept., Thames Wharf Studios,
Rainville Rd, London W6 9HA

Book title: _____

NEXUS NEW BOOKS

To be published in September 2007

LONGING FOR TOYS
Virginia Crowley

Robert and James are upstanding members of the community. They are young professionals with bigoted, conservative upper middle class girlfriends. When Michele – a gorgeous stripper at the notorious club Hot Summer's – sees Robert's shiny red new roadster, she is overcome by a desire to possess it. Manipulating his friends and neighbours with offerings of ever more sordid sexual delights, she engineers Robert's descent into a tangled world of erotic temptation. As his character degrades from that of an altruistic medical researcher into a drooling plaything around the manicured fingers of his keeper, Robert's fiancée and best friend try to help him; unfortunately, their involvement also subjects them to the irresistible lure of pretty toys.

£6.99   ISBN 978 0 352 34138 9

BEING A GIRL
Chloë Thurlow

Late for a vital interview on a sweltering day, casting agent Jean-Luc Cartier pours Milly some water and holds the glass to her lips. When the water soaks her blouse he instructs her to take it off. Milly is embarrassed but curious. As Milly strips off her clothes, more than her shapely body, it is her deepest nature that is slowly uncovered.

Jean-Luc puts her over his knee. He spanks her bottom and her virgin orgasm awakens her to the mysteries of discipline. Milly at 18 is at the beginning of an erotic journey from convent school to a black magic coven in the heart of Cambridge academia, to the secret world of fetishism and bondage on the dark side of the movie camera.

£6.99   ISBN 978 0 352 34139 6

If you would like more information about Nexus titles, please visit our website at www.nexus-books.com, or send a large stamped addressed envelope to:
    Nexus, Thames Wharf Studios,
    Rainville Road, London W6 9HA

NEXUS BOOKLIST

Information is correct at time of printing. To avoid disappointment, check availability before ordering. Go to www.nexus-books.com.

All books are priced at £6.99 unless another price is given.

NEXUS

☐ ABANDONED ALICE	Adriana Arden	ISBN 978 0 352 33969 0
☐ ALICE IN CHAINS	Adriana Arden	ISBN 978 0 352 33908 9
☐ AQUA DOMINATION	William Doughty	ISBN 978 0 352 34020 7
☐ THE ART OF CORRECTION	Tara Black	ISBN 978 0 352 33895 2
☐ THE ART OF SURRENDER	Madeline Bastinado	ISBN 978 0 352 34013 9
☐ BEASTLY BEHAVIOUR	Aishling Morgan	ISBN 978 0 352 34095 5
☐ BEHIND THE CURTAIN	Primula Bond	ISBN 978 0 352 34111 2
☐ BEING A GIRL	Chloë Thurlow	ISBN 978 0 352 34139 6
☐ BELINDA BARES UP	Yolanda Celbridge	ISBN 978 0 352 33926 3
☐ BENCH-MARKS	Tara Black	ISBN 978 0 352 33797 9
☐ BIDDING TO SIN	Rosita Varón	ISBN 978 0 352 34063 4
☐ BINDING PROMISES	G.C. Scott	ISBN 978 0 352 34014 6
☐ THE BOOK OF PUNISHMENT	Cat Scarlett	ISBN 978 0 352 33975 1
☐ BRUSH STROKES	Penny Birch	ISBN 978 0 352 34072 6
☐ BUTTER WOULDN'T MELT	Penny Birch	ISBN 978 0 352 34120 4
☐ CALLED TO THE WILD	Angel Blake	ISBN 978 0 352 34067 2
☐ CAPTIVES OF CHEYNER CLOSE	Adriana Arden	ISBN 978 0 352 34028 3
☐ CARNAL POSSESSION	Yvonne Strickland	ISBN 978 0 352 34062 7
☐ CITY MAID	Amelia Evangeline	ISBN 978 0 352 34096 2
☐ COLLEGE GIRLS	Cat Scarlett	ISBN 978 0 352 33942 3
☐ CONCEIT AND CONSEQUENCE	Aishling Morgan	ISBN 978 0 352 33965 2

□ FAIRGROUND ATTRACTION	Lisette Ashton	ISBN 978 0 352 33927 0
□ IN FOR A PENNY	Penny Birch	ISBN 978 0 352 34083 2
□ THE INSTITUTE	Maria Del Rey	ISBN 978 0 352 33352 0
□ NEW EROTICA 5	Various	ISBN 978 0 352 33956 0
□ THE NEXUS LETTERS	Various	ISBN 978 0 352 33955 3
□ PLAYTHING	Penny Birch	ISBN 978 0 352 33967 6
□ PLEASING THEM	William Doughty	ISBN 978 0 352 34015 3
□ RITES OF OBEDIENCE	Lindsay Gordon	ISBN 978 0 352 34005 4
□ SERVING TIME	Sarah Veitch	ISBN 978 0 352 33509 8
□ THE SUBMISSION GALLERY	Lindsay Gordon	ISBN 978 0 352 34026 9
□ TIE AND TEASE	Penny Birch	ISBN 978 0 352 33987 4
□ TIGHT WHITE COTTON	Penny Birch	ISBN 978 0 352 33970 6

NEXUS CONFESSIONS

□ NEXUS CONFESSIONS: VOLUME ONE	Ed. Lindsay Gordon	ISBN 978 0 352 34093 1

NEXUS ENTHUSIAST

□ BUSTY	Tom King	ISBN 978 0 352 34032 0
□ CUCKOLD	Amber Leigh	ISBN 978 0 352 34140 2
□ DERRIÈRE	Julius Culdrose	ISBN 978 0 352 34024 5
□ ENTHRALLED	Lance Porter	ISBN 978 0 352 34108 2
□ LEG LOVER	L.G. Denier	ISBN 978 0 352 34016 0
□ OVER THE KNEE	Fiona Locke	ISBN 978 0 352 34079 5
□ RUBBER GIRL	William Doughty	ISBN 978 0 352 34087 0
□ THE SECRET SELF	Christina Shelly	ISBN 978 0 352 34069 6
□ UNDER MY MASTER'S WINGS	Lauren Wissot	ISBN 978 0 352 34042 9
□ THE UPSKIRT EXHIBITIONIST	Ray Gordon	ISBN 978 0 352 34122 8
□ WIFE SWAP	Amber Leigh	ISBN 978 0 352 34097 9

- - - - - - ✂ -

Please send me the books I have ticked above.

Name   ....

Address   ....

                ....

                ....

                .... Post code ....

Send to: **Virgin Books Cash Sales, Thames Wharf Studios, Rainville Road, London W6 9HA**

US customers: for prices and details of how to order books for delivery by mail, call 888-330-8477.

Please enclose a cheque or postal order, made payable to **Nexus Books Ltd**, to the value of the books you have ordered plus postage and packing costs as follows:

UK and BFPO – £1.00 for the first book, 50p for each subsequent book.

Overseas (including Republic of Ireland) – £2.00 for the first book, £1.00 for each subsequent book.

If you would prefer to pay by VISA, ACCESS/MASTERCARD, AMEX, DINERS CLUB or SWITCH, please write your card number and expiry date here:

....

Please allow up to 28 days for delivery.

Signature ....

Our privacy policy

We will not disclose information you supply us to any other parties. We will not disclose any information which identifies you personally to any person without your express consent.

From time to time we may send out information about Nexus books and special offers. Please tick here if you do *not* wish to receive Nexus information. ☐

- - - - - - ✂ -